UNDER THE ARCH

St. Louis Stories

Edited with Introduction by Paul Thiel

Foreword by Mayor Francis G. Slay

ANTARES PRESS
Kirkwood, Missouri

Copyright © 2004 by Paul Thiel

All rights reserved. No part of this book may be reproduced in any form or by any mechanical or electronic means including photocopying or recording or otherwise, including information storage and retrieval systems, without permission in writing from the publisher. Antares Press is not authorized to grant permission for further use of copyrighted selections reprinted in this book without permission of their owners.

Published by Antares Press
P.O. Box 220122
Kirkwood, Missouri 63122

E-mail address: Antarespress@Yahoo.com

Library of Congress Control Number: 2004097831

ISBN 0-9745450-1-5

TABLE OF CONTENTS

Francis G. Slay, **FOREWORD**... 1
Paul Thiel, **INTRODUCTION**... 3
Dakin Williams, **TENNESSEE IN ST. LOUIS**... 7
Mary Troy, **THE ALIBI CAFÉ**... 18
Richard Burgin, **THE PARK**... 31
Daniel Stolar, **CITY MAP**... 45
Edmund de Chasca, **SHOPPING DAY**... 58
Michael Kahn, **THE CAVES**... 64
Harry Jackson Jr., **IN REMEMBRANCE OF TERRY A. LAWSON**... 73
James M. Huggins, **PETE GRAY**... 81
A.E. Hotchner, **THE CHRISTMAS CANARIES**... 88
William Gass, **WINSTON CHURCHILL**... 98
John Lutz, **SECOND STORY SUNLIGHT**... 106
Suzanne Rhodenbaugh, **YA GOTTA LOVE IT**... 125
Colleen McKee, **THE LURE OF ANNIHILATION**... 131
Rick Skwiot, **THE GRANDMOTHERS**... 136
Robert Earleywine, **FIDO THE TALKING DOG**... 149
Michael MacCambridge, **HEMAN PARK: THE URBAN TENNIS JUNGLE**... 155
Charles Wartts Jr., **BIG MUDDY BLUES**... 165
Richard Newman, **AWFUL**... 175
Robert Randisi, **KEOUGH'S CAREER**... 181
Eileen Dreyer, **SAFE AT HOME**... 191
Ryan Stone, **A STORY TO TELL**... 203
Margaret Hermes, **HER SECOND LOVER**... 213
David Carkeet, **PASSING THROUGH**... 227
BIOGRAPHICAL NOTES... 234
ACKNOWLEDGMENTS... 240

This book is dedicated to my high school teacher, Miss Esther Goff, who inspired her students at Normandy High School with a love for literature and a desire to reach beyond themselves.

FOREWORD
by Mayor Francis G. Slay

It might surprise a nation that knows St. Louis best for its smoky music, cold beer, and winning sports teams to learn that we have always cared as much or more for other things. Of course, we are proud of our contributions to America's vices and other recreations, but our Midwestern honesty requires us to note that St. Louis has also produced proudly more bricks and books than most other cities.

Ranging from the strictly utilitarian to the downright exotic, bricks fired from the unique clays discovered under the southern and western parts of the city built the neighborhoods of bungalows, mansions, and warehouses that make St. Louis one of the true superstars of the National Register of Historic Places, which identifies and protects our architectural heritage.

Living in these decorative homes and sturdy warehouses no doubt inspired by the example of the careful craftsmen who stacked the bricks in creative ways—St. Louisans have always toiled away with pen, typewriter, and word processor to place words and sentences in even more remarkable arrangements and exported their finished works to eager readers everywhere.

As this collection shows, St. Louis seems to sit atop an especially rich vein of inspiration. Is it our cultural and ethnic diversity? Our location in the country's very center? Is it our Indian mounds and old French cathedrals? The water or the weather? I don't know the answer.

But, perhaps a thoughtful reader of this volume, less occupied with municipal budgets and tables of organization, might hazard a guess.

St. Louis

... is the name Pierre Laclede and Auguste Chouteau chose for their outpost of civilization on a bluff south of where the muddy Missouri River merges into the clearer Mississippi. They christened that location in honor of their beatified king, Louis the Ninth. Their initial intention focused on the commercial possibilities of the site, especially trade with trappers from the upper reaches of those rivers. Over time their outpost developed into a formidable city. For a while in the early nineteenth century it was supposed it would become the greatest city in the new nation. But then train transportation became the norm, Chicago became its center, and river use rapidly declined. Mighty expectations arose again when in 1904 the "Greatest of World Fairs" brought the world to St. Louis. But a fair, alas, ends—however memorable.

The City and the burgeoning St. Louis County did go on to become one of the country's larger metropolitan areas, home to a wide array of industry and a virtual explosion of immigrant talent in every field. And St. Louis has become a modern city, symbolized by Eero Saarinen's shiny arch. This was accomplished without tearing down so much of the nineteenth and early twentieth century brick homes and public buildings that almost define it with their charm. Renovation of the many brick buildings is fairly common now. And yet, St. Louis is still a very affordable city, traffic is tenable, and it has remained a family town.

It's also my home town. My great-grandfather came here to work as a contractor on that architectural wonder, the Eads Bridge. My mother, bless her Irish soul, is buried with him in the Catholic cemetery of St. Louis, Calvary. This fact, like virtually everything in a town relating to people's lives, involves a story. When my father died, he was supposed to be interred on top of Uncle Francis. With limited space, relatives are often buried in tandem. But Calvary mistakenly buried him on top of Grandpa McCaffrey. "That will never do," my mother told them. "You'll just have to unplant him and put him back where he's supposed to be. He'll never get along with that old buzzard. I'm the only one who can get along with Grandpa." They did it. Dug him up and replanted him. So when she died, we put her there on top of Grandpa McCaffrey. I presume all is well. General Tecumseh Sherman is right next door, keeping an eye on things, and it's only a hop, skip and a jump to the Tennessee Williams family plot.

When Williams wrote the "Glass Menagerie," he had a St. Louis apartment in mind. The city's been a formative influence on a large number of writers, as widely diverse as T.S. Eliot, Eugene Field, William Burroughs and Kate Chopin. Mark Twain was affected by it, and a whole raft of musicians as well, from W.C. Handy, author of "The St. Louis Blues," to Scott Joplin, Miles Davis, Chuck Berry and today's rap artist, Nelly.

It's been my grateful task to assemble writing from some of today's St. Louis writers. I include here fiction, because there's so much truth in it. And non-fiction because, colored as it is by the writer's perceptions, it has its own element of fantasy.

The anthology begins with an account of Tennessee Williams entering the city for the first time, as related by his brother, Dakin. It goes on to include work by William Gass and A.E. Hotchner as well as enticing pieces from many other established writers. These are tales that range in St. Louis settings from the giant Forest Park to a supermarket, a police station, a skyscraper, the Eads Bridge and caves under the city which the first German biermeisters used to store their products. So let's raise a brew in toast to this great city and some of the writers calling it home.

Paul Thiel
St. Louis
2004

TENNESSEE IN ST. LOUIS
by Dakin Williams
(from the biography, *My Brother's Keeper*)

Tom and his mother, Edwina, arrived at Union Station in downtown St. Louis on a blazing hot day in July 1918, the last summer of the war. They were met by Cornelius, Tom's father, who had gone on ahead. Rose, Tom's sister, was still in Mississippi with her grandparents.

Tom's memory of that day was of passing a fruit stand on the way out of the station where he plucked a grape. His father gave him a stinging slap on the hand, shouting that he must never steal again. For all his other faults, Cornelius was an honest man.

St. Louis at that time was flooded with war workers, and it was not easy to find an apartment. They went first to a boarding house on Lindell Boulevard, which Edwina described as "fashionable." With Edwina all things seemed to mature, like wine, and became more fashionable. A boarding house seemed a good idea then because Edwina had never actually cooked a meal. She said she could make angel food cake, and that was all.

The boarding-house period didn't last long. Edwina saw an advertisement for an apartment to be rented to anyone who would buy all the furniture. This sounded perfect because they had none of their own. So Edwina answered the ad, and when she arrived at the apartment, she found a sad young man sitting in the midst of his nice furniture. His wife had left him, and he didn't want any of it, so Edwina bought it all; some she kept for more than half a century.

The apartment was at 4633 Westminster Place. It had six rooms and a bath and was, with some artistic license, the setting of *The Glass Menagerie*. Most probably it was less fashionable than Edwina remembered but also less frightful than Tom's recollection. To Tom the apartment was dismal, with walls the color of dried blood and mustard. The back looked out on a dark alley where cats were frequently cornered and disemboweled by dogs.

In addition to a new home (and new furniture), Tom and Rose were soon introduced to a new brother. On February 21, 1919, they were brought to St. Anthony's Hospital, where they found their mother holding a small bundle, a baby named Walter Dakin after Edwina's father. He was to be Edwina's last child. The Reverend Mr. Dakin came up from Clarksdale, Mississippi, to baptize him.

Some of the St. Louis elite still lived in Westminster Place, and Tom and Rose had their children as playmates. This was a mixed blessing, since the Williams children were attending Eugene Field public school, whereas most of the other children went to private schools, Mary Institute for girls and Country Day for boys. The Williams' southern accents, so foreign sounding in St. Louis, made them seem like poor immigrants, whereas in Mississippi, as the grandchildren of the Episcopal minister, they were used to being regarded as among the best people. The haughty children, whom they met only at Sunday school, treated them like white trash. They would throw Tom's cap out the window when the teacher wasn't looking, and they gave Rose the silent treatment. "The girls snub me," she told her mother. As a result, Tom and Rose would stop at Masserang's drugstore across from the Sunday school and spend their time, as well as their offering money of twenty-five cents, at the soda fountain.

The artificially rigged social barriers of St. Louis were frightful for the Williams family. In spite of them, Tom made friends with two Mary Institute girls, Mary Louise Aide and Hazel Kramer. Hazel, a plump red-headed girl, remained Tom's close friend for years. In his *Memoirs* he wrote that she was the greatest love of his life, even greater than his later manly loves. Sketches of Hazel appear throughout Tom's writing. In one of

Tom's short stories, "Three Players of a Summer Game," there is a fine self-portrait of a very young boy with a girl like Hazel. In the story she spends a great deal of time waiting in an electric car while her mother makes love in the house. The story has elements that were later to develop into parts of *Cat on a Hot Tin Roof.*

Edwina then committed a grave offense against the tribal customs of St. Louis. She wanted to get out of that dark apartment and into a bit of sunshine, so they moved from Westminster Place to a brighter apartment at less fashionable South Taylor. The children were dropped immediately by all their "friends," except for Hazel. And because they were left alone, Tom and Rose grew closer, "aliens in an alien world," as Edwina wrote.

Edwina tried to make the best of it. She learned to cook, to make sandwiches and deviled eggs, and she would take the children for picnics into beautiful Forest Park, which still had lagoons and ponds and pagodas left over from the St. Louis World's Fair of 1904. They also spent hours at the famous St. Louis Zoo and at Shaw's Botanical Garden. Tom and Rose often swam at the Lorelei Pool. Swimming would later become Tom's favorite exercise.

But the parents' marriage was heading for trouble. Since Cornelius wrote no memoirs, there is only Edwina's side. By her account, she was long-suffering and brave. Her friends bragged about having their husbands bring them coffee in bed, but she rose at six to cook Cornelius a big breakfast, and, "no matter how difficult the drudgery all day, I always took a bath in the evening and changed to a dainty dress for dinner, as did Rose."

Edwina thought Cornelius was becoming a monster. It's likely that, for the first time, he felt fenced in. The free-ranging salesman now had an office and an apartment. And in the office he was the dreaded sales manager who had to hire and fire salesmen. "Sometimes that makes a man want to take a drink."

"Before we arrived in St. Louis," Edwina said, "I saw only the charming, gallant, cheerful side of Cornelius. For a while he tried to keep the Mr. Hyde from me. But he could hardly hold secret his excessive drinking, not when he would come home emitting fumes of alcohol, and in a cross and ugly mood."

At first Cornelius had his cronies in for poker, and Edwina said the game sometimes lasted "the whole weekend." She then told him to take his games elsewhere. He would go off to his club or to hotels. But he always made it to the office on time on Monday mornings.

Edwina wasn't the only one who suffered under Cornelius' moods; he was also quite hard on Tom. Cornelius saw Tom as a delicate, non-athletic, sissy. He even called him "Miss Nancy." These sentiments were echoed by Tom's peers.

Tom had rheumatic fever as a young child and could walk but not run. On the playground, the other children used his condition to ostracize him. He was no good at team games, and since the pecking order was based on that, he was bullied. One day he came home with his ankles black and blue. He had been sitting on a bench watching the game, and each boy who went by had kicked him on the ankles.

So for Tom, friends were hard to come by, and even if they hadn't been, it's unlikely they would have earned Edwina's approval. In her eyes, all the boys were "too rough" for her delicate son, and the girls were too "common," even Tom's closest friend, Hazel.

Edwina felt the same way about Rose's friends. They were a "bad moral influence." Therefore, Rose, too, was lonely, and she and Tom moved closer emotionally. But something came between them. Rose became a woman. She came down to breakfast one morning after her first menstruation, and Tom's mother and grandmother helped her gently to the table, handing everything to her that she could not reach.

Tom was also beginning to have feelings he could not understand. He wrote about them years later in a sensitive and beautiful short story called "The Resemblance Between a Violin Case and a Coffin." In his story, a sister and her young male friend were practicing for a piano-violin duet. The narrator of the story watched through an opening of the door as they played. He found himself watching Richard, the young man, and this troubled him. Richard seemed beautiful, as the sunlight shone through the sheer white cloth of his shirt, revealing his torso and his nipples. Tom's narrator was falling in love with Richard at the time the real Tom didn't know what the word homosexual meant. And his mother would not have told him. It was not a word in Edwina's entire vocabulary. In those days the word sex was simply taboo to most well-bred women.

When Tom was eleven, Edwina took ten dollars out of the household money and bought him a second-hand typewriter. She said, "It was large and clumsy and sounded like a threshing machine, but Tom was delighted with it. I could hear him hitting the keys for hours." Tom said, "I forgot to write longhand after that." Much later, after he graduated from high school, he took a typing course. His letters and the *Memoirs* are full of anecdotes of renting, buying, borrowing and hauling typewriters.

His first known composition, preserved by Dakin, was a contest entry, for a flour company, signed with his mother's name. An ode to crisp, brown muffins, it could scarcely have been better written, but the Jenny Wren flour company was not impressed and gave him no prize money.

Tom was twelve when he wrote his first literary piece. The teacher told the students to look around the classroom at the framed pictures, and to pick out a subject for a theme. He chose the Lady of Shalott, drifting down the river on a boat. He read the theme in front of the class, "and it had a very good reception. From that time on I knew I was going to be a writer."

His first known published works are two poems written for the junior high school paper, one called "Nature's Thanksgiving," about the woods in autumn, and the other titled "Old Things," about the lovely old contents of an attic. They are signed "Thomas Williams, 9th Gr." and are quite extraordinary. Poetry was always his first love, and he had written it all his life, in addition to the poetry that runs through his plays.

The situation between Edwina and Cornelius continued to deteriorate, but they still attended the annual picnics of the International Shoe Company. They would travel to Creve Coeur (locally pronounced "creeve core") Lake, which was then out in the country, at the end of the electric trolly-car line. There, among the dogwoods and the lilacs and the daffodils, they would enjoy a fine day of near beer and lemonade and boat rides—and, of course, company politics. Many of the company people were from Tennessee, and at first, Cornelius and Edwina were very popular with them. But all that was to end with their crumbling marriage. They had slept in separate bedrooms for a long time.

Both sons remember violent arguments, usually about money or Cornelius' drinking. Edwina recalled one time when she did not have enough money to buy food for the weekend. Cornelius, who was making $7,500 a year—a good salary in those days— threw $6 on the kitchen table and said, "There, take it all and go to hell!"

Perhaps the final blow to their already battered marriage came on one of Cornelius' many weekends away from home, when he and two of his younger cronies from International Shoe arranged a supper party. They rented a room in a downtown hotel, brought in bootleg booze, set up a green-topped table with cards and poker chips, and also brought in a couple of what Tom would have called "light ladies."

One of the young salesmen caught a social disease from a light lady and passed it on to his wife. She was highly displeased, and went straight to the boss who called Cornelius and the two salesmen on the carpet. The two young men denied everything. The always truthful Cornelius admitted it.

The two young men were fired; Cornelius was kept on as sales manager because of his honesty—and because he was so good at his job. But his upward progress at International Shoe was finished. This episode also destroyed whatever was left of the marriage. Edwina became ill and had two major operations, including a hysterectomy.

Tom, already a neurotic and introverted child, was having all kinds of psychological problems. He was even terrified to go to sleep at night, because he thought sleep was similar to death. As he grew into his teens, he became almost pathologically shy. He blushed when anyone looked him in the eye, particularly when women looked at him, even his own girlfriend, Hazel Kramer. She told him she would certainly never say anything to hurt him. They were in love, and her mother, "Miss Florence," regarded him almost as a son. All three would drive around St. Louis, often in the evening, sometimes to the places where couples parked and "necked"—like the top of Art Hill (near the equestrian statue of St. Louis) and in a low, woodsy road called Lovers Lane.

If this mild voyeurism was intended to suggest anything to Tom, it apparently didn't work. He wrote that he liked being shocked. There is no indication that Tom and Hazel were physical. Apparently he was most attracted to her shoulders, and his first "genital stirring" was when he saw them, bare, in the West End Lyric movie house on Delmar Boulevard. Later they went on the Mississippi River on the excursion steamer *J.S.* On the top deck, in the dark, he put his arm around her "delicious" shoulders and ejaculated in his white flannels. He was quite embarrassed. Hazel decided they'd better not dance any more after that.

In his *Memoirs*, Tom suggests that there were already conflicting temptations. In the summer of 1928 he went with his grandfather to Europe. The Reverend Mr. Dakin was shepherding a group of Episcopalians on the grand tour. On the boat Tom sometimes waltzed with a dancing teacher, a woman of about twenty-seven, who was having a flirtation with a man much older than Tom. He remembered a conversation the three of them had in the ship's bar. They were talking about him, discussing what his future would be. The man was quite certain, but the woman said that, at seventeen, it was too early to tell. Tom concluded later, when he wrote his *Memoirs*, that they were talking about whether he was heterosexual or homosexual, though at the time he was totally mystified.

While he was in Europe, Tom had an odd psychological crisis apparently having little to do with the trip or his companions. It was a kind of wide-awake nightmare so intense that it left him shaking and drenched with sweat. He was terrified by the thought of thought, by the concept of the process of human thinking, as a mystery in human life, and it made him think he was going mad. The panic struck him while he was walking in Paris and followed him in travels down the Rhine. It was resolved by an experience that he thought was supernatural. He was kneeling in prayer in the cathedral of Cologne and felt an unseen hand on his head. Suddenly his phobia was lifted. He was sure then that it was the hand of Jesus.

The phobia returned again in Amsterdam and this time he cured it by writing a poem, a lovely one about strangers passing in the street. It made him recognize he was not alone but a part of humanity. The phobia left him for good.

In 1928 he returned to University City Public High School for his final semester and wrote an account of his travels for the school paper. It was serialized in many issues, with no mention of the phobia. He remained the most bashful boy in school, so shy that he could not even answer questions aloud in class. But he had something special. He had been abroad, the only one.

Tom was always writing. He entered many advertising contests. He won his first writing prize at sixteen. Smart Set magazine held a contest: "Can a Good Wife be a Good Sport?" The fact that Tom had never had a wife, good or bad, didn't stop him. With a straight face he invented his own marital adventures, and told how, after their third wedding anniversary, he discovered his wife was unfaithful and how they were divorced a year later. Competing with thousands of people who knew what they were talking about, Tom won third prize—five dollars.

The following year he sold his first short story, called "The Vengeance of Nitocris," to *Weird Tales*, a pulp magazine. Nitocris was an Egyptian queen who rated only a paragraph or two in Herodotus, but Tom expanded her story into a minor epic. He made thirty-five dollars for it, his first big writing money. The story ended with Nitocris' smoke-filled suicide. The scene's inspiration may have been a contest Tom had just won. It was sponsored by the St. Louis Citizens Smoke Abatement League, whose slogan was SMOKE MUST GO. In his story, Tom compared the smoke to a dragon engulfing the city. And in those days, St. Louis was engulfed in industrial smoke. Sometimes in winter you couldn't see across the street.

Tom wrote his first play long before the "Tennessee" pen name was invented. Stopping at nothing, he decided to take on Shakespeare and improve him. The family was spending a vacation at a YMCA camp at a lake near Springfield, Missouri. For amateur night Tom contributed a play, the first draft of which had already been roughed out by Shakespeare: *Romeo and Juliet*. Tom noticed that W.S. had not taken the trouble to rhyme the poetry, and decided to do it up right.

In addition to being a prolific writer, Tom read constantly. He spent "endless hours" at the library and continually brought home books. Nevertheless, his mother noticed when he brought home D.H. Lawrence's *Lady Chatterley's Lover*. She opened it to a rather sexy passage. "Tom said I had a veritable genius for opening to the most lurid pages." She thereupon "marched Tom and the book to the library, where I gave the librarian a piece of my mind." From then on, Edwina crossed Lawrence off her list, and resolutely refused to see or read Tom's one-act play *I Rise in Flame, Cried the Phoenix*, his youthful (1941) poetic account of the death of Lawrence. However, Tom remained an admirer of Lawrence's work.

During this period in the last months of high school his relationship with Hazel Kramer had a profound effect on his whole personality. Tom and Hazel were close emotionally, yet their physical relationship was almost prim. He wrote that Hazel allowed him to kiss her on the lips only twice a year, on Christmas and her birthday. He was never sure whether this was from frigidity on her part, or simply a coquettish ploy to bring out a more aggressive attitude on his part. In any case, it didn't work. However, he does say that the episode of the fig leaf in his "Three Players of a Summer Game" really took place with Hazel at the St. Louis Art Museum, that she did indeed lift a fig leaf on a male statue (*The Dying Gaul*) and did ask him, "Is yours like that?" The *New Yorker* cut this line from the story, and Williams later put it back. And who cares if there are no hinged fig leaves in the Art Museum? Fig leaf or no, the implication was that Hazel wasn't as cold as all that, and maybe Tom was not getting the whole message.

Sadly, the relationship did break up, possibly due to Cornelius. Tom and Hazel both graduated from high school in 1929, Hazel from Mary Institute and Tom from University City Public High School (with a B average). Cornelius knew that Tom and Hazel were very close, and he was determined to prevent an early marriage. Hazel's grandfather, who worked for International Shoe under Cornelius, was persuaded to send Hazel to the University of Wisconsin. Tom, meanwhile, had decided to go to the University of Missouri in Columbia instead of to nearby Washington University.

Edwina accompanied Tom to Columbia to help him find a place to stay. The very first night, in the hotel, he wrote a letter to Hazel at the University of Wisconsin proposing marriage. A week later she replied that they were too young to think about anything like that. Tom saw Hazel again, but the romance was over.

Years later, Hazel's divorced mother, Miss Florence, dropped in on the Williams family. Flamboyant as ever, she sashayed in and went to the piano, as was her custom, and started to spank out a popular tune.

"Not so loudly!" said Edwina, fearful of the landlady.

Miss Florence stopped abruptly, and said she was leading up to the fact that Hazel would be singing on the radio that very night. Hazel had a good voice, and had found a number of professional singing jobs. But Miss Florence saved the big news for Tom. When he came into the living room she kissed him on the lips and said, "I've got news for you, sonny boy. Hazel has gone and got herself engaged to be married."

Tom was shattered and couldn't believe it, but Miss Florence showed him a letter proving it. She also said that Hazel was coming back to St. Louis, and she invited the family to come over on Sunday for tea to meet Hazel's fiancé, a young man named Terrence McCabe.

They went to tea and noticed that Terry McCabe, quite different from Tom, was a tall, extroverted, back-slapping fellow who was the life of the party. Tom, quiet, shy, and heartbroken, listened as Terry told a joke. "Did you hear this one about the stockbroker? He was telling his new client, 'Hold your gas, let your water go, sit on your American Can! Scott tissues went down three points. Thousands were wiped clean!'" Great guffaws from Miss Florence. Tom never asked another woman to marry.

Hazel's marriage ended years later, and this affected Miss Florence so much that she committed suicide. Hazel died mysteriously on a trip to Mexico, of alleged food poisoning. And Tom became Tennessee.

THE ALIBI CAFÉ
by Mary Troy

Bev was at the counter filling salt shakers, and I was in the back doctoring my barbeque sauce when Joseph Patrick Sweeney entered the Alibi Café for the first time. He was nine years old and on his way home from St. Hedwig's, two blocks south, where he was in the fourth grade. We had been opened only two months and had not quite caught on in the neighborhood yet, so the place was empty. Joseph Patrick, JP as he called himself, walked up to the counter, hoisted himself and his backpack onto a stool, and asked Bev if she wanted to buy candy bars, caramel or almond, at a dollar a piece.

"Hmmmm," she said. She put down the box of salt and looked at his full moon-shaped face covered with big freckles, the kind that are reddish and seem to run together. He had little dark eyes and what was probably brown hair in so short a crew cut the color was gone. He smiled at her, and I noticed his teeth were yellow, though later when I saw the smile close up, I decided they were more green than yellow, especially at the roots. "It's for St. Hedwig's science lab," he said.

Bev bought four candy bars, two of each kind, and I came out from the sauce and bought four more. I did it because JP was ugly, and being kind of pretty myself—some say I'm a reincarnated Natalie Wood—I have always had a soft spot for the less fortunate.

Of the four dollars Bev gave him, one was in dimes she counted from the register drawer, causing his mouth to gape open and giving us a view of his moss-colored teeth way in the back. "Wow," he said. "Where are your fingers?"

Bev laughed. "I didn't get as many as you to begin with." On her two hands put together, she had only two fingers and one thumb. She had stumps in all the right places, which throughout her thirty years she had used as if they were fingers. She was able to count change and even to type. She had also been born with only one leg, or rather, one and a half, as what was missing was from just above where the right knee should be. So she did have two thighs. It was all the result of morning sickness medicine her mother, my Aunt Josie, had taken while carrying Bev, what my mother called our "main family tragedy." Mom spoke of Aunt Josie's mistake with a tinge of relief in her voice, because she believed each family had an allotment of tragedies, and she believed Bev was living proof that we already had had a good portion of ours. The money from the lawsuit against the pharmaceutical company that made Mother's Help was what paid for the Alibi Café and what enabled Bev to go into business for herself and give me, her woebegone cousin, a job and more.

Bev was also born with yellow hair as thin and limp as fringe, wide-set eyes, and not much of a chin, all of which could not be laid at the pharmaceutical company's door, but would have to be blamed on genes our mothers carried. Recessive ones, thank God.

I was thirty-six and had just been divorced from my second husband after sixteen years. He was a man who sold and installed siding for his family's business. Instead of children, we had dogs, two border collies named the owl and the pussycat who now lived with my second ex-husband. My first marriage which lasted less than a year had been to a guitar-playing data processor who decided marriage was too confining. My second husband was the one I thought would stay, and he would have been enough, too. I mean, I really believed I did not need children with him around to make me feel complete. His falling for the veterinarian's receptionist, a woman not much younger than I and certainly not as pretty, was a shock, one I was still recovering from when Bev opened her café and, my work in the siding business at an end, I needed a job.

Bev claimed owning a café had long been a dream of hers, though she was the one with the college education, the one who had had good grades all her life, the one who had been a history teacher for eight years at Agnus Dei High School for girls too rich to know how dumb they were. Still, once the appeals were over and the lawsuit money came through, she quit her job, bought the lease on an old diner, and ordered a sign reading Alibi Café. She had been in trouble at Agnus Dei anyway for telling her girls they did not have to confide in their parents, not totally anyway. "You're happier not knowing," she told the parents at the emergency meeting cum inquisition that followed. The wealthiest parents wanted her fired, but the principal persuaded them to accept a formal apology. Bev, though, decided that quitting made the most sense.

Four days after JP sold us eight candy bars, he showed up with an order form for Girl Scout cookies. His sister was a scout, and Bev and I bought a dozen boxes each, thinking we could add them to the menu in the "as-long-as they-last" category. Bev gave him a glass of milk and a slice of her specialty, banana cream pie, and rolled up her right pant leg to let him feel the smoothness of her prosthesis.

"Wow," he said, rubbing his hand along the shiny part that was the shin. "My sister should feel this."

The following Saturday, he brought his sister in at noon, but our eight customers kept Bev too busy to roll up her pants. JP's sister, Mary Kate, did not seem eager for a demonstration anyway. She was a pale girl with only a few washed-out-looking freckles, but the familiar small eyes. She hung her head in what I first took to be embarrassment, assuming she had been taught not to ogle the handicapped.

"At least look at her hands," I heard JP say as they stood at the end of the counter by the cash register. "See?" he said. "No fingers."

"It gives me the creeps," Mary Kate said. "Let's get out of here."

"I bet she gives us pie in a minute."

"I wouldn't eat it," Mary Kate said. "And you better stay away from here." Then she dragged JP out, pulling at the neck of his sweatshirt until he was on the sidewalk.

The following Tuesday, JP sold ten two-dollar raffle tickets on a handmade quilt to Bev and me and one each to the two sewer workers who were drinking coffee at the table right in the center of the front window.

Bev teased JP before she gave him the money, asking if he was really a student or a salesman, asking him if he was studying commerce and finance.

His face became a quivering red fist as he scrunched it up at her laughter, preparing to squeeze tears through the teeny ducts. He recovered, though, when she handed him the twenty.

"It's awful hard sometimes," she said "to produce even one tear."

Bev was free with her money, taking it out of the register not only for JP, but also for heart association, cancer society, and March of Dimes collectors. She told me the settlement was obscenely large, certainly more than a leg, six fingers, and a thumb were worth, and the café did not have to make a profit, or for that matter, even cover expenses for quite a while. She just wanted it to be fun, an easy place to be for the customers and me, and something tangible for her. "With teaching, you never know if you've succeeded or not, if you've done anything. But a grilled cheese sandwich is not relative."

When Bev leased the diner, she took the two-bedroom apartment upstairs, too, and invited me to live with her, probably at our mothers' urgings. My ex-husband and I had made the amicable, adult decision that we would sell our home and split the profit, if any. I had been living in it while it was for sale, though, living in it alone and worrying my mother by keeping lights on day and night. A minimum of one light per room. I was not afraid of the dark, not exactly, but it seemed to spread out indefinitely, to be stronger than light. I was afraid it would be permanent, that if I let things go dark, they may never be light again. But that is another story, and has little to do with Bev, who gave me not only a job, but also a place to live.

So I wanted the Alibi Café to succeed, even if she did not care. I daydreamed about restaurant critics praising us, about the line that would form outside and around the block, about bottling and selling my knock-your-socks-off barbecue sauce with my picture on the label.

Our menu was a list of what each of us did well, or at least could do OK. Because of my barbecue sauce—fresh, juicy garlic was my secret—we offered ribs, barbecued beef on a bun, and oven-barbecued chicken. I made a pretty spicy chili, too, and a good pickle-less potato salad. Bev did an open-faced tuna salad with melted cheddar on top, a BLT, and the grilled cheese. She also made deep dish pies with flaky crusts, and big, soft biscuits for breakfast. We scrambled eggs with bacon along with the biscuits, and I made a passable but pasty sausage gravy.

We had six four-person tables, and four deuces, as well as six swivel stools across the counter. We could have seated thirty-six at once, but the two of us could not have cooked for, served, and cleaned up after all thirty-six and remained cheerful. Bev, though, could serve six plates at a time without a tray, and even with her artificial leg could lurch and stomp across the floor as fast as I could walk. Our main meal was lunch, and our main customers were utility workers or city employees, the ones who were continually tearing up the streets and sidewalks in our neighborhood, one so old it was labeled historic.

For about two weeks, a gas man was in the area, working on a crew that was digging up first one corner, then another, and he would come in alone for a three o'clock break, sit at the counter, and flirt with me over his pie and coffee. I knew he was flirting because he talked about himself all the time, telling me what a hard luck life he had, but laughing quietly so I'd know he really thought both his life and he, himself, were pretty special.

He was in the day JP came in selling costume jewelry: the enamel poodle and daisy brooches, the glass-bead chokers, and earrings with the backs missing. The gas man was relating one humorous piece of his life—"So naturally the boss thought I was the brains behind it all..."—but I was only sort of smiling, not paying much attention. For one thing, women like me, good-looking ones I mean, can get tired of being flirted with, and for another, the mole on the inside of my arm, right below the elbow, had developed bumps on it. I was trying to decide if I should worry, have it checked, or ignore it. Bev said it was my divorce that made me afraid, just as I had been about the dark, and I figured it was my age, too. I had lately become frightened by my body, by its power to ruin me, by how irrevocably I was attached to it. I checked myself twice a day for breast cancer; I flossed my teeth morning and night; I tried to eat calcium-rich foods, low in cholesterol; I tried to memorize things like the names of the U.S. presidents in order of terms to ward off Alzheimer's. Now I had this changing mole.

"I can give you a good deal on this jewelry," JP said. "I made it in Scouts."

"Hey kid," the gas man said after being interrupted in the midst of his story. "It's great. I love the way you made it look so old and broken."

"Huh?" JP said.

"The poodle doesn't have a face anymore," the gas man said. "My mom had a pin like that years ago, and the dog's supposed to be smiling."

"Not this one," JP said, his ears turning red. "Where's Bev?"

"If you made that junk, kid, I'm the King of Persia." The gas man winked at me.

JP balled up his face again, actually forcing a few tears to his little eyes. "Oh for heaven's sake," I said. "You're certainly not the sensitive type."

"Beeeeeeev," he wailed to prove me wrong. He had had practice in showing hurt.

Bev rushed out of the kitchen and told him crocodile tears wouldn't work. She said he was too old to let his feelings get bruised so easily, and told him to shape up. "I'm running a café here, not a nursery school,' she said. Then she examined the jewelry. She held some pieces up to the light and pinned a daisy on her chest, using her stumps as fingers to do so and once again eliciting a "Wow" from JP.

Of course, she bought the entire shoebox full, as both JP and I knew she would. She gave JP two dollars and threw in a glass of milk and a slice of pie.

"Cuz," I said later. "You know he's just using you to supplement his allowance."

"I taught high school,' she said. "I'm not naïve."

"Then you're deliberately encouraging his lies?"

"Well, I imagine he had that habit long before he met me. Besides, I don't like to see people picked on." She pointed a whole finger at me. "Tell your boyfriend to stop it."

Naturally, I was mad at the boyfriend crack, especially as she was not above teasing JP herself, but was also ashamed at myself for forgetting Bev was special. I pictured the other kids teasing her in that way that is cruel and can bring tears that do not have to be forced. I imagined older people, too, thoughtlessly perhaps, making her feel like a freak. "You've been there," I said, touching her shoulder, about to hug her.

"Don't indulge your fantasies of pathos and cruelty on my account. I was the most popular kid in school when the others learned my leg could float, and when they figured out that if I liked them, I'd let them hang on it all summer in the deep end."

I stumbled on my words for a moment or two then, talking the way I do when I can't think of what to say, wishing I would shut up. I said I knew she had probably been luckier than the rest of us, that after all, it was only a leg, only fingers; the chin problem was what Great Uncle Herbert contributed to the family, and he had been a high liver if the stories were to be believed. And I said so what, and who cares, and I guess I never did understand, until she interrupted me.

"It's like this," she said. "You're temporary. You'll probably get married again, as you do seem to like it so. I had a roommate before you, a friend from Agnus Dei. She lived with me for two years and then got married. Before that was another girl, an ex-neighbor who stayed for a year before moving in with her boyfriend." She shrugged. "That's how it is, how it goes. When I see them now, we have only the old days in common. The only date I ever had was when Aunt Rose made Cousin Chuck take me to my senior prom." She had moved to the other side of the counter, and now plopped herself down on a stool. She swiveled back and forth as she continued. "I have a dream often. I dream the phone rings. It's night and I'm home alone. I answer it and say 'Hello, hello?' There's no response. Just the silence of wires across the night sky. Dead air. Nothing. I think it's important."

"It is," I said, remembering how the dark tried to destroy the light in my house.

During the next three months, Bev bought more raffle tickets to furnish St. Hedwig's computer room, bought pizzas for band uniforms, and Christmas ornaments for the library. She also bought green spray-painted rocks, a woman's moth-eaten mink pillbox hat, a scratched 45 of Fess Parker singing "The Ballad of Davy Crockett,' an eagle feather, and a dusty plastic fruit arrangement. One afternoon, she changed into a skirt so when JP came by she could raise it slightly and show him where and how the leg was connected.

"Did you know it floats?" he asked me as he drank his milk later and waited for Bev to come up from the basement storage room.

We laughed about JP then, each time he brought in his junk to sell. "He's such a little con man," Bev said one evening as I was cleaning the grill.

"He has a great future," I said. "As a junk man."

"He's good at selling it." Bev was filling the tin napkin dispensers, but she stopped, leaned against the counter, and laughed. "And I'm the idiot that buys it all. I guess I have a great future as a sucker."

"It's called a consumer," I said, and then asked what I had wanted to for months. "Why?"

"It's only money,' she said. "Besides, I've seldom had my body so admired."

After a while, we did more than laugh about JP and his money-making schemes. We both told him at different times and as gently as we could to brush his teeth. Bev reminded him to button up his jacket, too, and she sometimes stood at the window and watched him cross the street, watched him walk away until, a block down, he turned at the hardware store and disappeared. She knew the name of his teacher and what he studied, and would talk to me or some of the customers about his school work, wondering out loud how the math test went, if he managed to finish his book report. She listened to him spell the words assigned each week, and taught him some of her favorite mnemonic devices. "Parallel has a ladder in it," she said, though she couldn't spell mnemonic when he asked. And twice that I know of, she removed her leg for him, then let him help strap it back on by working one of the buckles.

During the same three months, I increased our business by about ten percent by adding a codfish sandwich and a quarter-pound burger to the menu, and by offering the buy-one-sandwich-get one-at-half-price Monday and Tuesday special. I also grew two new moles on the side of my right breast, and noticed a new wrinkle—I watched it deepen daily—alongside my mouth.

One rainy morning in February, JP brought a dog in, and I told him to take it right back out, especially as there was a woman with smeared mascara and matted hair at the corner deuce who seemed to be barely easing her eggs down, and who looked as if she were testing her system with each bite. My own stomach had grown queasy in response, and I figured a wet dog wouldn't help either of us.

"Bev is the boss," JP said. "Not you. I want her to see Ninja."

And as Bev came from behind the counter with the coffee pot, he dragged the dog to her, pulling hard at the rope knotted at its throat. "My spoon stuck in your gravy," she said to me as I passed them.

I went back to add milk to the gravy, and from the kitchen saw Bev, the coffee pot still grasped firmly by her stumps, bend over and pet the stiff-haired black mutt. Then when I took the order from the two policemen who had just come in, I saw her give JP a five-dollar bill. When she looked at me, we both rolled our eyes.

"His mother's making him get rid of that dog because they can't afford to feed it," she said after he left, laughing at how poor that story was.

"I bet it's a big eater," I said. "Probably eats five dollars worth a week, maybe ten."

Bev agreed. "I wonder where he got it. It didn't seem to know him," she said, but added, "It's really not such a bad story for a nine-year-old. He's a budding entrepreneur."

"No doubt," I said, and as I started slicing onions for my barbecue sauce, I thought that in spite of being ugly, JP could lose his appeal. And on top of the faint nausea I picked up from the customer who had managed only four tastes before letting her eggs grow cold, I had another problem. My thick and normally shiny blue-black hair had turned dull recently, and now seemed to be falling out faster than usual. I did not know whether to see a doctor or a hairdresser.

When April came, JP signed up for a little league softball team and said we should come to the games on Sundays, the only day the Alibi Café was closed, though we did shut down at 2:00 P.M. on Saturdays. He was the shortstop, he told us, and had a five hundred batting average. "What?" I said. "You're not going to sell us tickets?"

"No," he said innocently, as if he had not sold Bev a weathered bicycle horn just three days earlier. "Little league games are free. You could be a sponsor, though. Or work the concessions."

Though Bev told JP with only one finger on each hand she could still catch and throw a ball, I doubted she had ever tried that trick. Sure, she had often had opportunities to participate in "special" or "handicapped" events, but had declined each time. Her lack of interest was almost genetic. No one in our family was athletic, no one competed in anything physical. Bev's father bragged that he had never played on a team of any kind, not even in neighborhood games as a child, and my father did not even watch TV sports. In fact, I was considered the family athlete because I had once participated in a race. It was a five-mile run actually, and I had signed up because I liked to run and knew five miles would be easy. As I came down the final hill, though, I saw a crowd at the bottom and heard its cheers. People I had never met and probably never would meet were waving me on. I stopped about halfway down the hill. I thought how odd it was that they would care whether or not I finished. Then I turned around and walked back up the hill, down the other side, and went home. I am still not sure why the cheers of strangers stopped me. It was my first and last competition.

Nevertheless, as Bev got caught up in the spirit of the Bear Cubs' first game, rooting especially for JP, but also for all the Bear Cubs, I got caught up watching her. She booed the opponents, the Pirates, with vigor, too, and she lurched up and down the third base line in front of JP's team's bleachers, her yellow hair flying behind like streamers, and shouted advice. Of course she knew little about softball, but as she said to me, what did you need to know. What she shouted was "hit the ball," "run fast," "catch it," and "throw it."

In the third inning, JP got a home run by hitting a grounder between the pitcher's legs, and Bev made herself hoarse by shouting his name. "I'm so proud of him," Bev said to some of the parents nearby.

In the fifth inning, JP was on second when the batter hit a grounder to the pitcher again, but this time it was caught by an outfielder who threw it to second base, and the second baseman, rather than risk another throw, ran across the diamond and tagged JP as he reached home plate. JP was pronounced out, and Bev was thrown out of the park soon after for poking the umpire in the chest with her sole index finger, telling him how blind and stupid he was. I got involved then, too, and cursed the umpire along with her, asking him how much the Pirates had paid him, because I finally recognized the appeal of athletics. Screaming and booing is tremendous fun.

After the Pirates won 16 to 12, Bev was allowed to return. She was there for the lineup, the part when the losers parade before the winners, slapping hands like friends and saying "good game." By that time most of the parents and assorted relatives from the stands were either staring at her or trying not to, and after the lineup, some players from both teams were giggling and pointing at Bev and JP. Bev seemed oblivious, though, as she stood there smiling, waiting, I knew, for JP to come over for a hug or a hand slap. But JP's sister, Mary Kate, came up to us instead, leading a moon-faced blonde with tiny eyes. "This is the one," Mary Kate said to the woman. "She showed JP how her leg fit on."

"I'm JP's mother," the woman said. "I'll be blunt. Leave my son alone."

"He's a nice kid,' Bev said. "We talk a little. Mainly I just give him pie. There's nothing to be upset about."

"Sometimes he doesn't feel too good after the pie," Mary Kate said.

"I'm not discussing it," Mrs. Sweeney said. "I'm telling you. I have to protect him. He's showing an unhealthy interest in deformity." She said deformity as if it were a synonym for perversity or pornography. "A mother can't be too careful. Not today."

"Look," Bev said. "I'm not contagious."

"I know you told high school girls to lie to their parents. If you don't leave my son alone, I'll call the police."

I saw JP then, standing behind his mother, looking at Bev and me, listening. When he saw I was watching him, he gave me his green-toothed smile. I assume Bev saw him, too. We went home in silence, and for quite a while did not speak of the incident, of JP or Mary Kate, or even softball.

It was more than three weeks later, on a Thursday afternoon, that I saw JP in the Alibi Café again, sitting on his usual stool near the cash register, eating a giant slice of banana cream pie. I had been at the butcher's, trying to work a better deal on ground beef, and I acted natural when I saw JP, just nodded my head to him on the way into the kitchen. We had three other customers at the time; two of the women who worked in the drug store across the street were having pie and coffee, and one of the salesmen from the used car lot at the other end of the block was working on a quarter pounder with cheese. I could tell Bev was busy watching JP eat, smiling at him as if he had just escaped from a POW camp, so I took over her customers, gave them free refills and wrote up their checks.

When I opened the register drawer for the salesman's change, Bev reached in and took out a five. She gave it to JP, and I looked at her quickly enough to see her blush. It was the first time in my memory I had seen that, so I decided to ask. "What's the five for now? Another money-making idea from St. Hedwig's?"

"It's for JP," Bev said quietly.

"Who else?" I said, but she just shrugged and looked down at her hands spread out flat on the counter. She wiggled her stumps. I looked at JP then, and he gave me the same old green grin.

He stuffed the five in his front pocket and slid off the stool. "I just hope my mom doesn't find out I've been here. Or Mary Kate."

Later that evening as we wiped the tables and cleaned the grill, put the potato salad and sauce up for the next day, Bev said, "having a holiday to celebrate motherhood is like having a day just for rich people."

One of my bottom molars had felt loose since afternoon, and I tried to stop worrying it so I could answer her. I had been thinking that blackmail was probably an advanced type of entrepreneurship, and was about to say it, when I decided what she really wanted was agreement. She deserved it, too. "Yes," I said. "That's absolutely right."

She sighed, and I went back to testing my tooth with my tongue.

THE PARK
by Richard Burgin

> *Don't think I leave for the outer dark,*
> *Like Adam and Eve put out of the park.*
> —Robert Frost

At first it was like an invitation from the sky which there was no possibility of refusing. He began going to the park every day knowing something important would happen. He found a favorite pond, later a favorite bench facing the pond, and waited surrounded by a group of delicate, oriental-looking trees with their red and green, gold and orange leaves. Then her image appeared before him one day like a delicate little tree itself. It was as if she were born in the park, as if that were her true home and her life at the travel agency a mere illusion. Vince wasn't even surprised or disappointed when the image left him a few moments later—he already knew what to do.

The next afternoon he returned to the agency where he'd met her just the week before. He'd gone there twice, once to buy a ticket to Chicago, then to buy one to New York. At the time he figured he needed to travel since it had gotten so quiet in his apartment building where he hadn't yet met anyone.

This time he didn't go inside but watched her through the street-level window, seeing mostly the crown of her yellowish hair. When she was ready to leave work, he followed from a safe distance 'til she got to the Metrolink stop, pressing himself against the side of a lamppost and waiting until she got on her train heading west.

He began going to the agency on the pretext of planning a winter vacation in Bermuda or Jamaica and soon started finding out some things about her. Her name was Janice and she was twenty-five, quite young, but not necessarily too young for him. She lived alone near the airport outside the city and seemingly had traveled everywhere, taking advantage of her reduced travel rates, she'd said, laughing. Her teeth protruded a little, yet this didn't inhibit her from having a full smile, which Vince found extremely appealing.

On his third or fourth visit Janice started asking Vince some questions, too. What exactly did he do? He told her that after his mother died he'd inherited some money and eventually had come to St. Louis a month ago to start a small business. "Why here?" she asked. There were so many better places to start a business back East, she would think. Because he'd had some happy years here before his parents moved, he said. Also, he knew it was a buyer's real estate market in St. Louis and he was interested in buying a house and settling down. His parents had bought a wonderful house here, but then they sold it to make money and moved East. He wanted to buy a house and *stay* in it, he said. She seemed impressed by that and by the time he left her office he wished he'd asked her to lunch.

He went directly home and watched the sunset over the park, seeing an image of Janice's toothy smile above the multicolored trees, then later the interplay of moon and clouds like a mother holding a child. When he looked more closely, he saw Janice's profile in the moon and knew he would have to talk to her tomorrow and certainly, this time, invite her to lunch.

While he was shaving the next morning, he wondered what he would say when she'd inevitably ask him some more questions about his life. Since he wasn't working now and hadn't had a history of remarkable jobs, there wasn't much to talk about there. He'd been one of those students whose ambition was genuinely intellectual, and even spiritual, but definitely not material. He was like his parents that way: they had had only minimal experience with the working world. Their money, like his, had been inherited. They were fearful and suspicious of society in general and the business world in particular. That much Vince knew. But he couldn't tell if they created his own similar fears, or simply had the ability to understand them. They'd had him late in life, after a miscarriage and years of trying for a child, and seemed to guard him like a jewel. Yet he loved them deeply and often thought they were the only truly kindred spirits he'd ever met. Should he talk to Janice about them or focus more on his own life (since his parents were both dead now) and his plans for the future?

Perhaps there was one thing he definitely should tell Janice about his past—"the genius hour." The few people he had told seemed to find it quite intriguing. Every day, beginning with his freshman year in high school, his parents insisted he have at least one hour of contact a day with a great mind. It was one of the few things, besides basic honesty and not driving while drunk, they ever demanded of him. The hour could be served, as it were, in a variety of ways. He could listen to an hour of Beethoven or Bach, or go to a first-rate museum and look at Rembrandts or Picassos, or he could read an hour of Kant, Shakespeare, Spinoza, etc. The important thing was developing the discipline to do it every day until it became a habit. Though his parents checked on him, and two or three times a week listened to music or read and discussed philosophy with him, much of the genius hour was done on the honor system. But there were few times he didn't do it on his own, even during his college years while he was away from home. It was only after his father's heart attack that he stopped doing it regularly. Yes, he would definitely tell Janice about that, if she agreed to have lunch with him.

Inviting her wasn't as easy as Vince had hoped. He hesitated on the phone until he could sense Janice beginning to get exasperated, then blurted it out. She surprised him by suggesting they meet in an hour and a half during her lunch break. But this was said in such a casual way, as if he were her college roommate, that he felt deflated and wondered if she wanted him to know that in her mind this meeting had absolutely no romantic potential.

He remembered thinking there was no time to indulge such worries, no time for anything other than to shower, shampoo, and get dressed. He decided to wear a blue shirt, because his mother had always said it set off his blue eyes to great advantage, and having decided that much, he continued to pick blue as the color of his jeans and sports jacket.

He felt that he was racing too much, getting too nervous, so he stopped and gazed at the park for a moment from his bedroom window. It looked wise under the full sun. "That's where it all began," Vince said to himself. Then he left for the Greek-style diner that she'd suggested. She couldn't have picked a more pedestrian place but he tried not to interpret that as a bad sign. He had to stay strong and positive and reassure himself. At least I'm tall, he thought, as he approached the door of the restaurant, and that's almost always something. And wasn't it also true that he was intelligent and relatively well-read and, for now, financially independent, and that he had slept with a number of attractive women? The problem there had been his always wanting it to lead to something emotionally important and his pressing for that goal too quickly. His parents had told him that even geniuses don't matter much unless their gift helps or sustains people in a lasting way, and Vince felt the same about relationships. He made a mental note not to demand too much of Janice too fast, were he lucky enough to get involved with her.

She arrived a few minutes later, in a shortish black dress with gold hoop earrings and a matching necklace. She looked smart—she always looked smart and acted calm. She didn't seem to be the slightest bit nervous as she slid into the booth the way she slid into her swivel chair at work. He noticed, too, that she spoke to him in the same voice she used on the agency phone. Was she still thinking of him as a client, and of this as some kind of business lunch? He closed his eyes for a moment and concentrated on the image of her he had seen in the park when she appeared as an Eve-like figure of destiny in his life. When he opened his eyes she had a puzzled look on her face and he wondered how long his eyes had been closed. "Is something the matter?" she asked.

Vince felt nonplused. He had to explain but how could he without lying? He said he'd been visualizing part of Forest Park because it made him feel good to do that.

"Are you a nature lover?" she said, still in her pleasant professional voice. Her Greek salad had arrived and she was already eating it in a perfectly relaxed way, whereas he felt befuddled by his Gyro plate and wished he had ordered something easier to eat. "Do you know the names of the different trees and flowers and what not?"

"Some of them, not many. That's not really why I go to the park." She raised her eyebrows as if still puzzled, and he explained that he went to the park to get ideas.

"What kind of ideas?" she said.

"Ideas and...feelings about myself and life in general, and how I fit into it. That's what the park gives me."

She momentarily looked away. and he began thinking it might all be over with her, all be vanishing as her image did that day in the park.

Suddenly she turned toward him and looked him straight in the eyes. "I know what you mean about wanting to know how to fit into life. When I first started working in the agency, I couldn't stop flying."

For a moment he thought she knew how to fly like a bird or an angel, but she meant traveling in planes, of course. It began with her trying to take advantage of her reduced employee rates by flying a lot to the Caribbean but continued because she was lonely then and traveling was something to do that could give her life structure. "That's what I thought you were doing, too, when you kept buying plane tickets."

"I did that before I really discovered the park...but I used to do something else to give myself structure," he said, and then began telling her about the genius hour.

She followed him closely with her eyes while he spoke, which made him feel oddly important, then looked unusually animated when she answered him. "That's really neat the way they wanted you to develop your mind and all, and the way you stuck with it. Maybe you should keep doing it. I mean, why stop?"

Vince looked at her closely, himself, and felt transfixed.

"Would you consider the park? Would you consider going there with me sometime and just seeing what happens?"

"Thanks, that sounds nice, but I'm just so busy lately."

"I know it sounds a little odd. I know there's always a resistance to trying new things that we have to overcome, but believe me the rewards are immeasurable. There's a wonderful world in the park, a magical world where you can transcend the normal fog we walk around in, and pierce through to a different level of perception. There's a..."

"There's something else," she said, cutting him off. "There's a special guy in my life and he might have trouble understanding why I'd go to the park with you, you know? See, I spend almost all my free time with him."

"I see."

He felt a pressure shoot up near his eyes, stopping perhaps a quarter inch from his eyeballs. It was all he could do not to scream. Somehow, five minutes later, after she'd finished her pecan pie, he walked her back to the agency. He could scarcely feel his feet, while a pins-and-needles sensation was resonating everywhere in his body, as if it had replaced his blood and flesh and he was all discordant nerve now.

She didn't comment on the way he walked or looked, but he turned his head away slightly so she wouldn't get a direct view of his eyes. He said good-bye and turned into an almost blinding sun streaming directly at him as he started to walk home.

So she had someone else. He'd never had a chance then. He stopped walking around his living room and sat down on the sofa, so lost in thought he barely noticed the park, though it was shimmering under the full sun. Then he got up from the sofa. What if she merely said she had a boyfriend just to get rid of him. Was that possible? Foolish to wonder about that now, though. Either way, she'd made it clear she wanted little to do with him. And was there such a great wonder there? He was tall (sometimes in the park he felt like a tree himself) which would be good for a tall woman, but she wasn't tall. Besides his height there was probably nothing outstanding about his appearance. His mother had loved his blue eyes and told him he was handsome, but that hardly meant other people thought so. The women he'd slept with had not said as much as he wanted (though he always yearned for a lot, he knew), and when they did he couldn't tell if they were merely flattering him. He could believe only in his parents' praise, but paradoxically, that was why you could also grow to distrust your parents. For what did their love do but paint a false or distorted picture of the world, since no one else would ever love you half, or a quarter, as much. And what was the purpose of this great early love in your life if they were going to die while you were still young, as his parents had before he was thirty? How was he to fill up all the years that were left him?

He was glad when the dark came. He was glad when he could lie in his bed and close his eyes at last and let sleep come. He fell asleep easily enough, but woke up with a jolt at 2:30 in the morning. It was as if he had been dreaming a long, puzzle-like dream and had woken up with the knowledge of the final piece. His lunch with Janice had not been in vain. The purpose of meeting her was not simply his own humiliation and defeat—far from it! Instead, it was that she might tell him, as she had during lunch, to resume the genius hour. That she should be so emphatic about its value and the importance of his returning to it instead of the park, which she scarcely mentioned, that she should say to him, "Why ever stop?" Why indeed? Stopping the genius hour was the worst thing he had ever done to himself, and now this message was sent through Janice, as if by some higher force, to set him back on the right path.

Tears came to his eyes as he thought about why he *had* stopped. In essence, he hadn't thought he could do the genius hour without his father being alive. It seemed to be something that was so connected to his parents that, when one of them died, the spell was broken and he lacked the will to continue. Then after his mother died, his will to do it left him completely. It was a step he was incapable of taking, but now a step he suddenly needed to take again.

How much time had he lost? It hadn't been part of his daily life for at least five years. Well, now that he wasn't working, now that he had the time and money for at least a year before he would have to work, he'd spend six genius hours a day, everyday, to make up for the lost years.

He began turning on all the lights in his apartment. He hardly knew where to start. Finally he decided to continue where he thought he'd left off, by finishing *The World as Will and Representation* by Schopenhauer, which he'd abandoned around page 100 five years ago, just after his father's heart attack. Certainly it wasn't easy reading (he had forgotten, for example, what the "Principle of Sufficient Reason" was), yet his concentration was so unusually intense that he was able to understand most of what he was reading and to read for two straight hours before he felt the need to stop.

After Schopenhauer, he listened to three of Bach's unaccompanied cello suites, then to Mahler's "Das Lied von der Erde," whose haunting finale seemed to recreate in musical terms the experience of dying. He grieved for his parents, then, seemed to see them smiling at him in the sunrise's silver-white points of light. After that he fell asleep, but resumed reading Schopenhauer after lunch in his kitchen until he reached his six hours. He repeated the routine of reading, music, and reading for the next two weeks, always pushing himself until he finished his hours.

Meanwhile, the leaves were still mostly out and full of color, but he'd stopped going to the park. He seldom even looked at it through his windows. It was as if one night it had gotten up and moved away from him, so that when he did look now the park seemed to be quite far away. Only occasionally would he wonder why he didn't go there anymore, and when he did, the reasons came to him quickly. If the park had a purpose, it was to lead him to Janice, whose purpose, in turn, had been to lead him back to the genius hour. That purpose had been served. Moreover, it hurt him to remember the look on her face when he told her about the park and finally her rejection when he asked her to go there with him. Perhaps in addition to telling him to resume the genius hour, she was also trying to tell him to stop putting his faith in the park. To move on. What had the park really ever done for him? The park didn't love or educate him, the way his parents had, the way the genius hour was doing now.

It seemed easy not to think of the park, but at night he couldn't help dreaming about it. He might read all day, but at night he dreamed about the park. He would be on the bench by the pond, or walking deeper into the forest with the bright leaves blowing around him. Sometimes one of his parents would be with him. In one dream both of them were sitting on the bench laughing at a dog that was doing tricks in the pond. Whenever he had such dreams they would make him think much more about the park than he wanted to the next day. One afternoon while he was reading he found he couldn't stop looking at the park through the living room windows, until finally he got up from his chair and pulled down the venetian blinds. Then he pulled the blinds shut in each of his other two rooms. There had been way too much light in his apartment, anyway. Now with a few flicks of his wrist he could keep the park out almost completely.

But that night, he had his most powerful dream yet of the park. He was walking in the woods when he heard his mother's voice calling from a field up ahead. "We're here," she said, referring to herself and his father. "We're here." It was so strong a dream that when it was over it seemed to pull him out of bed, until the next thing he knew he had put his clothes on and was walking past the quizzical-looking doorman, across the street toward the park.

It was almost completely dark, except for the half moon, and there were hardly any cars on the highway. He knew he should walk slowly to avoid falling but he could hardly keep from hurrying, moving as much by memory as by sight, while trying to keep alive the sound of his mother's voice in his mind.

There was a field near the pond, above and to the left of it, which he had sometimes walked through. Of course there were several—perhaps many—fields in the park, but it would make sense for his parents to choose the one nearest his favorite spot in the park if there were going to be any sort of meeting or communion. Besides, it would be impossible for him to find, much less explore, the other fields tonight.

He was walking through a clearing toward the bridge that led to the pond, when he heard a rustling sound. The shock of it made him stumble and almost fall. He stood still and, looking toward his right, heard, then half-saw, someone walking his dog and talking to it. It was a man with a flashlight (which Vince wished he, himself, had taken), very possibly someone from his building. It surprised Vince that he was not alone, that other people, even at 4:00 in the morning, were also in the park. He stared in the direction of the man (who had been keeping a steady stream of chatter going at the dog) until his voice faded away. Then slowly, vigilantly, Vince crossed the bridge that hung over the highway. Stepping off it, he slipped and fell to one knee near a rock, his hands pressing against the leaf-covered ground. He got up slowly, checked to hear his mother's voice, then kept walking. Somewhere up ahead was his bench, where he yearned to rest for awhile. He took a few more steps, then saw the moonlight reflected on the water. With the pond in sight, he knew his bench was near; in fact, he appeared to be walking directly toward it. It was only when it seemed no more than a few yards away that he realized there were people on it who were having some form of sex. One appeared to be seated on the bench, the other standing. It was probably two men, but he couldn't be sure, their genders being erased in the dark. Vince began backpedaling, then turned around. "It's a good thing I saw that dog walker earlier or I would have been really startled," he thought, and it was a good thing in a way that the bench was occupied, since his purpose was to go to the field and he really had no time for rest or diversion.

    He walked more quickly then. The voice was beginning to fade and he wanted to still be hearing it when he reached the field. The clearing grew wider, the moon more visible. He could feel the ground become smoother under his feet and knew he was finally in the field. At first he circled and walked across it several times. It was very quiet. There was no sign. He sat down in what he imagined was the center of the field and waited. The ground was cold and slightly wet and Vince closed his eyes tightly to recapture the sense of his dream and his mother's voice.

    Once, while he sat, he almost felt the ground give way and open up, could almost feel himself tunneling down to where his parents were waiting to embrace him in a world of light below the earth. But it didn't happen. There were always signs like the feel and smell of the wet, bumpy ground that reminded him he had gone nowhere.

    Sometime later, he gave up and began to walk toward his apartment. "So that's the park," Vince thought, "a place where dogs shit, people screw, and the dead make false promises to rejoin the living."

    Still, when he was back in his room, in the half light of early morning, he missed the park and wished he had been there when he could have seen it in the daylight. After all, he had gone there on a mission filled with desperate hope. He shouldn't judge the park too harshly in light of those conditions. The park, itself, was not to blame, nor was there any point in trying not to see the park if he still saw it in his dreams. No point in keeping his blinds shut either and walking with his head down if he *thought* about the park while he was walking. It would be better to acknowledge it, to even walk through it every now and then, as he had an hour ago, as long as he divested it of its former significance. Yes, the key was not to believe that it had any special powers. The key was to simply let it be a park.

Twenty minutes later he got out of bed and opened the blinds in his bedroom, then in the living room and study. The park looked as it did in his dreams—immense, serene, and, under the pebble-pink patches in the early morning sky, slightly mysterious. He thought he would go to it after eating breakfast, perhaps before all the dogs and dog walkers got there. Later, thinking about the park so much, he had trouble reading Schopenhauer. He kept rereading the same paragraph, which no longer made any sense to him. In his mind he heard again, though faintly, his mother's voice from his last dream—"We're here. We're here." Then he grabbed his jacket and left his apartment, not even remembering to lock his door.

The elevator stopped three times before it reached the lobby. Four people got on. They seemed to ignore him but small-talked with each other. Small matter; he yearned to get to the park and hoped for no more delays. The doorman was not at his desk in the lobby as Vince walked as briskly as he could toward the door, nearly bumping into an elderly lady with a large bag of groceries who was standing outside the building by the doorway. She looked at him with slightly stunned, saucer eyes. He apologized, then realized she was waiting for the doorman to help her with her overly full grocery bag.

"Would you like some help with that bag?" he said. It wouldn't kill him to help this poor woman for a minute. She looked at him doubtfully. It had been a long time, if ever, since Vince had seen a person with such a vulnerable expression. Perhaps he had had such an expression in his eyes when he first met Janice for lunch and it had scared her away.

"Oh thank you, so much. That's very kind of you. I'm afraid my shopping cart broke down...I wonder where Walter is," she said, referring to the doorman.

Vince opened the door, picked up the bag, and carried it to the elevator. It occurred to him that it would still be difficult for her to carry it into her apartment. The woman was so small and frail, and at least seventy years old. Now that she had opened her navy blue coat she was even skinnier than he realized. He asked her if he could bring the bundle to her apartment and she thanked him profusely and told him she lived on the eleventh floor—one floor above him.

"I wonder why I haven't seen you before," he said to her in the elevator. Her eyes were friendly looking now, he decided. They were warm and blue.

"I don't get out much, but I've seen you. You always looked like you were thinking about something."

"I guess I was."

The elevator door opened and he walked her to the door.

"Could I bring it in for you?"

"Why, thank you. You're being very nice," she said, fidgeting with her key. "Would you like a cup of tea?"

"Yes, thanks, I'd like that." He set the bundle down on the counter by her sink and began unpacking it and putting the perishables in her refrigerator. When he was finished, she thanked him again and invited him to sit at the table in her living room. Her apartment was filled with rose and green furniture and paintings. They were ordinary enough colors on the one hand, yet heavenly in a way because they were so appropriate to her life. He thought he could feel a part of her life in each piece of furniture. Her table was in the same place as his was, just in front of her long counter top. He noticed that her living room window also faced the park and turning his head he looked at it briefly. It was just a park. A pretty, though muted-looking, group of trees now that most of their leaves had fallen and their color gone. He sat down with his back to it. He was vaguely aware that he was smiling. The woman was wearing a blue dress that matched her coat and was smiling at him, too, as she brought in the tea and cookies.

"Well, we're here," she said. "I hope you like oatmeal cookies. I made them yesterday."

"Thanks, I do. I haven't had any homemade food in a long time."

She looked concerned for a moment. "Really? Well that's a shame. You're such a kind young man to help me the way you did. My name's Gertrude," she said, extending her skinny arm to shake hands with him.

He felt he was feeling the touch of destiny at last.

"I'm Vince," he said, smiling widely now and grasping her small hand in his.

CITY MAP
by Daniel Stolar

I turn left out of Kingsbury Place, through the turn-of-the-century stone gates, and head north on Union. Soon I cross Delmar, and the change in scenery indicates the line in St. Louis's social geography which I have just crossed. There is a flatness to the streetscape, a two-dimensionality to the buildings which front Union north of Delmar, an absence of lawns, a proliferation of liquor stores and drive-thru's. There are groups of black men hovering on corners, front stoops. Further north, I turn right on Natural Bridge, then left on Shreve and right on San Francisco. From the time I was born until I turned sixteen I rode with my mother and sister to take Lillie home. Since I have been able to drive, I have taken her home myself.

Often, I go inside and sit downstairs in the two family flat where Lillie lives, visiting with Janice, her daughter, and Gemila, her baby granddaughter. The entry hall slants to the far corner where a yellow box of mouse poison spills out its grey pellets. There is a proud, dusty display of glassware in the armoir. The kitchen beyond is a dank and close place. It is wallpapered halfway around where Lillie's son James left it unfinished fifteen years ago. The wallpaper ends in a vertical line, the end of one day's work to be taken up the next. The exposed wall is gray cement with a jagged crack running diagonally like a scar across it. In twenty-seven years, I have never seen the upstairs of Lillie's house.

I know this drive as well as I know anything. If we could somehow tease apart the neuronal connections which let us know what we know, the map of this drive would be found in thick relief on my brain, a part of me. In fact, the whole neighborhood around Kingsbury Place and the house where I grew up (and where my father still lives) has a history which is tangled inseparably with my own personal history: my father was alderman of the 25th ward for four years; my mother succeeded him and held the post for eight years after that. For twelve years the battles of the old 25th ward were my dinnertime introduction to the adult world. It was a ward of both the best and worst-urban St. Louis could offer: a unique pocket of majestic 1904 World's Fair Era private streets, dismal boarded-up slums and tenements, a chunk of the second largest urban park in the country, a street of fledgling cafes and boutiques. A ward of subtle and not-so-subtle boundary lines between white and black, safe and dangerous, developing and forgotten. And it was a ward which experienced unparalleled growth during my parents' time in office—regentrification, rehabilitation, redevelopment—for which both my parents, and particularly my mother, received a handsome amount of credit and local celebrity. Into this ward, into our home, Lillie came three times a week from her home in the heart of Black North St. Louis, a part of the city which otherwise I probably never would have known existed.

• • •

I was raised, in large part, by Lillie Bausley. I have played at giving her titles—maid, housekeeper, nanny, even good-friend-of-the-family, or adopted aunt, surrogate mother—in my inability to explain her role in my life and my embarassment about it. But these are not titles which clarify. In their very inadequacy, they point to the underlying cliche. It is a cliche colored perhaps with racist underpinnings and assumptions: Jewish white boy and girl raised in a tiny pocket of inner-city private streets surrounded by black slums, raised by professional parents with a black maid coming Monday, Tuesday, and Friday, and whenever my parents were on vacation. She was hired a week before I was born and works for my family to this day. And, cliché as it may be, there can be little doubt that there are only a handful of people on this earth with whom I have spent more time than I've spent with Lillie Bausley.

For the first twelve years of my life, Lillie's son James was also a fixture in our house. And even more, in my young imagination. He was like no one else I knew. Seven years older than I, he treated me inconsistently. Sometimes he would brush by without a word, his eyes fixed in the distance. But sometimes he would grab my hand in his and pull me to him to whisper in my ear. To me, he was eight feet tall, black as night, rippled with muscles. I remember the thick raised cheloid on his neck—mean and dangerous, dizzying. At the age of sixteen, he'd had a tryout with the baseball Cardinals; he was a catcher with a rifle arm, a year or two away, they told him. It was the same year he taught me to pitch.

When James was aloof, I felt painfully little and awkward, and, something more, I felt painfully white, as if this were a part of my awkwardness. He was all power and confidence striding into our kitchen twirling a toothpick in his mouth and I literally paled in comparison. But more often, he would call me "partner" as he pulled me to him and our kitchen became charged with his presence. I couldn't help but try to mimic his speech when we were together: "no" became "naw," "isn't" became "ain't;" I dropped words and conjugated verbs incorrectly.

Lillie will always tell the story of the time she went out back and tore a switch off the hedge "to get after" James and me. She tells the story as if this singular incident happened regularly, once a week, her putting us boys back in line and to this day, she'll threaten to do it again if I give her a hard time. But the truth was she indulged us. When my parents were away on vacation, I stayed up to all hours watching movies on television while Lillie dozed on the couch. If James was out of school, he would stay with us too. I stayed awake for the movie while they slept, their heads lolling slackjawed on the other's shoulder. Together, James and I could get away with murder.

James was her only son of four children, and though he looked the invincible part of a star highschool athlete, his life had been a precarious one. He had juvenile-onset diabetes, and on a couple of occasions had been near death in a diabetic coma. When he picked Lillie up at our house, he guided her gently to the car, two fingers and his thumb on her elbow, and Lillie, who needed no help walking, let herself be guided. When I think of their relationship, this is the image I see; it was the way they were with each other. None of this thought was conscious at the time, of course, but I could feel what they brought into my house: in a place as familiar as my own kitchen, they not only brought warmth, but the excitement—danger, even—of another world, a poor and black world which I heard about on the news, which I heard in James's slang and which I thought I saw in his hard, aloof walk. Sitting with them around the kitchen table, watching the afternoon soaps on TV, it was a world to which I was allowed the illusion of belonging.

• • •

The years 1978 and 1979 brought great, unwanted change to both my family and Lillie's. In the spring of 1978, when I was ten years old, my mother was diagnosed with breast cancer. Though she would live the remaining nine and a half years of her life mostly free of symptoms, she (and we) would never be free of the prognosis which accompanied her cancer, already present in four lymph nodes at the time of her mastectomy. We lived many of those years wondering if they would be her last.

A little more than a year later, in the summer of 1979, Mr. Jules Gordon, a middle-aged Jewish man, a fixture at the handball courts in Forest Park for over twenty years, was shot dead there as he stopped for a drink between games. It was a brutal, headline-making murder, occurring within the boundaries of my mother's ward. It was a murder which terrified and outraged all of us, not simply because of its proximity, but also because of its sheer gall: the black man who shot Mr. Gordon walked up to less than ten feet away from him in broad daylight with dozens of people watching, and shot him twice. There was another black man waiting behind the wheel of a car, and together the two men sped off. With plenty of witnesses to describe the make, model and license number of the car, the police needed only a couple of days to make the arrests. One of the men arrested was James Bausley; he drove the car. It is likely that he drove North on Union, past the gates to Kingsbury Place, across Delmar and back into North St. Louis—the same route I have taken myself so many times with Lillie.

The details of the following weeks and months, of James's trial and conviction are no longer clear to me nearly two decades later. There was no question that James was driving the car, and no question that the other man had pulled the trigger. Apparently robbery was his intent, though the eight dollars in Mr. Gordon's pocket and the hundred dollars in his car were untouched. What lay in doubt was James's intent. He testified that he did not know why his friend wanted to stop at the handball courts, that he did not know his friend was carrying a gun. James said that he drove away because he was scared. He said that a black teenage man in North St. Louis does not go to the police after being involved in a murder. A black teenage man does not seek out the police for anything, James said.

Eighteen years old, James was tried as an adult, and convicted of second degree murder. He was sentenced to ten years. With a call to the Lieutenant Governor of Missouri, a fellow Democrat and a member of our temple, my mother was able to ensure that James was imprisoned in a minimum security prison, instead of the maximum security penitentiary in Jefferson City. It was a small victory, but one we were proud of at the time—something, finally, that we could do.

More than anything, I remember the conversations I had with my mother during that time. (How I must have tormented her.) I knew James. He had hung around my house for as long as I could remember. He had taught me how to pitch—as a ten year old and for three or four years to come, it was my most prized ability. And, of course, I knew Lillie. I could not reconcile what I knew and what had happened. And so my twelve year-old mind stopped on this question: what, really, had James done? Yes, he drove the getaway car from a murder. Yes, he hid what he knew from the police. But did he want to kill that man? What did he think as he drove to the park that day, as he slowed the car and his friend got out? As his friend rushed back in and they sped away?

Over and over I asked my mother these questions. (I would not dare ask Lillie.) Did my mother believe James? Did she think he knew what his friend had planned? At the dinner table or traipsing into my parents' bedroom in the middle of the night, I asked her. For a time, my mother sidestepped my questions—somehow it wasn't the vital issue to her. Probably, more hardened to the city, she did not want to tell me what she really thought. We would never know the truth, I said incessantly, we would never know what James knew. Finally my mom settled on an answer: someday, she told me, we would know. If James was able to put his life together after prison in a good and moral way, if he was able to stay out of trouble, that would be our answer.

• • •

The black vote was one that my parents as liberal democrats depended on. The dynamics of urban black poverty, the tension of black and white relations, these were part and parcel of my parents' daily work. And there is no question in my mind that they felt themselves to be enlightened (as I confess to feel now) advocates of the poor and discriminated. I still believe—will always believe—that it was a cause to which they were truly dedicated. But it was a cause decidedly more likely to be met with frustration than success. A complex cause confounded endlessly by personal interest and human frailty, not to mention centuries of social, economic and political inequality. I imagine now that more often than not, my parents came home from City Hall convinced of the futility of their work, and that, even as they ate the dinner prepared by a black maid, they searched for ways to steel themselves against this futility.

I wonder at the role of innuendo at our supposedly liberal dinner table. Between them, my parents spent twelve years on the Board of Alderman, and a lifetime in the city, and I came to understand that this time in the trenches gave them license to make pronouncements which they would never have tolerated in their suburban peers. It was a sort of calloused conservatism born of the wounds of a raw and frustrated liberalism, still tender at its center. An "I've been there" conservatism, "I know how it is." Our dinner-table conversations were often heady and heated. How well I remember their gentle condescension: "It's good that you feel that way while you're young." And, etched permanently in my memory as a further point on this same continuum were the subtle suggestions that Lillie's lenience and indulgence—the same indulgence she always showed me when my parents were away—were somehow responsible for James's demise. What exactly was said? I am not sure. My parents would not dare suggest it openly—perhaps not even to themselves. "He should have been working," I may have heard at some point. "Major league baseball—that was a pipe dream. I don't know why she encouraged it." I could not swear to either of these quoted sentences, only to the felt truth of their implication. Something, somewhere had gone deathly wrong. And quietly, in the spaces between words, blame inevitably settled in around us on 59 Kingsbury Place.

• • •

"Come on, white boy, you ain't got a bad arm," James would say. "Focus on my glove." Like a Zen master, James would tell me to focus only on the details of the thing: his glove hovering over the bare spot of earth which served as our plate, the hard, cracked grip of the ball, its dry seams under my fingers. "Forget everything else," he would tell me, until, at last I could do it. There was only his glove, the ball, and my body moving smoothly through the wind-up he taught me: the step back, the kick, my weight flying forward, propelling my arm like a whip, my back bending into the pitch, a moment of glorious silence and frozen time when only the ball moved, and then the satisfying pop of the baseball hitting leather. Pitch after pitch, only this pop of ball in leather punctuated the hot stillness of those St. Louis summer days. Over and over, I brought my focus back to his glove, my target, like a mantra until everything else fell away and experience became purely sensory, purely experiential. Maybe in those moments of athletic Zen, we were able to play ball on some common field.

Ten years old, I had a flawless wind-up.

But what lay behind our pitching sessions in the parkway outside my house? Had Lillie asked him to play catch with me? Coerced him? Forced him to play with this geeky white kid seven years younger than him? I imagine now that this is the case, and I imagine furthermore that she did it partly out of pity for this skinny kid who spent his afternoons watching television and whose father's fatherly gifts were obvious earlier and later in life but not at this vulnerable age. (To this day my dad loves to tease me when I am watching baseball on television by asking me who's winning the Superbowl.) It is, indeed, a short leap to cynicism: was James teaching me to pitch nothing more than an extension of the servant-employer relationship his mother had with my parents? Was this childhood idol of mine, this mentor, merely working for me?

I think now that this is the question that I was really asking my mother. The reality of what had happened—of murder, of prison—shed new light on the afternoons sitting around my kitchen, the late nights watching television, the pitching sessions in the parkway. Suddenly, the utter inequality of our two worlds and the relationship between them was as clear, as boldly black and white, as the newspaper headline and underlying photograph of James in handcuffs. Here was truth irreducible, the subtext lain bare. (How well I can see that photograph to this day: his head lowered in shame, the thick scar on his neck as mean and expressive as his face was blank.) Now the enlightened talk of my liberal politician parents seemed nothing more than talk, hollow and false. The line between us and them was as solid and fixed as Delmar Boulevard.

I hardly dared to ask myself the questions which logically followed from those I asked my mother. If James had done it, if he had gone to the park that day with the intention of helping his friend kill Jules Gordon, what then? How was it possible? I imagined James gripping my hand, holding Lillie by the elbow. How could he be led to such brutality? What had happened on the streets of North St. Louis? Or, maybe, in the house at 59 Kingsbury Place? If, somehow, I could only believe that James had gone there innocently, unknowingly. Then maybe I could reconcile it all. It could happen to anybody, this mistake, this lack of judgment. I saw my own pale hands on the steering wheel of James's Cutlass. I felt the presence next to me of that other black man whose face I knew from the newspaper. I think now that this is what I so desperately wanted to believe. That James and I were not so different. That I too could have followed the path which took James to that place on that day.

• • •

Each day for years after James went to prison, I brought home a dollar's worth of change. I set it on my mantel and Lillie collected it every two weeks. In prison, she told me, you needed change for everything. At the time, I allowed myself to think that I was really helping out. Now, I realize, of course, that Lillie could have gotten change anywhere, that she took it for me. Every other week she left bills on my mantel and took my dimes, nickels and quarters to James in prison. It was my only connection to him. (I thought of the English class assignment of following the life of a penny, and I imagined my nickels, dimes and quarters, leaving my house on Kingsbury Place, taking the familiar drive into North St. Louis, then another longer drive and finally passing beyond the prison walls to James. I imagined them in James's hands, being traded for soda, food, cigarettes.) In exchange for my silver, Lillie brought me statistics from James's games in the prison baseball league. She scribbled the numbers on the back of an envelope—otherwise, she said, she would never remember "all that nonsense." James was tearing up the league, hitting homers and doubles, throwing out ten consecutive base-stealers at one point. Lillie always said that he asked after me, but he never returned the notes I sent with her and eventually I stopped writing.

Lillie continued to come Monday, Tuesday, Friday, just as I continued to make my way through school, summer camps, little league. Every other weekend Lillie visited her son in prison. And the new given of my life was that my mother was dying of cancer. It permeated our house. My mother continued to work—finishing law school during her second aldermanic term, leaving politics for a law practice and then, for the last two years of her life, returning to public office as the appointed director of Forest Park. But the cancer and, more importantly, the doomsday prognosis were ever-present in the countless chemotherapy and radiation treatments, the three major surgeries, the wigs and scarves and hats. I wouldn't dare leave dishes in the sink—not because my mom worked hard and deserved better, but because my mom had *cancer*.

On the most basic level, Lillie kept our household running smoothly as it suddenly became a thing of the utmost importance. But there was more. My mother took on an almost untouchable presence in our family—cancer having greatly upped the ante of disturbing her. If my sister and I needed last minute help with a term paper, or got in trouble at school or just came home grumpy, my mother would always be our last resort, the final defense. But short of crisis, we would no longer bother her. We went instead to my father or to each other. Or to Lillie, who was there three times a week sitting in the kitchen—her thick elbow on the table, her chin in hand—ready to talk, when we came home from school. She cooked our dinners and helped with math; she knew our friends by name; she told us that our mother was a strong woman, that she would keep fighting.

The question of James stayed lodged in my mind. Eventually, I stopped asking my mother. By now I knew her exasperated response: only his life after prison could really prove his innocence to us. (I realize now, how much she probably wanted to believe this herself.) And, as time passed, and the murder and conviction receded further into the past, the questions burned less fiercely. New routine developed, took precedence. Even as I depended more on Lillie daily, the questions about her son, and all that they stood for, faded.

But in the end, there would be no long moral life after prison for James to prove his innocence. Five years after he was convicted, a year shy of his probable release, he was stabbed to death in prison. Apparently another inmate tried to steal a small color television from him, there was a fight, and James was stabbed. I knew that television: I sat next to Lillie on the couch in our den as she picked it out of a catalogue. We had given it to her for Christmas. She, in turn, gave it to James.

• • •

I did not go to James's funeral. I cannot remember why. Recently, I asked my father and my sister and they are likewise at a loss to explain why I was not there. My father vaguely recalls taking the trip with my mother into North St. Louis to the funeral home during the wake. They went to see Lillie, he says, and she was not there when they went. In black communities, he explains still, it is customary to have a very long period of formal mourning, and nobody stays the entire time. I was sixteen years old and it was during a time shortly after my mother's cancer had reappeared in some new part of her body, a time when things looked particularly bad. But I know that this is at best a partial explanation for why I was not at this man's funeral.

At my mother's funeral, four years later, Lillie stood in the row behind me in United Hebrew Temple on Skinker Boulevard, the western boundary of Forest Park. The rabbi motioned over our heads to the doors of the Temple and invoked the image of that shining park beyond—at the time of her death, my mother was still the Director of Forest Park. Its restoration would be my mother's legacy, the rabbi said. Lillie squeezed my hand while the rabbi spoke. At the time of his death, James was serving a prison sentence for a murder committed in that park. Lillie's palm was warm and moist. Tears streamed down her face. She would tell me later that she was crying for both of us, as I was not yet able.

• • •

Lillie Bausley still works for my family. She is seventy-six years old and she comes only Mondays and Fridays now. She cooks dinner, washes the clothes and goes on a weekly grocery shopping trip. A professional maid service comes once a week to do what my father and step-mother call "the real cleaning." I still look for clues as to what exactly Lillie's role has been in my life. Yes, I love her. Yes, I have depended on and confided in her. But have I ever really known her? Have we ever met on equal ground? She flew to Boston with my family for my college graduation. On her own, she came to see me at medical school, clutching my mother's old flight bag as she came off the plane which terrified her. And when I visit St. Louis now as a young adult, she gets roughly the same amount of face-time as my three grandparents, more than my aunts, uncles and cousins, less than my father, sister and girlfriend.

We still sit around the kitchen talking. If my Dad and step-mother happen to be out of town, Lillie still stays at our house (she says she likes the peace and quiet) and I pretend to feel indulged as we sit up late watching movies. I cannot help but cringe as she calls me "my only boy, now."

Silent tears still fall down her face if we talk about James. She is peaceful as she talks, resolved. She has gone to the same church every Sunday for as long as I can remember (and with her, all of my outgrown clothes) and she has a religious fatalism which I can only envy. "It was his time," she says. "When God calls, there's nothing we can do. Everybody's got their time to go. Just like when God called your mother. Maybe if he'd have gotten out of that prison he'd be running the streets on crack. You know how them streets are where I live. All that matters is I know in my heart that he was a good boy. I never did howl and carry on at his funeral like all the rest."

• • •

My parents were responsible for the bike paths in Forest Park. The original loop, 6.2 miles around the perimeter was my father's idea during his aldermanic term; the later addition, slicing through the center of the park, my mother's. I ride or run or walk these paths with great pride. They are invariably crowded, and in St. Louis, they represent one of the most culturally and racially mixed assemblages of our population. Moving along these real-life manifestations of my parents' vision, I fall easily into reverie, the progress of my physical body symbolic of the metaphysical journey these paths afford me. The newer path invokes my mother in its every turn and twist. The original path, my father's, passes by the handball courts where James helped kill a man. They are paths that permit remembering and contemplation, but they seem to defy arrival. Surely there is symbolism in this unending series of loops and circles lain down for me by my parents.

No matter how I try to approach the subject now, I could never have arrived at the handball courts that afternoon. It never, ever could have been me in the car with the black man who became a murderer that day. This is the real answer to the questions that lodged permanently in my twelve-year-old mind. The reality of living 24 hours a day in a black man's skin in North St. Louis is unimaginable to me. How could it be otherwise? Even as I pictured my own hands on James's steering wheel, I could not hear the conversation in the car. I could not feel the expression on his face or see the look in his friend's. The simple truth is that I can never know what was on James's mind that day as he drove to and from Forest Park.

But at my mother's funeral I hold Lillie's hand. She cries my tears. A cynic would deride this moment, this relationship. It is false, he would say, a servant-employer relationship, rich boy-poor woman relationship, what can you share? This logic is convincing, but wrong. At some point we do come together. It may not be a complete union but what union between people is? The lines dividing us are deep and complex. I may not go upstairs in Lillie's house, but I do come inside and sit a while.

Shopping Day
by Edmund de Chasca

Herbert Woolf worked in his apartment in the Central West End, so the weekly trip to the supermarket was an "out" as well as a necessity; just like walking his two small dogs, or going to the post office, or making the daily visit to the Schlafly Branch of the library to read the Wall Street Journal. He usually did not change clothes for the occasion. He did pause before the mirror in his bathroom, however, lit by a single dusty bulb, to make sure that his appearance showed the proper degree of neglect. It was fine to be unshaven for a day; two would not do. If he had not bathed recently, he would pat some cologne on his cheeks and neck. He might clip a few nostril hairs. Then, weather permitting, he would put on his leather jacket, stuffing his coupons and perhaps an old utility bill into the torn pocket. The jacket was scuffed and had lost its lustre, but when he put it on, it was possible to have an adventure.

He always went to the Schnuck's in Richmond Heights. The store was huge, the produce section alone as big as a schoolyard. He surveyed the rows of fruits and vegetables and was disappointed to find that his girlfriend was not working that day. She stocked the bins with such grace, her reddish-blonde hair gathered up behind her head. Still, here was a ripe brunette handling the heads of lettuce. Woolf smiled at her ever so slightly as she glanced up at him. The tiny black holes of her eyes swung away. He was undismayed and, indeed, his next encounter was more rewarding. He had blocked an aisle with his cart while picking out a zucchini squash. When he turned around, it gave him the opportunity to apologize profusely to a woman with a tight, gymnast's body waiting to get by. Her own denial was accompanied by a tense smile. Woolf backed up his cart gallantly, all aglow.

How beautiful the bins of fresh produce now seemed: plump oranges and grapefruits, pert lemons, stolid acorn squash, stocky cantaloupes, clownish bananas, exotic pineapples and coconuts, homely brussel sprouts, knobby potatoes, all declaring nature's abundance in subtle shades of gold, green and red. They gladdened his soul. They were his allies. Their juices flowed through him.

A rounded young woman passed. She sensed his joy and acknowledged him with a caress of her eyes. Woolf swooned with pleasure. He reached for a pineapple and inhaled the scent of its spiny leaves. Even though he never ate them, he threw the cone into his basket. Here was a matron leaning over whose flesh had spoiled, like an overripe banana. Woolf forgave her.

The two fish women were not worthy of his finest efforts and the deli workers tended to be an earnest lot. He had a girlfriend at the meat counter and she was on duty, as usual, on Thursday. He noticed that she had dyed her hair a darker red. He would compliment her on it after they chatted for a few minutes. He waited until she finished with an order, then slid up to the counter. She greeted him cheerfully—no change there—but two other customers were at his elbows before he could make any personal remarks. He had to restrain himself while she wrapped his pork chops and turkey wings.

He had much better luck at the bakery section. His "steady" was there, instructing a new worker. When he approached, he was introduced as a regular, and the new girl was told that they always had ready for him two loaves of unsliced buttercrust bread. Her teeth glistened and she turned her head at an excited angle. Woolf could tell that she adored him, and already looked ahead to next week when they could further their acquaintance.

He simpered down the aisles in his leather jacket, bargain hunting, scowling over his list. If his head was in the sale ad, he lifted it at the sound of another shopper. If it was a woman, he let their souls brush. It was a moderately successful day: three or four smiles, only two rebuffs, a few measured appraisals, one significant verbal exchange ("Excuse me's" did not count).

Saving frozen foods and refrigerated items for last, he pushed his cart toward the rear of the store. The section was relatively empty. A male stocker was putting up cartons of eggs; an old lady was attempting to read a label. The chill from the cases of products reached into a remote part of him. In spite of their bright packaging, the cylinders of ice cream and the boxes of frozen dinners appeared tired and still. He was ready to finish up and leave.

A whirring sound distracted him. A motorized wheel chair— a scooter, really—had come up beside him. The woman in it seemed small, almost a part of the chair. Her head was bent at an unnatural angle, like the broken stalk of a flower.

"Cayouh eech dere?" She lifted a loose arm and tried to point toward a shelf, but her arm shook.

She spoke again and this time the words were more distinct. Woolf attended closely to her. He saw shiny hair and a pleasant smile, but these traits seemed isolated, as if they belonged somewhere else, to womanhood in general, not to this disordered being whose flesh had lost its form. He tried to control his fear.

"Which one do you want?" She was pointing in the direction of the yogurt cups.

"Aad un." Again the arm attempted to lift itself.

Woolf removed a container of Yoplait Light and held it before her. "This?"

"Noowh!" she cried out with surprising vigor. Again she pointed. "Reyeh un. I ont ryeal one."

He removed a regular yogurt and handed it to her. Then she said something resembling "two" and he reached for another. She thanked him and her scooter whirred away.

Woolf chose a couple of "light" yogurt cups for himself. That thing—the woman in the wheelchair—had wanted a "real" one. He supposed she was entitled to the sugar and fat. What else did she have?

He patrolled the frozen food cases, but he had lost interest. He kept seeing the woman twisted in her chair, kept hearing her inhuman speech. When a housewife rumped by, he jerked his head automatically, but her flesh had no bite.

Back in the salty snack and soda section he revived. This part of the store was a carnival of bright party colors, unnatural reds, blues, and yellows, designed to cheer the shopper into a buying mood. Woolf seized a can of mixed nuts that were on sale, even though they weren't on his list, then grabbed a two-liter bottle of orange soda to go with it. He went an aisle over to the toilet paper. Even these aids for a lower function were given an agreeable appearance, with designer print rolls and pastel colors. By the time he picked up some spaghetti sauce, he was buoyant again. He perked at a youngish female who, in spite of a "generic" face, like the plain yellow boxes, had solid haunches. He beamed at a bosomy mother of two.

As he swung his cart toward the check out lines, he saw her again. She was seated in her chair with her basket of groceries at the end of a line, lower than the people ahead of her. Woolf instinctively headed toward the counter furthermost away. Then he noticed an almost perfect beauty in the line next to her. An idea struck him. He redirected his cart and stopped behind the disabled woman.

Her head flopped around and she recognized him. Woolf responded noisily to her grotesque smile. He held up his own yogurt cup, as if crediting her for giving him the notion to buy it. He stole a glance toward the next line. He had succeeded in arousing at least the mild interest of the beauty, and others were approving. The chair whirred forward, almost tunefully. Now she was alongside the counter and began, with her rubber bands of arms, to try to transfer the groceries from her basket onto the counter. Woolf leaned over. "May I be of help?"

"Huank oou." Her eyes sparkled.

With grand gestures, Woolf pulled her goods from the basket and placed them on the counter. He was a nurse, a minister, a social worker. Surely the others were observing him, noting how naturally such a kind deed came to him. "What a fine man," they were saying to themselves. He pictured his girlfriends in the produce, meat and bakery sections nodding their heads and pointing to him, as if they too were witnessing the scene.

The bagger tied her plastic bags with a knot and placed them in her basket. The woman whirred off. Woolf enjoyed the aftermath of his victory. He held his head high, as befitted a person surrounded with an aura. After he checked out, he lingered by the bench along the wall, studying his receipt. The woman with the classical profile was paying her bill now. She would pass by him and perhaps say, "I noticed how kind you were to that poor thing."

She glided by without a word, almost without a glance, then stopped at the customer service window. Woolf cursed under his breath. Some people were too cold to appreciate an act of kindness. But he would not let her spoil his hour. He unwrapped a candy bar and chewed off a large bite. He pushed his cart through the automatic doors, whistling a jaunty tune.

Outside, the disabled woman was stopped not far from him, her scooter half on and half off the sidewalk. One of her bags had spilled onto the pavement and she was struggling to pick it up. No one was around. To hell with it, Woolf thought. I've done enough for her already today. He struck a diagonal away from her toward his car. As he opened his trunk, he turned his back on her.

"Let me help you," a voice said. He swiveled his head. The beauty was picking up the groceries and placing them back in her basket. Bitterness filled his mouth. What a bad piece of luck! He might have figured she would be following him out. If he had helped this final time, she would have stopped. They might even have introduced themselves. Perhaps even now ... no, it was too late, for a van was pulling up by the curb.

A well-formed young man got out. At first, Woolf thought he was an attendant, but the van wasn't marked and he was not in any kind of uniform. He was thanking the woman who had helped. It might be the handicap's brother. He appeared clean and strong and Woolf envied him, for the beauty was obviously taken with him. She might offer to help his sister with her shopping some day. They would exchange telephone numbers. They chatted briefly, and then she left. The man opened the rear of the van and pulled down a ramp. He leaned down and kissed the disabled woman on the lips. Woolf could hear him distinctly.

"I'm sorry I'm late, darling. How was your shopping?"

He kissed her again, this time on the forehead, and tousled her shiny hair. Woolf caught a fleck of gold on his hand. Now he helped her up from her scooter. She held onto the edge of the van while he ran it up the ramp. Then she took her husband's arm and walked around to the other side. Woolf was astonished to see that she had a womanly form.

A sense of desolation came over him. He buttoned his leather jacket against the November chill. He could not account for the feeling, except that it grew out of a sense that the world had been unfair to him. He got into his car and sat there awhile. Finally, he started it up and left.

By the time he got home, it had passed. He thought of the new bakery girl and tried to remember her name. Not that he would call her by it next time. He would wait until the following week for that.

THE CAVES
by Michael Kahn
(from chapter 28 of Due Diligence)

St. Louis sits atop a thick bedrock of limestone. For hundreds of millions of years, surface water percolated through fissures in that bedrock and created a vast latticework of streams within the limestone, like arteries within a body. During the wetter millennia, the added water pressure drilled larger and ever larger tunnels through the rock. Gradually, those trickling streams became mighty underground rivers.

Then came the drier millennia. The water table dropped, the surface waters receded to the current channel of the Mississippi River, and the landscape became familiar. By the time New Orleans merchant Pierre Laclede and his fourteen-year-old stepson, Auguste Chouteau, clambered up the west bank of the Mississippi in 1764 to admire the fertile landscape spread before them, the underground rivers had long since run dry. On Valentine's Day, 1764, Pierre Laclede announced that he would erect a settlement on this good land—little realizing that this good land rested, like a massive green carpet, over an extraordinary network of cool limestone caves.

The caves of St. Louis were a provincial curiosity until Gottfried Duden arrived in St. Louis in 1822. Duden was, quite literally, an industrial scout, sent to America by various brewing and manufacturing concerns in the Rhineland who were looking for business opportunities in the New World. Back in the days before electric refrigeration, every brewer the world over dreamed of access to vast natural cooling cellars where the climate remained a dry, constant fifty-two degrees year-round—the perfect temperature for storing and fermenting beer. Accordingly, when Duden discovered what was spread out beneath the streets of that booming town along the Mississippi River, he immediately understood the opportunities it held for his German clients. I have found your Garden of Eden in the New World, he eagerly reported.

Within twenty years, St. Louis had become the largest beer-brewing center in North America. By 1860, there were more than forty breweries in St. Louis, most owned by German immigrants, each operating directly over a limestone cave. There was the Gast Brewery Cave and the Winkelmeyer Brewery Cave and the Clausman Brewery Cave and the Minnehaha Brewery Cave and the Cherokee Brewery Cave.

And then there were the celebrity caves.

There was the Bavarian Brewery Cave, which sat directly below Joseph Schneider's Bavarian Brewery on Pestalozzi Street. When the Bavarian Brewery went bankrupt in 1859, one of its major creditors, Eberhard Anheuser, bought the brewery and changed the company name to his name. A few years later, another German immigrant married Eberhard's beautiful daughter, Lilly. When old man Anheuser died, his son-in-law, Adolphus Busch, assumed control of the brewery and made one final addition to the company name.

And there was English Cave, nestled beneath Benton Park in south St. Louis. Used as a malt liquor brewery from 1826 to 1847, it was better known for the legend of the beautiful Indian maiden and her lover, who fled from the lecherous tribal chief and hid out in English Cave. The jealous chief posted a guard at the entrance to the cave to make sure she didn't escape. She didn't. The lovers died of starvation, and their skeletons were found wrapped in each other's arms. Or so went the legend.

And there was Uhrig's Cave, an underground saloon and nightclub near the corner of Washington and Jefferson, connected to Joseph and Ignatz Uhrig's brewery by a one-half-mile tunnel in which the brothers had installed a narrow-gauge railroad for movement of beer between the two locations. The brothers held concerts and plays in their converted cave and sold rides on the underground railroad. By the turn of the century, Uhrig's Cave was a prominent national entertainment spot and the site of the North American premières of The Mikado and Cavalleria Rusticana.

But of all the caves of St. Louis, none approaches the fabulous story of Gutmann Caverns. In 1846, a German immigrant named Gregor Gutmann purchased a cave near Gravois south of Chippewa. It was an ideal brewery cave. Fifty feet below ground with a constant temperature of fifty-two degrees, the caverns included an enormous main chamber with tunnels at either end, one of which connected to another large chamber that could serve as additional storage space for the enormous casks in which the Gutmann Special Lager would age.

Aboveground, Gutmann built his brewery at one end of the cave. As business expanded and his fortunes grew, he erected a huge family mansion above another portion of the cave. By the turn of the century, Gregor Gutmann's wealthy descendants had bricked and smoothed more than two hundred yards of the family portion of the cave and had installed a variety of opulent underground additions, including, among other things, a full ballroom, a swimming pool, a gymnasium, a miniature railroad, and a theater.

Alas, poor management and constant shareholder battles among the grandchildren mortally weakened the company during the early years of the twentieth century, and Prohibition sounded the death knell. The Gutmann Brewery ended in a liquidating receivership. The last St. Louis remnants of the Gutmann family were evicted from the mansion in 1932, and the structure was condemned two years later. All that remains of the three-story Gutmann Mansion are a series of stunning black-and-white photographs that hang in the main gallery of the Missouri Historical Society. The abandoned brewery building lingered on as a vacant eyesore until the city fathers, spurred into action by a newspaper campaign against urban blight, razed the structure in 1947 and converted part of the property, including the former mansion grounds, into a small city park named after Gregor Gutmann.

The old entrance to the brewery portion of the cave, which was just east of Gutmann Park, was used primarily as a neighborhood garbage dump until 1958. That's when a colorful local entrepreneur and history buff by the name of Mordecai Jacobs entered the picture. He purchased a parcel of property east of the park that included what the neighbors then called the Gutmann Dump.

Jacobs brought in a crew of men to clean out the rubbish and excavate the clay and gook that clogged the first fifty feet into the cave. To his delight, he discovered that the old storage channel was actually the front end of yet another large cave that meandered north and featured a dazzling variety of rooms of many sizes, each festooned with stalactites, stalagmites, and other formations. Even more incredible, two of the workmen exploring some of the smaller branches of the cave stumbled into a room that contained what appeared to be the bones of a large mammal. Jacobs was able to convince the Field Museum of Natural History in Chicago to send down a paleontological crew, which identified the find as a large saber-toothed cat. The crew spent six heavily publicized months in the cave and exhumed more than two thousand bones of prehistoric animals, including three full skeletons of an immense, long-extinct species of saber-toothed cat. As part of his deal with the Field Museum, Jacobs selected one of the skeletons and the museum reconstructed it in a ferocious attack position. Using the lighting director of the St. Louis Muny Opera, Jacobs dramatically spotlighted the skeleton in the original excavation chamber, which he renamed Saber Tooth Cemetery.

Jacobs had the soul of a carnival barker. He installed electric lights and advertised heavily, not only on local radio and television, but on billboards on every major highway within a 300-mile radius of St. Louis: COME SEE GUTMANN'S CAVERNS-THE EIGHTH WONDER OF THE WORLD! He lured them in from all over the country. During its brief but brilliant heyday, Gutmann Caverns was in the top ten of St. Louis tourist attractions, right up there with the zoo and the riverfront. A visit to Gutmann Caverns included guided tours of all the natural formations (with Satan's Waterfall as the highlight), the family portion of the cave, the beer storage process used by the brewery, and, of course, the Saber Tooth Cemetery.

Unfortunately, the reborn Gutmann Caverns lasted less than a decade. In 1965, the Highway Department purchased the aboveground portion as part of the parcel needed to construct a section of I-55. Gutmann Caverns closed on December 1, 1965, and highway construction began the following spring.

One normally would have assumed that the entrance had long since been sealed off, and perhaps it was. But given the recollections of Clara Jacobs' housekeeper, it was definitely worth a trip down to south St. Louis to search for a way into the cave.

We dressed optimistically, i.e., for cave exploration. I wore my running shoes and my jogging sweats—the closest I could come to appropriate attire given the grabbag of outfits Benny had selected for me. Flo put on jeans, a Kansas City Monarchs sweatshirt, and hiking boots. Benny had arrived wearing a Chicago Bulls T-shirt, baggy khakis, and high-top Converse All-Stars. Although the T-shirt wasn't warm enough for cave temperatures, he had a windbreaker in the trunk of his car.

On the drive toward south St. Louis, we stopped at a hardware store for a high-powered flashlight, plenty of fresh batteries, and the sorts of odds and ends that three rookie spelunkers thought might come in handy in a cave, including metal cutters, twenty-five feet of rope, several rolls of film for Flo's 35-millimeter camera, and a backpack in which to carry it all.

Flo drove while Benny and I tried to navigate from the backseat. I had a St. Louis street map open on my lap and Benny had the old cave map on his. We got onto Gravois and stayed with it past the Cherokee intersection. We went several more blocks, turned left at the light and weaved our way through several more intersections as the neighborhood changed from purely residential to a shabbier mix of bungalows, two-flats, and an occasional warehouse or storefront.

Flo slowed the car. "Here we are," she said.

There was a city park up ahead on the right. I looked down at the map for a moment and then back up. "You're right. Gutmann Park."

We peered at it through the windshield.

"Drive around it once," Benny said.

Gutmann Park was, by any standard, entirely unexceptional. It was a rectangle three blocks long and two blocks wide. There were two ball fields, each with a rusting backstop, and a half-court basketball blacktop with several bent and netless hoops. The picnic area consisted of three picnic tables, two metal grills, and a small shelter with restrooms in back. There was a playground with a set of clunky, old-fashioned equipment: swings, slides, jungle gym, merry-go-round. Unfortunately, the one thing we didn't see was a huge flashing red arrow with the message, "This Way to Cave Entrance."

The three of us got out of the car and walked the length and width of the park while Benny and I tried to coordinate the surface with the cave map. Although it was hard to be certain, since the map predated the park by at least a decade, it appeared that the cave ran directly beneath the middle of the park. We hadn't expected to stumble across an actual entrance, of course. Nevertheless, given that the Gutmann Mansion had stood roughly between the two ball fields, I had hoped to find some evidence, although faint, of what had once been. We moved carefully through the entire outfield, but found no sign of the mansion or the cave below. Just the patchy grass and weeds of a poorly maintained field. We even checked out both restrooms, but found nothing to suggest any subterranean access.

"Where was the other cave entrance?" Flo asked. "The one the brewery used?"

I checked the map, got my bearings, and pointed east. "A few blocks over."

Across the street from the park was a row of rundown bungalows. Visible beyond the bungalows were several warehouses and, rising above the warehouses to the right, the long, looping exit ramp off the highway.

We got back in the car. This time I sat in the passenger seat up front. As we drove toward the warehouses, I tried to trace our path on the cave map.

"Stop here," I said.

We were midway down a narrow street. There was a warehouse to our left and another to our right. Visible in the distance and slightly to the right was the descending curve of the exit ramp. The highway itself was beyond and above the tops of the warehouses. You could hear the sounds of cars and trucks rumbling along.

I got out of the car with both maps in my hands. I handed the cave map to Benny. Flo came around to study them with us.

"Nu?" Benny said, studying the street map.

I compared locations on Benny's map and mine. "Come on, guys." I walked toward the end of the block.

"Where are we?" Flo asked.

"Here," I said, pausing to point to the spot on the street map Benny was holding. "The tourist entrance was off Grolier Avenue." We were almost at the end of the block. I checked the cave map again, then the street map. "That means the entrance would have been—let's see—about a block further east."

We both looked up slowly.

"Shit," Benny groaned.

Exactly one block further east was the descending curve of the exit ramp. The ground beneath the entire length of the exit ramp was paved with broad concrete slabs. There wasn't even a hint of what had once been there. It was all covered by cold gray cement.

"Rats," I said in frustration. "It's gone."

"Not gone," Flo said. "Just covered."

"Great." I gave her a look. "Unless you have access to a twenty-man jackhammer crew, it's as good as gone."

We stared in silence.

"Come on," I finally said with a weary sigh. "Back to the drawing board."

The three of us walked slowly toward the car.

Benny paused as he opened the car door and looked around. "This area is the pits," he said. "Talk about urban decay."

I looked up at the warehouse across the street. It clearly was long abandoned: half of the windows were broken, and the rest were filthy. It looked like a rundown building out of a horror film. The sign above the door was battered and grimy. I squinted, trying to read it.

"What do you know," I said with surprise. I could barely make out the legend:

M. JACOBS & COMPANY, INC.

Flo turned to look at the sign. "How about that? Old Mordecai must have owned it."

We got in the car to leave, but as Flo started the engine I grabbed her arm.

"Wait."

She gave me a curious look and turned off the engine.

I pointed to the exit ramp in the distance. "If that's over the cave, then so is this warehouse."

"So?" Benny said.

I looked at him impatiently. "Think about it, Benny. If Mordecai Jacobs was storing business records in the cave even after the Highway Department sealed off the tourist entrance to Gutmann Caverns, then he had to have another access to the cave. Maybe that access was through his warehouse."

Flo looked at the warehouse and then back at me. "Let me see that cave map."

I handed it to her.

Benny leaned over to look, too. After a moment, he grumbled, "How do you read this goddam thing?"

"Here." I pointed to the area that appeared to be located below the exit ramp. "You see, the cave splits down there. One branch runs due north, the other runs northwest. Look at the position of the warehouse. It's due north."

They frowned at the map, and then Flo turned to stare up at the warehouse.

"You're not serious, are you?" Benny asked incredulously.

"It's worth a shot," I said.

Flo turned back and winked. "It sure is."

"Hold it," Benny said. "Are you saying you actually intend to go in there?"

I looked at Flo. She smiled at me and nodded. I turned to Benny. "Come on, stud. Let's do it."

"Jesus H. Christ, Rachel," he growled at me under his breath as we got out of the car," and you actually have the nerve to wonder why I prefer the company of bimbos."

In Remembrance of Terry A. Lawson
by Harry Jackson Jr.

I once watched a man die.

Not the hospice sort of death, a homicide sort of death that no one knew had happened—until the man died.

Once there was a bouncer in a gambling house in what was then a red light district in Gary, Indiana. I was a police reporter at the Post-Tribune, and covering the police beat meant deep investigation. I'd made points with a lot of the street cops and detectives—which was why I was in the building leaning against a wall watching everyone pretend this was a bar fight and not violence at an illegal casino. It was 1979 or 80 or something; gambling wasn't legal in Indiana then—at least not without secret permission.

The bouncer was an enormous man—maybe 400 pounds—fat folding from him like the Pillsbury Doughboy. He sat on a high stool and answered questions from the uniforms. Some little guy with a bad temper lost more than he could afford while playing dice on a hardwood floor. His temper tantrum got him thrown out, but not before the little bastard pulled a .22 short pistol and fired three or four shots as the bouncer slammed him around like a fisherman would do an unruly carp. The gun flew away and the sore loser landed in an alley.

The bouncer finished the story, got light-headed, blacked out and cascaded to the floor, so flabby that when he landed he sloshed.

An autopsy found one of the .22 short bullets had bored beneath a fold of fat and into a vital organ, the liver, I think. He bled inside and didn't feel the pain.

The word is that when you look into the face of a man who dies, you never forget him. I guess I'd spent too much time in the streets. I forgot the bouncer's face before bed that night.

The face I can't forget is Terry Lawson's. This day in the mid-80s I was on the exit interviews of a story to tell East St. Louis and St. Louis it had a street gang problem. I was on the story because I'd recognized the signs of organized street gang activity before the Metro East and St. Louis governments would admit they had a problem.

Terry Lawson was at the center. He was an angry man and he stood before me ranting. His age then was 21 or 23 or 19. He was angry because no one of proper breeding could understand the need for the Park Avenue Players, one of two street gangs on the law enforcement hit list. Politicians eventually found that admitting the problem meant photo opportunities and a chance for press conferences where they could talk tough about their own citizens and how they'd crush the problem.

The problem: Young black men were shooting each other, and sometimes innocent bystanders. Officials blamed drugs. Politicians saw the young men as weapons of mass distraction or photo opportunities and threw around the word "gangs" the same as they do now with the name al Qaeda. Police saw the young black men as nuisances with one—or two—solutions.

If they only knew.

Terry Lawson was one of those young black men. But guns and riches weren't his center. He saw himself as a sentinel. His guardians were the only line between safety and an evil force trying to invade East St. Louis. He thundered as he spoke to me while I sat in the front room of his drafty, rented home. He flung his arms about with Spartan ferocity. He pointed to his daughter, a sweet little girl, quiet, shyly clinging to her mother's arms, not trying to hide the healed-over eye, shot out by the enemy gang's bullet meant for her father.

Something about him made me gaze. I was taller, but I remember him as much taller than me. The muscles of his coal-black arms glistened from the sweat. They rippled like some sculpture from antiquity. He wore only a vest with no shirt and his washboard abs tightened as if modeling for a cologne maker.

Terry Lawson's Park Avenue Players saw themselves as the force stopping the insurgence of the Black Gangster Disciple Nation, a Chicago exporter of criminal organizations across the Midwest and a prototype for the groups such as the "Crips" and "Bloods" of Los Angeles.

I wrote about the St. Louis version; no one else had. No one wanted to admit St. Louis had a gang problem, least of all the people who were responsible for the conditions that spawned the gangs. I'd just arrived from Gary, Indiana, the only person who ever joined the *Post-Dispatch* and actually asked to work night police, 6 p.m. to 2 a.m. Tuesday through Saturday. Night police. Carnage. Lives of the night people. That was my specialty. I'd honed my skills and my nerve during a drug war in Gary, Indiana, the year it won the name, murder capitol of America. By the time I got to St. Louis, the faces of homicide victims didn't haunt me. My specialty was to go where other reporters didn't—or didn't want to go.

But the *Globe-Democrat* closed, the police beat was crowded and I was assigned to cover the Metro East below the bluffs, which was mostly East St. Louis and its suburbs.

That's how I met Terry Lawson, the man whose face I can't forget.

A few weeks of following these guys around gave me a deep respect for their principles, although their methods were upsetting. They were each a ticking bomb of indirection.

I never really knew how many young men belonged to the Park Avenue Players, only that Terry Lawson was the leader. He wasn't the largest or nose-to-nose the most fearsome. I'd heard of his legendary temper, but I never was afraid of him. I was awed by him.

But that's why he was the leader. Not the largest, not the most violent of his group, I'm not sure he could defeat every member of his group in hand-to-hand combat. But that's the nature of leadership. The Park Avenue Players followed his command. They once obeyed his command—I heard later—not to wreck me after I wrote the articles on East St. Louis' problems with street gangs.

His was the nature of leadership in the context of his community, hell, in any context. He knew what everyone knew but feared to say. The problem wasn't the gangs; the problem was the unaddressed poverty that spawned the gangs. Of course, those weren't the words he used, nor did he realize he knew.

"Gangs fighting for turf? What turf? The garbage cans, these old-assed houses and fucked-up streets?" His voice rose and the baby cried. "The cops ain't gonna do nothing. If it wasn't for us, the Gangsters would take over this city."

That was the man standing between me and the siege that had befallen his neighborhood. His neighborhood was called the Lansdowne district. I once wrote a story that quoted an alderman who called it a war zone because the violence had gotten so out of hand. Young men who thought they were at war died. Those who didn't die were maimed; others were scarred in much more heinous ways. Others to this day languish in prison, older men now, hopelessly paying for their boyhood pranks.

Terry Lawson might as well have been Hector defending the walls of Troy. He was the good; the Gangsters were the evil.

The East St. Louis auxiliary of the Gangsters had started when two East St. Louis youngsters returned from the youth prison in St. Charles, Illinois. They brought the Chicago tentacles with them, about the same time that I was learning East St. Louis and saw the emblems, codes and signs written in public bathrooms, on garage doors and on walls of vacant buildings. They were the exact emblems I'd seen before Gary, Indiana, became a war zone.

The star of David was in the middle of each vandalism. That was the emblem for the founder of the Black Gangster Disciple Nation. His name was David something, nicknamed King David, thus the star. Last I heard, he was either still in the Illinois State Penitentiary in Chester, Illinois, or had died there.

I needed to find out how the gang got into East St. Louis. The answer was prisons, child and adult prisons. Kids went in for stealing hubcaps, shoplifting, skipping school and came out officers in a crime syndicate.

A minister introduced me to Terry Lawson and his caretakers. For them, it wasn't about drugs, it wasn't about vice, it wasn't about guns. They fought for home, family and the sanctity of the land. None of Terry Lawson's regiment rode about in fancy cars like the black bad guys in the movies; they walked everywhere. No one wore fancy suits; they wore worn out sweat suits that hadn't been washed, seemingly for days. No one had lots of money to spread around and give to kids if they did their homework; they were broke. Their girlfriends and children were on Aid to Dependent Children. Their mothers were on welfare. Their children did without the things that made children happy.

These weren't thieves or extortionists or pushers. They were sentinels.

The Park Avenue Players pulled together once they saw the sadistic nature of the interloping Black Gangster Disciple Nation. The Gangsters violated the community ethic and broke the laws of the streets. Their members beat up old people to take their social security cash; they extorted money from school children and neighborhood stores, they dealt drugs on school sidewalks and killed those who dealt drugs without permission from the Gangsters. They intimidated innocent bystanders who had the misfortune to live in the midst of their mischief.

Terry Lawson and the Park Avenue Players would have nothing to do with it.

I couldn't write that because at that time at the Post I was a reporter. Reporters couldn't write the truth they realized; they wrote the facts they recorded. Someone had to say all this, and no one would.

Still, the scene that day in Terry Lawson's home was so stirring—almost like a Shakespearean soliloquy of a truth manufactured in a place even I had to struggle to understand. It was a logic that escaped me, but with a foundation more the stuff of Greek classical literature than newspaper fodder.

"They comin' in here from Chicago to take over, and all that stuff the cops are talking about ain't shit compared to what it will be like then. And ain't nobody else doing nothing!"

I wasn't as smart as I'd been or would be. Gary's street gangs weren't so introspective. So I asked the stupid question. "Could anything be done? What about jobs, to ..."

That's when I saw the face I can't forget.

This sinewed titan who in a different millennium would have competed with Achilles for ink, suddenly melted. His arms dropped to his side; the onyx upper arms softened to clay; the angry warrior became a child, the snarling teeth disappeared behind hopeful lips.

The room fell silent. The women stopped talking, the baby stopped crying, Terry Lawson's mother stopped chanting behind her son. They looked at me and I felt so useless for having asked a question that might stir hope. Terry Lawson's growled voice humbly pitched and cleared.

And Terry Lawson spoke.

"You got a job?"

I don't know what I said, but the answer was as stupid as my attempt at sociology. I just remember the intensity of his eyes. The slant of his eyebrows. He was no longer the commanding general as his expression begged me to say I might be able to help him find work. A job, so his child could dress better. A job, so his woman could buy cosmetics. A job, so his mom could prepare good food.

I was just a reporter. I had nothing to offer.

I guess he was used to that, the heat was gone, and, frankly, there was nothing left to discuss.

That episode probably was the last of the hardcore street reporting that I had held so dear for so many years. More and more I'd be called away because some politician wanted to make a promise in public that he had no intention of keeping when in office. I'd be the stenographer for something that relied on voters being naïve enough to believe.

No matter how I prodded, no politician ever addressed the issues of poverty, not the unemployment and certainly not the federal policy of ignoring communities hidden behind the pretty main streets so efficiently that the invisible citizens developed a culture apart from the mainstream; cultures that generated values, rules, truths, legends, language, rewards, consequences and heroes.

Despite Terry Lawson's mythic stature, he was, after all, human. Years ago, an enemy's bullet claimed his life in an argument about nothing, only a half block from his home, according to neighbors. Police knew he was dead, but provided few details.

I recall that Terry Lawson didn't read much. Ironically, that lack of literacy misdirected his anger. Lawson's downfall was his subculture's inability to grasp the real threat.

Lucky for America—if luck had anything to do with it. Had Terry Lawson and the other Terry Lawsons ever read the books and magazines that I'd read, the politicians had read, their organizations could have turned American cities into a bunch of Beiruts.

But they didn't. Instead, the young men, in their isolation, stole from each other. They sold drugs to each other. They killed each other. Until there was no one left to die. All that was left was a sad aesthetic.

The last contact I had with this story three or four years ago was when I ran across one of Terry Lawson's cousins. He'd been one of the junior members of the Park Avenue Players.

What was left of him was intoxicated, glassy-eyed and old beyond his years. He wasn't the soldier I'd met more than 10 years earlier. Instead he was a beggar. He begged for money for food and he told me he slept beneath the Eads Bridge. And he told me how Terry Lawson had died; how other members of the Park Avenue Players had died.

He was the end of the memory .

The men of the urban war zones had self-destructed. The

leaders of those days—those who lived through it—were neutralized by chemical weapons like crack cocaine, heroin, alcohol, sugar-shock cola, chips, cigarettes, marijuana; with germ warfare like HIV, hepatitis, VD; and psychological warfare like unemployment, underemployment, arrest warrants for child support, prisons. These tools had done more to quell the danger of angry, young black sentinels than all of the guns and tough talk the federal, state and local authorities could muster.

I gave the young cousin a few dollars and watched him stumble away. It was winter and he had to rush to claim a spot beneath the bridge, out of the wind.

Pete Gray
by James M. Huggins

"What's happened?" Helen was standing in the doorway to the hall. She had her dressing gown on and her hair was tousled from sleep. She looked irritable. Helen was ten years younger than Martin and very attractive when she wanted to be, but not so much at the moment.

"What do you mean?" Martin said.

"Whenever you make all that noise with the paper you're upset about something."

"I wasn't aware of that."

"So what happened?"

"Pete Gray died."

She studied the front of her gown, picked something off. "Am I supposed to know him?"

"No, I suppose not. He was before your time, I guess."

"Who was he?"

"A one-armed baseball player."

"Never mind," she said, and came over to get some of the paper that he'd finished reading.

"No, really. He played for the St. Louis Browns for a season back in 1945." She gave him the wry look that he'd learned meant trouble in the offing. Martin didn't want her to get angry over Pete. He wanted her to listen, to understand Pete had been someone important to him.

"He played center field, Helen, and I'd sit in the bleachers behind him. Kind of to the side a bit, so I could watch him handle the ball when it came to him."

"You think I'm a fool? It's impossible to play baseball with only one arm."

Helen stared at him a moment, her eyes narrowed, and then she went back into the hall toward the bedroom. Once Helen took a mindset on something the subject dead-ended. It had taken a couple of decades of quarrels for Martin to understand that, but he had it figured now. It didn't matter, he guessed. He'd almost always gone to ball games by himself back when Pete played and he could feel sorry for his passing alone, too.

Pete had been a wonder to watch. He snagged anything hit into his position. Then he'd tuck his glove under the stump of his right arm, palm the ball, and if a player were running, or trying to steal, he'd make the throw so straight and hard that even the catcher at home plate staggered at the impact. Pete batted one-armed too, and they never put a pinch hitter in for him. His bat would meet the ball with a crack that snapped about the park like a whip. The crowd would go nuts. Pete would be on first base before the roar could fade. He was fast.

It seemed that any power and talent that had been in his lost arm had piled into the arm he had left and more than doubled what it could have done. The obit said he'd batted 218 with six doubles and two triples scattered in among fifty-one hits. You couldn't watch Pete play baseball and doubt that all things are possible.

Martin put the paper down. He felt the loss of the man to an extent that surprised him. It came to him to send flowers, but he let that notion go. There was no point. It wouldn't mean anything to Pete, or to him.

Such things as flowers, and cards, and all the other things people give at times of loss seemed useless and a little maudlin to Martin. He favored making an appearance at such services with an empty-handed, straight forward, and sincere expression of sympathy for the bereaved, then leaving. But he hadn't considered what would serve when someone like Pete passed.

Pete had been a special person. Martin hated labels, and in this case what came to mind seemed kind of unmanly, but there was no alternative for the right word. Pete had been his hero.

Martin hadn't had many heroes, and from thinking about it, he got the notion that the few he felt that way about might all be dead now. That set him back. When he thought of them, he visualized them in action, not old and slow like him. He could see Pete scooping up the ball and making his throw. He couldn't see Pete any other way, but then they all had gone away somewhere and left him with memories of only their good stuff. Heroes get some distance when they begin to slip.

You don't get an invitation to their funeral either. Martin had seen people on television piling flowers and mementos at some public place to honor their heroes. Pete had died in Pennsylvania, a long way from St. Louis, and Martin wondered if the people there would make a pile of flowers for him. Martin watched for some mention of this in the paper and on TV that week, but nothing was reported.

Ralph and his wife, Phyllis, came over from next door on Saturday evening to play pinochle on a card table set up in the living room. Ralph was a baseball fan and Martin could hardly wait to talk to him about Pete. When they put the cards aside, while Helen and Phyllis went into the kitchen to get some snacks, he got onto the subject with Ralph.

Ralph said, "Yeah, I saw that. Tuesday's paper, wasn't it? I never heard of him before."

"You never heard of Pete Gray? Played center field for the Browns? Only had one arm?"

"Which arm?"

"The left. He was great with that arm."

"Didn't the Browns send a midget in to bat once?" Ralph laughed. "I'd liked to have seen that."

This reminded Martin that Ralph could be a dodo sometimes. "That's a whole different thing, Ralph. Pete was a legitimate baseball player. He was great."

"Paper said he only batted 218, Martin. That ain't so great."

"Aw no, he covered center like a rug. They wouldn't run against him, because of his throwing."

"Are you talking about that crippled ball player again, Martin?" Helen and Phyllis had come in from the kitchen with a tray of snacks and some beers. "You been moping around the house all week about that man. Can't you get it out of your mind? I'm tired of it. Grow up. Get over it."

"We're just talking baseball is all. Besides, I don't want to grow up."

"You don't want to grow up?" Helen looked at Phyllis as if to say: What did I tell you about him?

"I don't not want to feel bad about Pete."

"Want to say that again?"

Martin stared back at her, right into her eyes. "I want to feel bad about Pete's passing. He was a hell of a guy and I want to be sorry about it."

Ralph said, "I grew up on the East Coast and that's probably why I don't know anything about him."

"It doesn't matter," Helen said, "let's talk about something else."

Ralph looked at Martin. "You didn't read the morning paper, today?"

"Oh, good grief," Helen said. "I hid it from him."

"Ted Williams died," Ralph said.

Martin couldn't think what to say with the double bump of dealing with Helen having hidden the paper, and Williams' passing. He'd thought the deliveryman had missed his house again, and Ted Williams had seemed indestructible—he'd survived two wars. Martin had watched him on a sports channel just a week or so ago casting a big, white, feathery lure for bonefish off the Florida coast.

"I guess now you're going to jump off a building."

"No, Helen, of course not."

"Why not? Everybody's heard of Ted Williams. Paper said he might be the greatest hitter that ever lived. You got to give him his due."

Martin studied her for a moment, bewildered by her attitude. "Ted was a great player, Helen, one of the greatest ever, but it's not the same as Pete."

"I'll say, he's got a hugely better record."

"He played for Boston."

"You don't like Boston?"

Ralph said, "Phyllis and I were in Boston. The traffic is unbelievable. Isn't it Phyllis?"

Phyllis nodded and said, "Unbelievable."

"It doesn't have anything to do with Boston. And I am really sorry about Ted's passing, but he didn't play for St. Louis."

"I see, if they don't play for St. Louis you don't give a damn how good they are, or what happens to them."

"If they play for your hometown you get to see them a lot. You get feelings."

"Seems peculiar to me." Helen picked up the cards and began to shuffle them.

Ralph said, "I didn't like Boston."

Martin didn't say anything more about Pete that evening, or ever again. The more he thought about it the more convinced he became that heroes are private matters. You couldn't share them except by chance, and then maybe it would be different. It bothered him to think of Helen, or Ralph, having Pete for a hero. The loss of Pete, his sadness about that, was something he didn't want to share, nor could anyone take his place.

He didn't go to baseball games anymore. It was too expensive, and from where Martin sat the last time he went the play had reminded him of those video games his grandson stuck into his VCR when he came to visit. All the players looked the same and would catch, throw, and bat predictably. About the sixth inning, Martin had begun to hope for something unusual to happen, a brawl maybe, just a couple of clumsy roundhouse swings, or even a shirttail hanging out would have been something, but it was all very matter of fact, businesslike—robots at play. He couldn't remember the score, or who won. Summers had emptied out.

The middle of August, on a Monday evening, Helen came out of the house while Martin was washing the car in the driveway.

"Martin, they just said on TV that Enos Slaughter died. They said he was a baseball player in St. Louis. A really good one."

Martin didn't look around. He finished pushing the sponge about the hood of the car, then rinsed the dirt and soap off with the hose. "He was one of the greats," he said.

"Did he play for the Browns like that other guy?"

"St. Louis Cardinals. Left field. The Cardinals and Browns played in the same ball park though."

"Left field is out by the bleachers, isn't it?"

"Yes."

She went back into the house.

Martin went over and turned the water off. He let the hose and everything else lie where he'd dropped them and went around to the backyard. He sat down on one of the wrought iron patio chairs they'd inherited from Helen's folks. The sun had gotten about half down on the horizon and the mosquitoes would be swarming soon.

Martin could see Enos Slaughter coming at a run into left field from the dugout. Enos always ran to his position. He was known for that. The bleacher people cheered him on. They kept a close eye on him. Once in a while, when the manager turned away, Enos would toss a ball over his shoulder into the bleachers. Martin got one. It came right to him. He grabbed it and ran. Some of the bleacher guys would take a ball away from you if they could. Martin ran right out of the ballpark as fast as he could, and most of the way home, too.

The house was too small for him when he got there. His mother grabbed his arms and forced him to quiet down. He'd wrapped the ball in wax paper and hidden it his room, then got it out again and put a cloth around it so the wax wouldn't get on it. Then he'd hidden it in the attic, but later that day took it back. He might not have been able to get to it if there was a fire. He'd ended up putting it in a shoebox in his closet.

Martin still had the ball in that same shoebox. It was on the shelf in their bedroom closet. He'd get it out and look at it when he went inside. Maybe he'd show it to Helen, and tell her about Enos throwing it to him. Maybe. Maybe, he'd tell her.

The Christmas Canaries
by A. E. Hotchner

It was the year that General Hugh Johnson's NRA eagles first began to fly. No one we knew had a job, and our own family fortunes had dwindled so much that we were reduced to living in one room at the Hotel De Luxe, at the corner of Kingshighway and Delmar in St. Louis.

The hotel, like us, had seen much better days. The electric sign that ran vertically along the Delmar side never had more than half its letters lighted, and the glass canopy over the entrance was pocked with small, jagged holes. The hotel's main revenue came from the taxi-dance hall that occupied part of the basement and had its own entrance, over which was this big, blinking sign that always had all its letters in operation: GOOD-TIMES DANCE HALL. But I was twelve that year and my brother Selwyn was only seven, so we didn't care much about the dance hall.

But Selly understood about the trouble we were having. He understood how my father suffered over not being able to find work, and he knew how badly my mother felt that we boys had to sleep behind a screen and no longer had a room of our own. Selwyn had been boarded with an aunt in Keokuk for almost a year (my father paid two dollars a week for his keep), and he had just come back to live with us when we moved into the De Luxe.

My mother cooked for us on a two-burner hot plate which the rich Mrs. Minnie Rosenthal, who lived down the hall in 316, had given us in exchange for eating with us every Friday evening. Mrs. Rosenthal, who later became Aunt Minnie, was considered rich because she was the only one on our floor who was not behind in her rent. Every Friday after supper I would go with her to her room and play cards for an hour. We played rummy, and I discovered the second time we played that she cheated by dropping cards in her lap.

It disturbed me that she cheated, but after thinking it over I decided not to say anything about it, because I figured that it didn't harm anyone, since I didn't care if I won or lost (I always lost, naturally). Also, at the end of each card game, she would announce happily, "Well, looks like I've had a lucky run tonight," and then she'd fish in her purse and find a half dollar which was for Selly and me to go to the movies. She cheated very awkwardly, and sometimes it was hard for me not to see the cards in her hand being exchanged for the cards in her lap.

Our only real possessions (the hot plate, we felt, would have been immediately reclaimed by Aunt Minnie if we had defaulted on a Friday-night dinner) were our cabinet-model radio and our canary, Skippy—eleven years old. Skippy was still with us because pawnshops, at least in those days, would accept no items that required feeding. The radio had survived because its passing would have been a symbol to my father of complete surrender.

Skippy was a splendid canary. He could both chop and roll, which is pretty unusual for a canary, and he sang loud and clear even during his molting period. During the day, his cage was put in the window, but at night he slept with us behind the screen. Selwyn spent a lot of time talking with Skippy, and they were such good friends that Skippy would take food that my brother held in his lips.

One afternoon Selly came home from school highly excited. He said, "I've just been over to Billy Tyzzer's house—he lives in a *real* house! And guess what he's got in his basement—the whole basement! Canaries. He breeds them. He's got twenty cages, and he breeds them and sells them to Mr. Farley who runs the pet shop. And do you know what he gets for them?" I had never seen my brother so excited about anything, not even when he found a bone-handled boy scout knife in the gutter outside of the drugstore. "He gets five dollars each, that's what he gets. Five dollars! Why, just think how much money we can make! By Christmas we can have enough to buy everybody *real* presents. Oh, you should just see how easy it is!"

The previous Christmas there had been no money for real presents. Selwyn had cut pictures from the newspaper of the things he would have like to have given each of us and pasted them on pieces of paper. It worried him that the coming Christmas might have to be another pretend one. I hated to be realistic about his canary enthusiasm, but trying to breed canaries in that little hotel room did not seem like a very good idea to me and I told him so.

"If you're *with* me Mom will let us do it," he said, "and don't forget, I was with you when you wanted to collect cigar bands."

"But we don't have a female canary," I said. "What about that?"

"Oh, that's easy," he answered. "Females aren't worth anything because they don't sing, and Billy's going to give me one."

"But we'll need to buy special food and things, won't we? Where will we get the money?"

Selwyn hadn't thought of that, and he sat down heavily on the edge of the bed. But only for a moment. "I know," he said, bounding up, "the money Aunt Minnie gives us to go to the movies."

"I don't know about that. You know how funny Aunt Minnie is. She may not like us to use the money for that."

"Well, why does she have to know? We can just go off like we're going to the movies and stay away for a couple of hours, and she'll never know the difference."

I almost said that that was cheating, but then it occurred to me that cheating was just the way to spend Aunt Minnie's card money.

The last thing my mother wanted in that hotel room was a canary-breeding enterprise, but this was the first interest Selly had shown in anything since his return from Keokuk, and my mother was more concerned about that than anything else. She knew that Selwyn had been unhappy at being separated from the family, but she had been ill and it was the only thing we could do. Selly had been very withdrawn since his return, but this outburst over the canary-breeding market looked like he was ready to rejoin the family. Much as my mother did not want to add canary-breeding to her other worries, she consented.

Selwyn brought home a pamphlet on how to breed canaries that was put out by the Mrs. Finch Birdseed people, and we read it carefully many times. It itemized the things we would have to get: a nest, special nesting materials, a breeding cage, special kinds of food—which items, of course, were all for sale in shops that carried Mrs. Finch's products. Our problem was to find substitutes that did not cost anything. We found an old tea strainer that made an excellent nest, and pieces of cotton and flannel were every bit as good as the contents of Mrs. Finch's carton of Sterilized Nesting Materials. But the breeding cage was not so easy to come by. It had to be more than twice the size of the average cage. Selly and I tried to make one out of wood slats and screen, but Billy Tyzzer said it would not do because the birds would butt themselves on the screen and unfinished wood pieces.

Selwyn had made friends with Ben, the De Luxe's asthmatic bellhop, who lived in a room down in that section of the basement that was not occupied by the Good-Times Dance Hall. Selly told Ben about our breeding-cage problem, and Ben gave it some thought.

"Now, who could I have locked out who might have had a cage like that?" Ben wondered. He began to think of all the people whom he had locked out of their rooms over the past few years, for nonpayment of rent (which entitled the hotel to all the belongings captured in the room). "By golly," Ben said, "Ginelli the Great."

I happened to be down in Ben's room with Selly when Ben thought of Ginelli the Great, who, he explained, was a magician who was six months in arrears when Mr. Wormser, the owner, ordered Ben to padlock his room. "He wasn't even magical enough to open my lock," Ben said, "and it was just an ordinary cylinder lock." You could tell he had no use for Ginelli the Great. "Well, as I recall it, he had a bunch of white mice he used in his act, and he kept them all in a cage that was pretty much like you want. Come along."

He led us into the storage section of the basement and we spent an hour going through a strange collection of junk, but Ben finally spotted a trunk with Ginelli's name on it, and, sure enough, there was the white-mice cage, and it was perfect. We scrubbed it up and Martin, the janitor, painted it white for us. "We'll have to hurry," Selly said, "to get these birds borned and sold by Christmas."

It was very cold the day Selwyn got the female bird from Billy Tyzzer, and he carried her home in a little cardboard box that he buttoned up inside his shirt. She was a wonderful-looking bird, bigger than Skippy, and all gold. Skippy had half-moons of gray on his wings. Selly named the female Sooky, which had something to do with a comic strip that was very popular in those days, and he put her in the breeding cage by herself when he took her out from under his shirt.

We read Mrs. Finch's guide very carefully. *When the male is placed in the breeding cage with the female,* it said, *the birds may evince no interest in each other at first. However, eventually a conquest of the female by the male will occur, if the breeding process is to be successful.*

The time had come to start the enterprise which both of us were convinced was going to free us from the grip of the depression, and we were very nervous. We put Skippy's cage next to Sooky's, opened the two doors, prodded Skippy, and he flew into the breeding cage. We shut the door and watched breathlessly. Skippy went over to the feed cup and started to crack seed. Sooky hopped around on the bottom, sorting out good seeds from opened ones. They paid no attention to each other.

We took turns watching them all that afternoon and until

ten o'clock that night, but nothing happened. Not a thing. They might have been in separate cages for all the attention they paid each other. When we covered the cage and turned out the lights and got in bed, Selwyn said, mostly to himself, "He doesn't like her, that's what's wrong. Such a pretty female bird, and Skippy doesn't like her."

Three o'clock the following morning we were all suddenly waked up by a shrieking, whirring racket that could not possibly have emanated from two canary birds but did. Bits of feather were flying out of the cage. I rushed over to pull the cover off to see what was wrong, but Selly caught me by my pajama coat and pulled me back. "Don't touch it! Don't touch it!" he shoulded. "He's conquesting her! He's conquesting her!"

My father was halfway across the room, but he stopped, wagged his head at the two of us, turned out the light and got back in bed. We lay there in the dark, all four of us, listening to the noisy battle and wondering which bird, if either, would survive the night, when, as suddenly as it had started, the racket subsided and quiet descended on the room. There was not one sound from the cage, not a peep. Selwyn was right. Skippy had conquested her.

The male will shower attention on the female as she starts building the nest, Mrs. Finch's booklet read. *He will feed her and caress her. The female will take bits of the sterilized nesting materials* (hunks of flannel and cotton) *and weave them into the bottom of your Mrs. Finch's Nest Cup* (the old tea strainer from my mother's scrap bag)

Skippy and Sooky followed these directions as though they had read them, and as soon as the delicately constructed nest was completed, Sooky settled herself in and accepted most of her meals from Skippy's beak. Mrs. Finch advised us to watch for the eggs, usually four in number. . . .

Selwyn discovered the eggs one morning when he uncovered the cage, and he was so excited that he could hardly talk. There were four of them, just as Mrs. Finch had predicted, but as we stood there admiring them, Sooky deposited a fifth egg, and then to our amazement a sixth.

"How much is six times five?" Selwyn asked, breathlessly. It was more money than he had every heard of.

No wait in my life can compare with the torture of the twenty-one days it took for the eggs to hatch. Our impatience even affected our parents, who found themselves nervously watching the cage along with us. The morning of the twenty-first day, my brother and I woke up before dawn and set up a vigil. Mrs. Finch had warned that the father often treats the offspring cruelly, and we were going to have none of that.

But by nightfall the eggs showed no sign of cracking, nor did they the following day, and my brother was so despondent that he couldn't eat.

On the morning of the twenty-third day, at six o'clock, an unmistakable chirp brought Selwin and me bounding out of bed. Ecstatically we watched one baby bird after another poke through its thin shell. All six babies looked absolutely fit. We had been feeding Sooky Mrs. Finch's Rich All-Purpose Vitamin Tonic for Motherhood, and now we put other special foods into the cage. Despite Mrs. Finch's ominous warnings, Skippy was an admirable father, and he took his duties seriously.

Selwyn had already had several discussions with Mr. Farley at the pet store, and he confirmed the price Billy Tyzzer had put on the bird. Mr. Farley said he would buy the birds when they were six weeks old, and that they should be brought into the store on a Friday when Mr. Yamo made his rounds. Mr. Yamo was a Japanese who was an expert on the condition and sex of canaries.

Eight canaries are a lot of work; they make a lot of noise, they eat a lot of food, and when they start pulling one another's feathers out, they require separate cages. We put special Mrs. Finch drops in the babies' water, kep them supplied with fresh cuttlebones, lettuce and hunks of fruit, and somehow managed it all on Aunt Minnie's movie money. . . .

The time schedule worked out perfectly. The babies would be six weeks old on Friday, December 22nd, the very day Mr. Yamo came to the pet shop. Selly and I would then have the 23rd for shopping. Selwyn went over his Christmas list several times every day. He kept changing it and substituting new items, and he window-shopped a great deal. He kept asking my mother what she wanted most in the whole world, but she would never tell him anything specific, and he worried over what to give her.

There was no school on the 22nd, so Selly and I were at the pet store precisely at two o'clock, which was when Mr. Yamo was supposed to arrive. It was very cold, and we had put all six canaries in the breeding cage and wrapped the cage in our blankets. We put them on the counter in the pet shop, and Mr. Farley said they looked like fine healthy birds. Selwyn was very nervous.

Mr. Yamo came in at two fifteen. He was very small and smiled all the time. He took off his overcoat and hung it in the back of Mr. Farley's store, then he blew on his hands and rubbed them together. Mr. Farley showed him a parrot and some other birds he had at the back of the shop, and they talked quite a bit about them. My brother kept one arm curved around an end of our cage, protectively, and he never took his eyes off Mr. Yamo.

It was almost three o'clock by the time Mr. Yamo was ready to look at our birds. Mr. Farley put two empty cages on the counter next to ours. Mr. Yamo put his hand into our cage and expertly plucked one of the birds from its perch. He held the bird in his left hand, on its back, and he examined it carefully. I felt a terrible pang of sorrow at seeing the little bird leave our care. Mr. Yamo put the bird into one of the two empty cages and repeated the process until all six of the canaries were in one of the cages. The other cage remained empty.

I looked at my brother. His face was flushed with hope. Mr. Yamo reached over and patted him on the head. "They very nice birds," he said. "Very healthy. All females."

I did not grasp the import of what Mr. Yamo had said, but Selwyn did. The color drained out of his face, and he just stood there. Mr. Farley took Mr. Yamo to the back of the store, got his coat for him, and then walked him to the door. He stood at the door for a moment and then came back to us.

"Now that's a tough break," he said.

My brother had tears in his eyes, and I was embarrassed. "Aren't they worth anything?" Selwyn asked. "We can't take them back home. We only live in one room."

Mr. Farley rubbed his hand along the side of his face. "There's so little market for females..." he said. "They don't sing. Maybe I could give you a dollar for them."

"Is that all right with you?" Selwyn asked me in a very quiet voice. I said it was.

Mr. Farley rang up the NO SALE on his cash register and handed Selwyn a dollar bill. "I'm sorry it can't be more," he said.

"That's all right," Selwyn said, and now the tears were running along his cheeks, although he had his chin pulled up tight to stop them. He walked slowly toward the front door, with me right behind him carrying the empty cage and blanket. Next to the door was a wooden pen full of puppies of indeterminate antecedents, yipping and scratching. Selwyn bent over the rail and watched them, then he reached in and picked one up. It was round and very furry with a smear of black across one eye. It stuck out its quick pink tongue and licked Selly across the nose a couple of times. My brother pulled the puppy against his cheek and held him there for a moment. He turned and walked back to Mr. Farley.

"Would you trade me the puppy for the birds?" he asked, putting the dollar down on the counter.

Mr. Farley looked at him for a second and then at the puppy snuggled against his neck. "Sure," he said.

Outside it had started to snow. Selwyn tucked the puppy inside his overcoat and held him snug up against his chest. He walked along the whitening sidewalk, not talking, listening to the street-corner bells being rung by emaciated Santas, and the far-off sound of a Salvation Army band.

"I've thought of a name for him," my brother said, "but you'll think it's dumb."

"Let's hear it," I said.

He ducked his head inside his overcoat and snuggled the puppy. "I'd like to call him Christmas," he said.

"That's a good enough name," I said.

"Chris for short," my brother said.

The policeman at the corner came over to walk us across Kingshighway, and Selly showed him the puppy inside his overcoat. I happened to look at my brother as the policeman said what a handsome puppy that was, and I guess that's the proudest look I ever saw on anybody's face.

WINSTON CHURCHILL
by William Gass

Behold the friendless boy as he stands in the prow of the great steamboat Louisiana of a scorching summer morning, and looks with something of a nameless disgust on the chocolate waters of the Mississippi.
—The Crisis

If, in the 1940s, you went to visit the novelist in the small New Hampshire town to which he had retired, you had to promise in advance never to mention the name of that other Churchill, then so much in the news. But if, as reporters sometimes did, you went to visit anyway, you would likely find the novelist painting watercolors and smoking his pipe. Did he know the other Winston watercolored too? and swallowed much unhealthy smoke? Had he understood the overshadowing to come, he would not have run as the Progressive Party's candidate for governor of New Hampshire, which drew his doppelganger nearer, nor would he have allowed President Woodrow Wilson to use his grand old mansion as a summer White House, increasing the chances of confusion. Nor would he have been so interested in history his whole life, nor been so committed to political movements, nor would he have chosen to end his life as a neglected sage—an immensely popular writer the fickle populace finally tossed aside despite his triumphs.

The Churchills came from old New England stock, and it was a stock that Winston regularly inventoried. His great grandfather made a fortune in Cuban sugar and shipbuilding and was elected mayor of Portland, Maine, in 1844. His son Edwin, because his father could afford it, developed a taste for the good life, which passed, as such pleasant things usually do, easily into the character of Winston Churchill's father, an "Edward," to mark the small difference. Robert Schneider, Churchill's biographer, characterizes the father as spoiled, lazy and a proficient drinker, although handsome and charming as well. The latter qualities attracted one Emma Bell Blaine of St. Louis, though there is no mention in the record of how they met. After the couple's marriage, they planned to make their home in Portland; however, Mrs. Churchill preferred to have her first child "at home" in St. Louis, as many women did. Emma died (as all too often sadly happened) scarcely two weeks after Winston was born on November 10, 1871. He was only briefly in the care of the poor mother's mother, for she herself succumbed in two more years, whereupon Winston was taken in and raised by James and Louisa Blaine Gazzam, Emma's half-sister, in a house at 2810 Pine Street.

The child doubtless did not know he was brought up in genteel poverty, though he later thought of his foster father as saintly and his foster mother as a self-effacing Southern Puritan who believed in bearing life's trials (and life was surely nothing else) with cheerful fortitude and forbearance. Success was to be sought, but success lay in strength of character, not in simple social esteem or wealth. This type of triumph is harder to measure than most. Churchill wrote in an unpublished, third-person autobiography:

> The prospect of growing up a nobody, an unsuccessful man whom nobody thought much of, alarmed him. An unsuccessful man meant a poor man. Now his mother was far from a snob; her ambition was not that he should make a large fortune. She wanted to give him culture, and he inevitably connected culture with work; and work was doing something you didn't want to do, in order to be somebody you didn't want to be.

Guilt grew along with all his other inner organs. If Winston lied, played sick in order to avoid going to school, spent his streetcar money on candy, he fell into evil's endless pit, a hole down which no rescuer's ladder could be lowered. He felt that his mostly absent father was finally a fundamentally worthless person, self-indulgent and superficial, and later in life Churchill omitted his father from any mention as thoroughly as his father had omitted himself from his son's life. At the same time, his other relatives saw in the boy his father's looks and other traits, whose presence they did not fail to remark on.

When Winston was twelve his father suddenly called him to spend his summer vacation in Maine with his father's new bride (a widow who brought four kids of her own to the family), and although that stretch seems to have gone off well enough, it was enough, and Winston never saw his father again.

So in 1879, Churchill was enrolled in Smith Academy, a local private school, and he remained there until he graduated with honors in 1888. He was thought to be "a polite and elegant little fellow." A schoolmate, James Yeatman, who would become a well-known St. Louis philanthropist, described him as "a bright boy, a good boy and a frank, manly little fellow"; but he "was not precocious and gave no sign of possessing the talent which he . . . developed" after he grew up.

The Gazzams got Winston through private school, but they could not afford college, so when his schoolmates went east to finish their education, he remained in St. Louis where a job was secured for him as a clerk in a wholesale paper store.

Fortune smiled its wry smile. Churchill bumped into a boy who had been forced to give up his appointment to the Naval Academy on account of poor health. He immediately waited upon his congressman, F. G. Niedringhaus, and persuaded him to nominate the eager and articulate young man Winston appeared to be as a replacement. After all, Winston came from a shipbuilding family, had loved building balsa boats as a child, and was under the romantic spell of the sea.

Annapolis, however, stands on dry land; it is only near the ocean; and the academy's concerns were academic and military. Winston worked hard, and after ups and downs, which did not resemble the movement of the bounding main, he graduated thirteenth in his class. But he saw the navy as a place for time servers, which he did not wish to be. He had, in addition, "no aptitude for mathematics, mechanics, seamanship or fighting." Instead, Churchill had drifted almost imperceptibly into the world of the writer's profession—in his case, a world more workmanlike than literary. The editor of the *Army and Navy Journal* offered him the naval half of its editorship. It was a job that paid poorly but took little of his time.

He was immediately bored by this job, however, and unhappy with the reaction of his adopted family to his abandonment of a naval career, so when fortune smiled again, and *Century* magazine took a story, and then the new *Cosmopolitan* magazine offered him a position, he began to think seriously of marriage to a wealthy St. Louis woman, Mabel Harlakenden Hall, whose position in life much resembled his own, since she was also without parents and in the care of a guardian.

However, Churchill could not stomach the *Cosmo* staff, and now that he had married his wife's fortune, he could afford to be particular. Afterward, he never left his desk, except, of course, to travel or to walk around the grounds of his cottage on Lake George or his mansion in New England.

Churchill's first novel, *The Celebrity* (1898), a lightly seasoned satire, was followed by a child, a baby daughter whom they took to Baltimore while he worked on the background for his next book, a historical novel, *Richard Carvel* (1899), a commercial success that sent Churchill properly on his way. In October of 1897 the family returned to St. Louis because his wife was slow recovering from childbirth and their daughter fragile. Here he wrote in an office in the Security Building. As soon as his wife's health was restored, they went back to upper New York.

Churchill set *Richard Carvel*, his story of derring-do, during the Revolutionary War and fed it to a public hungry for fictional history, especially military, because this was the time of America's conflict with Spain over its colonies. The book sold wildly; his bio popped up in papers all over the country; teenage girls penned him worshipful letters; women's clubs put on programs centered about his thrilling tale. The bemused British confused him with another young Winston, a confusion neither the American nor the British publishers did anything to dispel. Moreover, their Churchill had just published his own novel, *Savrola*, and was happy to receive congratulations on his masterful yarn spinning, only to have his pleasure extinguished when he learned these letters were directed to a namesake. Then their Churchill wrote ours to say that henceforth he would add his middle name, "Spencer" to the title page of his books; but our Churchill, though appreciative of the gesture, was a simple Winston, and could not follow suit. He also decided against the suggestion that he place a characterization such as "The American" below his name. Meanwhile, secure in the public's impervious ignorance of any mix-up, our Churchill became the sort of celebrity satirized in his own *Celebrity*.

An enterprising entrepreneur (read, "scoundrel") named Major J. B. Pond, who ran lecture tours, thought it a splendid idea to have our Churchill appear on the platform with their Churchill when their Churchill did his American tour. The American Churchill would then introduce the British Churchill to his American audience. "It will be a magnificent and unique occasion." One brilliant notion followed another. Perhaps Mark Twain could be persuaded—he could—to introduce our Churchill, who would then, after the laughter had subsided, introduce theirs. But our man said, repeatedly, no dice.

However, when their Churchill was lecturing in Boston, ours met theirs in their hotel, the cigar-chewing Winston receiving the pipe-puffing Winston while reclining—was it insolently?—on his bed. Later, they had dinner together. Robert Schneider writes that "a relationship of quiet hostility was established—a relationship that never changed."

While the construction of a grand mansion in Cornish, New Hampshire, was proceeding, Churchill returned to St. Louis and sat again at his desk in the Security Building to gather material for and compose his next novel, which was to be set in Civil War St. Louis. For the German background, he leaned upon *Revolution and Counter-Revolution in Germany* by Friedrich Engels, but for life in St. Louis he drew from the first-hand reminiscences of friends, or others recommended to him, who had lived in the city through his story's time. The St. Louis libraries—the Public and the Mercantile—were also an essential source.

The Crisis (1901) had a story that couldn't miss: it recounted the conflict between Blue and Gray and told of the love which would bring harmony to those colors. "At the conclusion of the novel the North and South are reconciled as the Union officer and his Confederate lady, Virginia Carvel, proclaim their love for each other in President Lincoln's office." The glorification of both sides—a strategy that had proved profitable in Churchill's novel about the Revolutionary War—worked equally well for this one, and reviewers from every region of the country praised it.

If our Churchill hadn't at first feared a confusion of identities, he would now, for on his next trip to England the mix-up was pronounced, and although their young MP invited our young best-seller to his club, our man thought theirs acted "like a cad." Moreover, it wasn't just the *Manchester Guardian* that couldn't keep them straight, American papers like the *Chicago Chronicle* began to congratulate the Winston who was Spencer on his understanding of our country.

A new novel on the acquisition of the Louisiana Territory began to occupy Churchill's mind (he was also campaigning for governor of New Hampshire), and this brought him back to St. Louis, where he traveled down the river to New Orleans. His friendship with Pierre Chouteau proved invaluable, since Chouteau was himself occupied with a bibliography of materials on the territory. The novel that resulted, called *The Crossing*

(1904), was another success, although perhaps not as huge as his previous ones. It is not clear when he decided to include the letter "c" in the title of his books, though it became an almost uniform practice. Maybe he did it just for luck, having by chance begun that way, or in order to leave the mark of his name on more than one bit of the title page. But there it was, for after *The Celebrity, Richard Carvel, The Crisis* and *The Crossing* (1904), there arrived *Coniston* (1906), *Mr. Crewe's Career* (1908), *A Modern Chronicle* (1910), *The Inside of the Cup* (1913) and *A Far Country* (1915).

Churchill would return to St. Louis to visit Joseph Gazzam from time to time and continue to use the city as a fictional location, but his principal interests were now elsewhere—in New England politics, and in his writing concerns:

> I have no patience with literary cant. Writing, it appears to me, is a business, and a direct means to the end. If people read, they want to read for their own entertainment or instruction and not to serve the author's pleasure or hobby. The lawyer prepares his brief to secure a verdict; so must the author. The judgment must be passed from a standpoint entirely apart from that of the author. I make a business of writing. Action and atmosphere, bone and blood are the things I try to put into books.

If critics ever trouble themselves to remember Winston Churchill, they might hold these remarks against him. As it is, fate's wry smile became sardonic, since Fulton, Missouri's Winston (and the celebrated "Iron Curtain" speech he gave there) have, by now, quite eclipsed St. Louis's once popular novelist and his output of some seventeen books, including poems and plays. For twenty years Churchill was the king of fiction in this country; his ten novels sold about 500,000 copies each and went into fifty-four editions as well as being translated into several foreign languages. Then, except for the publication of a philosophical and religious work, *The Uncharted Way* in 1940, he was silent, increasingly engrossed by his painting and in the semi-private solution of philosophical issues.

Churchill's Cornish, New Hampshire, life did not change much for twenty-five years (except that he was alone at its end). He wintered in Florida, and on March 12, 1947, when he took his customary mile walk through the woods in Winter Park to visit Mary Semple Scott, an old friend, it was another day of quiet routine. He seemed to Miss Scott quite animated and in good spirits. They were speaking of his plans to visit St. Louis when he simply sank back silent in his chair with so little change of expression his companion thought him lost in thought; consequently, she waited a bit before calling a doctor.

There are those who claim that Winston Churchill died in St. Louis. Not exactly. He was merely thinking about going there. When he did.

Second Story Sunlight
by John Lutz

Nudger didn't so much mind that he always found himself in the longest line, but he wondered why there was never anyone behind him. That was how it was now, while he waited to deposit the check he'd received for recovering a lost deer. The animal had been one of many removed from a wooded area in one of St. Louis's wealthier suburbs. The residents there resisted any effort to trap or shoot the animals, though they were problematic and a traffic hazard. So with the best of intentions and at great expense, they'd had scores of the deer tranquilized and transferred to various wilderness areas, where most of them died from the shock of relocation or were killed by hunters.

A problem arose when one of the community's leading families had looked on one of the transported deer as a family pet. They had fed it, named it Beamer, set out a salt lick, and the animal had begun hanging around and the children had become fond of it. The family missed the deer and had hired Nudger to get it back. Armed with a photograph of Beamer wearing a frivolous hat at an outdoor birthday party, Nudger had flown to Fargo, North Dakota, paid most of his promised fee to a scout and trapper, and had actually located the animal and had it transported back to St. Louis County, where it was struck by a car.

Now here was Nudger standing in line before a teller's cage in the Maplewood Bank. He had to get the Beamer check deposited so it would clear and he could mail his alimony check to his horrendous former wife Eileen. She and her lover-lawyer Henry Mercato were threatening to take Nudger to court again in an attempt to raise his monthly payments. How they could do this, since Eileen, at the apex of one of those barely legal home product pyramid schemes, earned more money then he did, was beyond Nudger. But then, he was always last in line with no one behind him. He loathed the idea of going back into court to do battle with Eileen and Mercato. He was afraid of the whole business and wanted nothing to do with it.

Eileen had left another message on his answering machine referring to him as "the turnip that would bleed." She and Mercato were a bad influence on each other. Matchmakers say there is someone for everyone, but it was amazing that those two had found each other.

Ah! Nudger was finally at the tellers window. As the man ahead of him moved to the side and left, the woman behind the marble counter moved the hands of a small mock clock to read 2:00. Beside the artificial clock was a sign declaring that deposits after that time wouldn't be posted until the next day's date. Nudger glanced at his wristwatch. Two o'clock.

"But I've been standing in line twenty minutes," he told the woman.

"I'm sorry, sir," she said with a sad shake of her head. "I can't make an exception. It's all done by computer now, you know."

Nudger knew. He made his deposit anyway. Eileen's check would be a day late and there would probably be another turnip message on his machine. There sure wasn't going to be much left of his Beamer fee, he thought, gazing at the deposit slip as he walked from the bank. Money wasn't going very far these days, especially since the area where his office was located was becoming gentrified.

Nudger still didn't know quite what to make of this gentrification, but it was undeniable and as insidious as flood water. First it had been a trendy Creole restaurant opening down the street, then several antique shops had appeared. So it continued, along with an article in the newspaper about how Maplewood real estate was appreciating so rapidly. Then along came a coffee shop, a cafe, a music shop, a health food store. The B&L

Diner, where Nudger sometimes used to have lunch or breakfast, he noticed was now called Tiffany's. Probably the food had improved, like a lot of other things in the area, but Nudger missed his old, down-at-the-heels neighborhood.

His office hadn't moved or improved, its ancient window air conditioner protruding from a second-floor window over Danny's Donuts. And at least Danny's was still there. Though Danny had made a concession to the march of progress by featuring a "Donut de'jour" every week.

As Nudger entered the aromatic doughnut shop, he saw that this week's spotlighted confection was the same as last week's, something called the Plowman's Feast that had cheese and vegetable bits imbedded in the dough. Nudger had been appalled when he'd first seen one of the things, but Danny had assured him that the "artsy types" who'd moved into the neighborhood saw them as brunch food and were buying them as fast as they could be deep fried. Nudger wasn't sure Danny was being completely honest, as there seemed to be the usual dearth of customers whenever he was in the shop.

"Hey, Nudge!" said the Basset hound-featured Danny, as he stood behind the counter wiping his hands on the gray towel always tucked in his belt. "You had lunch?"

"Just a while ago," Nudger said quickly. The thought of Danny's dark and turgid coffee, along with what he invariably offered Nudger, the always featured and unpopular Dunker Delite, made Nudger's delicate stomach kick and turn. Nudger swallowed and got up on a stool at the counter. "I'll take a glass of ice water, though."

Danny shoveled some crushed ice in a glass, then ran tap water. He set the glass on a square white paper napkin in front of Nudger. "You notice my mural, Nudge?" He motioned toward a side wall. "An artist fella just moved in a few blocks from here painted it for me in exchange for a gross of Plowman's Feasts last week."

Nudger hadn't noticed any mural. He turned on his stool to look. A mural, all right, covering most of the east wall, an undersea scene of whales swimming among smaller fish above exotic sea growth on the ocean floor. It wasn't half bad. "Beautiful," Nudger said. "And environmentally correct."

Danny was grinning. "You notice something?"

Nudger looked again. "Whales, mostly."

"You look close and you can see the other fish are just fish, but the whales ain't just whales. They're shaped like Dunker Delites."

"Um," Nudger said, turning away and sipping some water while his mind absorbed this. "Painter's a talented guy."

"Sure is. And generous, considering all the other work he's doing."

"He's got a job other than painting?" No surprise there.

"None as I know of, but he and his new bride are fixing up a house on Emler Avenue, one of them old Victrolians. That's what the Plowman's Feasts were for, their wedding. I went to it. They got married over in the park wearing clothes made completely out of leaves and stuff. Everything natural."

"Romantic," Nudger said, thinking maybe it was.

The door opened and Nudger and Danny were surprised to see the bulk of St. Louis Police Lieutenant Jack Hammersmith enter the doughnut shop. It was almost ninety degrees outside, but Hammersmith, as usual, appeared cool as a scoop of vanilla mint. He was wearing blue uniform pants and no cap. His sleek gray hair was unmussed by summer breezes, and his smooth pink chin and jowls bulged over a white shirt collar. Visible in his shirt pocket were two of the putrid greenish cigars that he loved to smoke when he wanted to be alone.

He said hello to Nudger and Danny, then stared at the new mural.

"What the hell are Dunker Delites doing with fins?"

"They're supposed to be whales," Danny said in an injured tone.

"Sort of a combination of each," Nudger said, trying to protect Danny's feelings.

"You're kinda out of your jurisdiction," Danny said, knowing Hammersmith was a city cop and this was the municipality of Maplewood.

"Got a Major Case Squad crime," Hammersmith said, easing his way up on a stool two over from Nudger so there'd be plenty of room. The Major Case Squad was made up of city and county cops and called into action whenever a serious crime was committed in the area. That way there would be less territorial squabbling, and the facilities of the largest departments were available.

"You want a Dunker Delite?" Danny asked.

Hammersmith looked at him suspiciously. "Yesterday's unsolds?"

Danny blushed. Odd in a man in his fifties.

"Just some water like Nudger's," Hammersmith said.

As he placed the glass of ice water on the counter before Hammersmith, Danny asked the question Nudger was considering. "So what kinda crime brought the Major Case Squad to Maplewood?"

"Homicide," Hammersmith said, sipping water then using his paper napkin to dab at his lips with the peculiar delicacy of the obese and graceful. "Guy named Lichtenberg, over on Emler Avenue."

Danny released his grip on his gray towel, letting it flop back over his crotch. "Huh? That's the artist did my mural!"

"I know he is," Hammersmith said. "That's how come I knew those whales were Dunker Delites."

• • •

For Danny it was a slam dunk. After Hammersmith had gone back out into the summer heat, Danny had easily talked Nudger into trying to find out who killed Lou Lichtenberg. That it was an open homicide case didn't dissuade Danny; being Nudger's ersatz receptionist and sometimes helper, he knew Nudger's occasional disregard for rules. And of course Nudger was breaking one of his rules he least liked to disregard. He tried never to get involved in homicides. Already one person was dead, so was it all that unlikely another would wind up in that state? And with his luck ...

"Just report to me whenever you want, Nudge," Danny was saying, as Nudger waved a limp goodbye and pushed out through the grease-stained glass door into the heat.

Later that day in his hotbox office, Nudger phoned Hammersmith and got the basics: Lou Lichtenberg and his bride Linda had bought an old Victorian house on Emler a couple of months ago and had been living in it while they fixed it up. Like many rehabbers, they couldn't afford to stay in their own digs and be eaten up by rent money along with the funds they were pouring into the project house.

Last night, while they were stripping paint from an old wooden bannister, Linda had taken a break and driven to Mr. Wizard to buy them a couple of chocolate strawberry concretes. She'd returned to find her husband sprawled at the base of the stairs. At first she assumed he'd accidentally fallen and was unconscious. The paramedics who responded to her 911 call saw immediately that he was dead. At St. Mary's Hospital emergency, it didn't take long for a nurse to notice the bullet hole behind his ear.

So, murder without a doubt.

"Any hint of motive?" Nudger asked.

Hammersmith chuckled on the other end of the connection. "Hear tell, everybody liked the dead guy. He was one of those free spirits, and a talented painter, according to his friends. Since he'd just turned forty, he decided to settle down, become a husband and homeowner."

"What about the wife?"

"Linda. Skinny, pretty, distraught. She isn't faking it, Nudge; she really is grieving over hubby. 'Course, I could be fooled."

Nudger doubted it.

"She and the painter lived together the past five years, dated a couple of years before that. She's a photographer, but her stuff doesn't sell."

"Did her husband's painting sell?"

"Yeah, but not for much."

"Should I ask if you found the murder weapon?"

"All we know about it," Hammersmith said, "is it was a twenty-two caliber."

"Could it have been a professional hit, Jack?"

"Crossed my mind—small caliber weapon, one shot behind the right ear, soft bullet that spread and tumbled inside the skull. I don't guess we can rule it out. Or maybe the killer's somebody who saw a movie about a professional hit man."

Nudger hoped the latter was the case. The idea of crossing paths with a pro made his sensitive stomach twitch and turn. He didn't like playing in somebody else's back yard, especially if the somebody was the sort of person who might bury him there.

"Nudge," Hammersmith said, "tell me you aren't going to be mucking around in this case."

"Can't do that, Jack."

"Danny hire you?"

"He was fond of the dead guy," Nudger said. "Went to his wedding, supplied Plowman's Feasts in exchange for the guy painting those Dunker Delite whales. Dead guy was a regular customer of Danny's, and how many of those are there?"

Hammersmith knew the last was a rhetorical question. He didn't give Nudger the usual stern warning about overstepping the line in an active case. Merely hung up without saying goodbye. Nudger wasn't surprised by this abruptness. Hammersmith insisted on being the one to terminate phone conversations, and he often acted suddenly so as not to lose the opportunity. Had a thing about it. Nudger didn't mind. Almost everybody had a thing.

After replacing the receiver on his desk phone, he sat in his tiny, stifling office above the doughnut shop and gazed out the window at pigeons roosting on a ledge of the building across Manchester. The pigeons seemed to sense his attention and gazed back at him. He had never liked the way pigeons looked at him, as if they took for granted something about him that he maybe didn't even know himself.

He turned away from the window, wincing as his swivel chair squealed like an enraged soprano. Bile lay bitter beneath his tongue. Something square and on fire seemed to be lodged low in his throat. The cloying scent of baked sugar from the shop below was making him nauseated. His stomach hurt. Really hurt. Wrong business, he told himself for the thousandth time, and reached for the roll of antacid tablets on his desk. I'm in the wrong business. Wrong world, maybe. He barely chewed several antacid tablets and almost choked swallowing the jagged pieces.

• • •

Lou Lichtenberg's obituary in the paper the next morning said that he would be cremated, his ashes spread over the Mississippi that he loved to paint, and that there would be a memorial service at a later date.

Nudger put down the *Post-Dispatch* and used the number Danny had given him to phone the widow. When he mentioned Danny, she agreed to talk with him.

Linda Lichtenberg was twenty pounds too thin to be healthy and had a long, wan face out of a Renaissance painting. Telling her how considerate she was to agree to see him at such a time in her life, Nudger thought she looked born to grieve.

They were in the spacious living room of the old house on Emler. It was a mess, with an attached living and dining room, rough hardwood floors, yellowed enameled woodwork partly stripped to its original oak, and bare plaster walls too rough for paint or paper. Beyond where Linda sat on a threadbare sofa was the stairway with the long wooden bannister she and her husband had been stripping. The upper part was paint-streaked bare wood, the lower the same yellowed white of the rest of the unstripped woodwork. A worn gray carpet ran up the stairs, the sort of thing easy to trip over.

"If Danny says you're okay, I want to talk to you," Linda said. Her pink-rimmed eyes were pale blue and bloodshot from crying. "I never thought I'd say this, but I'm beginning to believe in the death penalty. I gotta be honest—I want revenge. I want to see the bastard that killed Lou roasted alive!" Strong words from such a frail looking woman.

With Nudger gently urging her along, she related the simple story told to and by Hammersmith. She and Lou had been stripping paint from the bannister. She'd gone out to get ice cream. When she returned, she found Lou at the base of the stairs. She thought he'd fallen so she called 911. It was the paramedics who discovered he'd been shot to death.

When she was finished talking, Nudger glanced around the partly rehabbed living and dining rooms.

"I know it doesn't look like much now," Linda said, "but Lou and I had plans."

"I don't see any of his paintings. I mean the kind you do on canvas."

"His temporary studio was going to be upstairs. Some of his work is up there, if you want to see it."

Nudger told her that he did, then followed her up the steep flight of steps and along a hall to a large second-floor room that was part of an addition to the house. There were skylights set in the slanted ceiling.

"It would have been a good place to work," Linda said sadly. "Lou didn't even have a chance to get properly set up."

Nudger walked over to where two canvases leaned against a wooden railing at the top of the steps. "Mind if I look?"

Linda shrugged. "It's why we came."

Nudger examined each painting. One was an unremarkable woodsy landscape. The other was of a slender nude woman standing near a window and bathed in golden sunlight. Her head was bowed and her long arms hung languidly at her sides.

"Lou's *Woman in the Light*," Linda said. "his last painting. He did it here because of the skylights."

"You?"

She bit her lower lip. "Me."

"It's beautiful." Nudger meant it.

Linda turned away. "Lou was so talented. His death is such a damned shame."

"What made him paint the whale mural in Danny's?"

Nudger asked, thinking it was a long way from the elegant, glowing woman on the canvas before him.

"Doughnuts. He did it in exchange for doughnuts for our wedding. It isn't that good, and he knows it."

"Danny likes it."

"Danny is sweet."

"From all those doughnuts," Nudger said. Got him a smile. "Can you think of anybody your husband might have angered lately, anyone who might have wanted to get even with him?"

"No. I told the police no, too. Lou was an artist; he didn't have any real enemies. Hell, he didn't even live in this world."

Nudger told her he understood, but he wasn't sure if he did.

He found his own way out, leaving her with her grief, and the canvas image of herself in sunlight that no longer existed.

• • •

Nudger met a woman he knew named Roseanne. She was slim, attractive, and the director of a small, privately funded museum near Grand Avenue. She wasn't from New York, but she had been there and often dressed in black. He regarded her as his art expert.

"Lou Lichtenberg," he said, standing near a life-size bronze Apollo in the museum. It made him feel inadequate.

"Dead,' Roseanne said. She was a woman who got to the point.

"Did he have talent?"

"Yes."

"Was he going to make it as an artist?"

"Who knows? He didn't understand or accept the marriage of art and commerce."

"Meaning?"

"Look around you, Nudger."

He did, and saw several ordinary objects—a clock, a chunk of concrete with steel rods protruding from it, a toaster, a suitcase, a small refrigerator. Next to each object was an X-ray view of its insides.

"The museum has an exhibit running this week of work done by the Anti-Christo."

"Isn't Christo the guy who wraps unlikely things in cloth—I mean, like coastlines or whole buildings?"

"The same. But the Anti-Christo displays solid objects, along with their fluoroscopic images or X-rays. The idea is he shows them *un*wrapped, bare of any surface or subterfuge. His work sells for a fortune."

"Is it art?"

"The market says it is. Is he as talented as Lou Lichtenberg was? Not on your life! Is he more successful as an artist? Yes."

"I don't like your business," Nudger said. "It's full of phonies."

Roseanne smiled. "Yours isn't?"

• • •

Hammersmith had told Nudger the Lichtenbergs bought their aged Victorian lady from Norton Anston, the last of a family that had lived in the house for almost a hundred years. Once wealthy from the timber business, they'd fallen on hard times during the Depression and never gotten up. Anston had been reared in comparative poverty that he'd managed to raise only to bare sustenance through a struggling antique shop. He'd jumped at the Lichtenbergs' offer for the old house. The closing brought him the most liquidity he'd ever experienced.

Anston now lived in an expensive condo in West County, where he agreed to talk with Nudger.

"To tell you the truth," he said, "it was a relief to get rid of the old family house. It had become a costly and troublesome relic. Better somebody young battle the termites and mold, rather than a man my age."

That remark kind of bothered Nudger, because Anston seemed to be in his late forties, Nudger's age. Though he looked older, Nudger assured himself, assessing Anston's thin hair, double chin, thickened waist, crows feet. Nudger's hair wasn't all that thin. Except on top, bald spot the size of a—half dollar, quarter, or maybe a nickel.

"I understand you sold the house yourself," he said to Anston, "rather than go through a realtor."

Anston smiled with a kind of toothy avarice, reminding Nudger of someone he couldn't quite place. "Sure. Why pay a commission?"

Why indeed? Nudger thought.

"In my business—buying and selling antiques—there's not much profit margin. I've learned to squeeze a dollar till it bleeds, and I don't apologize."

This guy talked disturbingly like Eileen. "Were the Lichtenbergs satisfied with the deal?"

"They wouldn't have made it if they weren't," Anston said. "Matter of fact, I'd say they were overjoyed. You know, young people, first time homeowners. Kind of touching."

Nudger remembered when he and Eileen, as man and wife, had bought a subdivision house, how for a while it had seemed like a castle. Then a dungeon.

"They had big plans for the place," Anston said. "Talked of turning it into a bed and breakfast."

"Really?" That was the first Nudger had heard of a B&B plan.

Anston glanced at his wristwatch. "I hate to rush this," he said, "but I'm supposed to meet someone at the Gypsy Caravan."

Nudger raised an eyebrow.

"Big antique show comes to town every year. Dealers from all over the country. Nothing to do with real gypsies."

Nudger chuckled in a way that should let Anston know he wasn't that naive, then thanked him for his time.

Nudger had parked in the shade, but as usual, starting his old Honda was a struggle in the heat. When he finally was able to get the balky little engine running, he saw Anston pull from the condo driveway in an even older car, a rusty Ford station wagon. It was the proceeds from the sale of the family home,

Nudger decided, that had enabled Anston to afford such a nice condo, and maybe with cash left over. He probably hadn't yet gotten around to buying a new car.

Nudger's phone was ringing as he entered his apartment on Sutton, noticing how shabby it looked after Anston's condo. As he picked up the receiver, he reached out with his free hand and switched on the window air conditioner.

Hammersmith was on the phone. Nudger moved as far away from the humming, rattling window unit as the cord would allow so he could hear.

"What I hear," Hammersmith said, "is that you've been nosing around the Lichtenberg case like a pig digging for truffles." Hammersmith would know about truffles. Food. "What have you discovered, Nudge?"

"Facts or truffles?" Nudger asked. "I'll trade either or both."

"Make it both," Hammersmith said. "That way you might stay out of trouble."

"Facts: Lichtenberg was a genuinely talented painter. If he had any enemies, I haven't uncovered them. He and his wife were happy with their new home. And they were considering turning it into a B&B."

"Breaking and entering?"

"B and *B*. Bed and breakfast."

"Oh. And your truffles?"

"The house's previous owner, Norton Anston, needed the money when he sold the place. The wife, Linda, is genuinely grief-stricken, and my guess is she had nothing to do with her husband's death. And it seems to me that there aren't many Lichtenberg paintings lying around the place, considering what a dedicated artist he was. Of course, all truffles are subjective."

"Sometimes when a painter dies, his work suddenly is in demand and the price goes up," Hammersmith said.

"You thinking somebody with lots of Lichtenberg paintings might have killed him?"

"I admit it's only a truffle," Hammersmith admitted. "Here's another one: a real estate agent says Anston took advantage of the young, artistic and naive and sold the house for more than it was worth. Only opinion, of course."

"What about your facts?"

"Official cause of death was what you'd expect, Nudge—bullet to the brain, massive damage. No powder burns on the victim's hands, though he was shot from close range. So no chance of suicide. And whoever killed him was probably a smoker."

"Huh?"

"Fresh burn spot on the stairway carpet where the gunman must have stood, from a cigarette or cigar ember."

"Lou and Linda were stripping the bannister. Maybe they burned off some of the old paint and singed the carpet," Nudger suggested.

"A possibility," Hammersmith said grudgingly. "I'll check with the wife, who incidentally ran into some friends while buying ice cream at Mr. Wizard's at the time hubby was being shot. Not to mention the kid who waited on her. He lives across the street from the Lichtenberg house and remembered her being there. So her alibi checks out strong."

"Maybe she shot Lou before she left the house," Nudger said. "Or right after returning."

"Not according to people who heard the shot. Though they didn't know at the time that was what they heard. Also, there was no gunpowder residue on her hands."

"You still considering a hit man?" Nudger asked.

"Yeah, but one thing doesn't ring true. We got a misshapen .22 bullet like a pro might have left in a victim, only it's more misshapen than it oughta be, considering the soft tissue it went through once it entered the skull. There's no way we can ID the make of gun, or even match the bullet in ballistics tests."

"Did the killer leave a shell casing?"

"Nope. That sounds like a pro. Unless it was an amateur using a revolver and the casing stayed in the cylinder. That way the bullet doesn't provide a lead, or any potential court evidence through ballistics, it mighta been a pro with some new kind of gun that makes his job safer."

"Have you noticed how everything's become a battle with technology?" Nudger asked.

"Tell me about it, Nudge. I'm recording this conversation, gonna convert it into print then scan it into my electronic murder file. Might write a book someday."

"Is that legal, Jack?"

But Hammersmith had hung up.

• • •

"I heard you and your husband were going to convert the house into a B&B," Nudger said, standing on the Victorian home's wide gallery porch and enjoying the glass of lemonade Linda Lichtenberg had just handed him.

"Not right away," Linda said. "But yes, that was the plan. Eventually, we were going to convert the garage to Lou's studio and put in another garage under the house at basement level. He could work out there in peace and quiet while I was dealing with guests." She slumped down in an old wood glider hung on rusty chains, as if her energy had just left her in a rush, and was obviously trying not to cry. "It's awful, how everything can change in an instant. Now, without Lou's income, I won't even be able to afford to stay here."

"Will you sell the house?"

She shook her head no. "We owe so much it wouldn't make sense. I'm going to let the bank take it. People like me, like Lou, I think we just weren't born to be property owners, to live normal lives."

"What about your husband's paintings? Can't you sell some of them?"

"There aren't any left except the two upstairs. I won't part with *Woman in the Light*, and the landscape is old work and practically worthless. We sold Lou's backlog of work in order to make a down payment and pay closing costs on this place."

"Who bought Lou's paintings?"

"I couldn't tell you. You'd have to check with the Plato Gallery. That's who sold most of Lou's work. When it sold."

Standing on the porch and looking at the dejected figure in the glider, Nudger felt his eyes tear up. He turned away and swiped at them with a knuckle, then talked with Linda Lichtenberg about anything other than her dead husband until the lemonade glass was empty.

• • •

The Plato gallery was in the wealthy suburb of Clayton and displayed antiques as well as artwork. A gaunt man with a white Van Dyke beard approached Nudger just inside the door and asked if he could be of help. He was dressed in black except for a white handkerchief that flowered from his blazer pocket.

"Do you have any Lou Lichtenbergs?" Nudger asked.

The man smiled sadly and shook his head. "I wish we did. The artist died recently, you know, and the value of his work has risen. But we sold the last of his paintings over a month ago, cheaper than we should have even then because he needed the money."

"For his Victorian house," Nudger said.

The man's dark eyes brightened. "Oh, you knew Lou?"

"No," Nudger said, and explained.

The man in black turned out to be Plato Zorbak, the owner and manager of the gallery, and when Nudger was finished talking he said with surprising fervor, "I hope they catch the evil swine who shot Lou. He doesn't deserve any mercy."

"Who bought his paintings?" Nudger asked.

"Most of them sold to a dealer in New Orleans—he buys for a number of clients."

A well dressed man and woman entered the gallery, and before Zorbak excused himself to wait on them, Nudger asked a final question: "About how much have Lou Lichtenberg paintings appreciated since his death?"

"As of now," Zorbak said, "about three hundred percent. And climbing, because Lou was a bona fide talent." He backed away, eager to greet his clientele and escape Nudger, who was obviously no art buyer. "Please feel free to look around before you leave," Zorbak said politely.

Nudger thanked him and did stay for a few minutes. Something had caught his eye.

When he returned to his office, he stopped in Danny's for a cup of coffee to go. After climbing the steps in the stifling stairwell to his office door, he went inside, walked to the tiny half bath, and poured the horrible brew down the washbasin drain slowly so Danny wouldn't hear pipes gurgling below.

Then Nudger switched on the air conditioner and sat down behind his desk. There was a message on his machine. Eileen's voice: "Nudger, if you call the bank you'll see that your measly checking account has been frozen. If you don't—"

Quickly he pressed delete.

He slid the desk phone over and called Maplewood Bank, but he didn't ask about his account. He talked to someone he knew in the loan department and asked what would happen when the bank repossessed Lou and Linda Lichtenberg's house.

"Banks don't really want to foreclose on anyone's house," he was assured. "We're not in the real estate business and don't want to be. The house will be sold on the court house steps to the highest bidder."

Nudger said thank you, depressed the phone's cradle button for a dial tone, then called Hammersmith at the Third District.

"Nudge," Hammersmith said, "I don't have time for you. Crime in our fair city demands my constant attention."

"If you promise not to hang up on me," Nudger said, "I'll tell you who killed Lou Lichtenberg."

Now and then life provided a sweet moment outside the doughnut shop.

• • •

The next morning, Nudger sat at the counter in Danny's Donuts. Before him were two free Dunker Delites and a large foam cup of coffee. He was trying to figure a way not to consume any of it without bruising Danny's feelings. Next to Nudger sat Hammersmith. He'd devoured three Plowman's Feasts and was determinedly working on a third, drinking only ice water, pretending everything was delicious. Showing his human side, Nudger thought.

"So how'd you figure it out?" Danny asked Nudger..

"By putting together facts and truffles."

Hammersmith glared at him while chewing a mouthful of doughnut.

"Property values in Maplewood are skyrocketing. The Lichtenbergs were going to open a B&B and build a new garage at basement level. With Lou's death, the house will be foreclosed on and sold on the court house steps. A straw party from New Orleans bought up Lou's paintings at the Plato gallery. The guns at the Plato Gallery were the final tipoff."

"Yeah?" Danny asked, looking at Nudger like a curious basset hound.

"Shnot nishe to toy with people, Nudge," Hammersmith said around a large bite of featured pastry.

"I asked myself questions," Nudger said. "Who might have been surprised by increasing property values and want to buy the Lichtenberg house at auction? Who would know enough to buy Lou's paintings through a straw party as an investment if they planned on murdering him? Who had access to an antique flintlock gun that might shoot a chunk of lead pried from a .22 cartridge, leave a burnt spot on the carpet from powder dropping from the gun's flash pan, and leave a deliberately mutilated slug impossible to trace or match with modern weapons? Who might have left behind one of Lou's best and most valuable paintings because he'd know the subject was the painter's wife and having possession of it might draw suspicion to him? And who might have something to hide if the cellar in the old family home might be dug up to accommodate a basement garage?"

"The answer's pretty simple when you stop to think about it," Danny said.

"And the proof came," Hammersmith said, "when we dug beneath the house and found the bones of antique dealer Norton Anston's wife, who was supposed to have run away to Las Vegas twenty-five years ago."

"Poor woman didn't get any farther than the basement," Danny said.

"She's gotten even with Anston now. He's confessed to her murder, and to Lou Lichtenberg's. And he says he'd like to murder Nudger."

"Make sure he's locked up tight," Danny said.

Nudger didn't feel he had to second that. He gathered his complimentary Dunker Delites and coffee, along with a paper napkin, and slid off his stool.

"Where you going, Nudge?" Danny asked.

"Gonna eat breakfast upstairs," Nudger said. "Lots of paperwork to do, and I'm expecting a phone call."

"Lemme know if you're still hungry later," Danny said.

Hammersmith was grinning at Nudger as he went out.

Nudger hadn't mentioned the real reason he'd begun to suspect Anston of Lou Lichtenberg's murder. One of the barracudas swimming among the Dunker Delite whales in the mural Lou had painted for Danny looked amazingly like Norton Anston.

To Nudger, anyway.

YA GOTTA LOVE IT
by Suzanne Rhodenbaugh

St. Louis, where east meets west and north meets south and all bets are on because predictability IS part of its character. Yes it's lovable, but not because of its nineteenth century ward heeler politics, every pothole politicized. And not because it proceeds from principles—they can be gotten around, over or under, when they're even recognized or acknowledged, which frankly ain't all that often.

Also not because of a delightful climate, described in one letter to the editor as "Siberian in the winter, the Black Hole of Calcutta in the summer." Or because its homes are graceful—beautifully detailed and stolid in a Teutonic kind of way, but hardly graceful. Or because the landscape is extraordinary, this mainly flattish place where the woods nudge into the prairie, with a few mildly interesting limestone river bluffs and caves and modest hills. And not even because of its history, though that history is wide and deep as The Big River which here conjoins The Big Muddy. (That'd be The Mississippi and The Missouri to you, babe.) No, this place is lovable because it's full of people who say—of a whole continent, or a philosophy, or a single neighborhood beer joint—*ya gotta love it*.

This is just one of many Midwestern locuses, just one chunk of the vast American flyover country, but arguably the heart of The Heartland. It's one of the great old American cities that stretch across the shoulders of the country: Baltimore, Pittsburgh, Cleveland, Detroit, Indianapolis, Chicago, St. Louis, Kansas City, Omaha. It's definable, to a relative newcomer such as I, by an unaffected stoicism laced with deflating humor, an understated sidelook encapsulating whole regions of thought and feeling with the wholly forgiving, *ya gotta love it.*

Not that this is always a good thing. Whole mountaintops of moral weighings and intellectual distinctions and aesthetic subtleties can get lopped off or knocked sidewise or blunted with some implied summary *ya gotta love it.*

Not to mention The Nice Factor. It's probably true everywhere that people prefer Nice over justice, rationality, compassion or spirit. Most people, that is to say, want everyone not to raise a ruckus, and generally be devoid of any colorful or even noticeable qualities. This nice-leaning tendency is raised to the nth power when the setting is also dominated by (a) Midwesterners; (b) Catholics; and/or (c) people of German stock. (About thirty years ago I inadvertently fell in love with and married a German Catholic Midwesterner, so I've had a long time to ponder this matter.) St. Louis being dominated by folks who qualify on all three counts, The Nice Factor is almost overwhelming. This leads to some good things and some bad things. The bad thing can be, people veering toward the passive-aggressive, or The Big Honkin' Non-Response. The good thing is, St. Louis people are mostly nice.

In any case, nothing's crisp here. Triumph, defeat, daily living: all outlinable as clouds on a windy day. Achieving change of whatever ilk is like pushing jello uphill with a baby spoon.

On the other hand, St. Louis has given us Chuck Berry and T.S. Eliot and Betty Grable and Yogi Berra and Marianne Moore and Tina Turner and Tennessee Williams and Joseph Pulitzer and Lindbergh's flight and the stocking of westbound wagon trains and a long long list of more in the way of talent and heart and achievement deliciously important and memorable in all fields of human endeavor—ya gotta love that.

I myself landed in St. Louis in mid-January in the last year of the twentieth century, about a week after a major blizzard. The first things I noticed were many public buildings without landscaping, and a good many houses similarly without, and streets broader than I was used to Back East, as I eventually learned to say.

My husband and I did a weekend blitz of the real estate, aided by a six foot tall, six months pregnant agent, who drove fearlessly. We went for a house on what at that time appeared a quiet, lightly-traveled street. It turned out to be a raucous urban thoroughfare, and I don't love that, but I sort of love the linchpin for our decision: fleur de lis carved on the front of the house. Ya gotta love fleur de lis determining a major life decision!

The day we moved in, one neighbor brought flowers and newspapers, and an invitation to see her modern dance troupe perform. (She would become the first subject of a series of features I'd write under the rubric "Arts in the 'Hood," for the neighborhood turned out to be jampacked with your painters, musicians, sculptors, dancers, designers and suchlike.) A couple days later, the neighbor on the other side brought homemade bread and brochures on plants that grow well in Missouri.

In the next few months we got multiple welcomes. We were immediately drawn into the neighborhood association. Then my husband (and I, as wife of) were included in one of a series of informal dinners organized by two women who work for the city school system, and their husbands, a foundation officer and a lawyer. Their idea was to encourage cross-fertilization of ideas across many fields, for people who might contribute to the leadership of St. Louis. For me these folks also contacted a well-known local writer, who took me to lunch and sketched the literary scene in St. Lou. The only person I'd previously known anywhere in the state came here from Columbia, Missouri, to take me to a poetry reading at a university, and introduce me to writers there. Soon a local writer invited me to read and be interviewed on his poetry radio show. The editor of a literary magazine said I'd be welcome to work on his staff, which I soon did. It occurred to me I could write book reviews, though I never had, so with writing samples I applied cold to the newspaper and got back the answer: Sure, come on in.

I was welcomed to sweet St. Lou. Not effusively, for self-conscious hospitality isn't part of the St. Louis style. But welcomed nonetheless. Given a chance. The universities were an exception but hey, no place is perfect, and ya almost gotta love that.

But what won me over most about St. Louis that first year were the sweet, sometimes sentimental, sometimes seriously moxie moves that drew my attention. When the St. Louis Rams got into the Super Bowl, the nurses at Barnes-Jewish Hospitals, one of the country's great medical complexes, put gold and blue knit caps on all the newborns. Ya gotta love that! And in the tony border suburb of Clayton, with its steely highrise downtown, traffic was literally stopped, as a matter of conscious police policy, because a mother duck was taking a long time getting her ducklings across. Ya definitely gotta love that.

With time of course, I got to know a laundry list for civic pride, from the rich architectural store, to the mythic Mississippi, to the excellent Southern-fried chicken dinner sold for $3.99 every Thursday night in south St. Lou by a Serbian biker, which meal devolved into a new myth we helped create, Chicken Night. I came to love the Chain of Rocks footbridge—used to be ole Route 66—over the Mississippi; and the lavish Fox Theatre; and the exquisite Byzantine and Florentine mosaics of the Cathedral Basilica; and the plethora of venues for music, many of them free in the summertime. What's more, I began to store local lore in my brain. Maybe W.C. Handy didn't write "The St. Louis Blues" while standing on the Eads Bridge, watching the Mississippi flow by, but I read or heard somewhere he did, and it's a good story, and I'm stickin' to it. Well, naturally my fandom for St. Louis just grew.

I also got to know full bore some of the city's (and region's) stupidities and passivity and plain bad stuff. Often here I've wanted to shake folks—as in shake 'em up, but also just plain shake 'em. I'm conscious, though, this was never a center of political or religious idealism. The place began for fur trade, then developed as a river town, then became an industrial city. Like much of the Midwest, this region has been not only farmed but robbed blind and raped by every form of taking away, polluting and not caring: chemical and munitions manufacturing, lead mining and smelting among them. A lot isn't right, and environmentalism in particular has a hard row to hoe here. Even into the twenty-first century, river bottomland is being developed in mad hubris, despite the 1993 floods; the Army Corps of Engineers, barge owners, big farmers and state government are still actively in favor of using the rivers primarily as transportation ditches; and the biggest cement plant in the world is being built not too far south of the city. Casinos and levees continue to crowd the riverfronts, an enlightened long-term bedamned. As for making sense of the riot of political jurisdictions in the city and surrounding county (90+), no one should hold breath waiting for that wasteful, irrational peculiarity to change.

I go through hills and valleys of outrage, concern and trying, and grow more cynical and at times less hopeful. When I get involved with some issue, it often feels like a muddle that's never completely resolved, just back-burnered until a new muddle takes its foggy shape. Still, I could live here the rest of my days, and hope to.

I live in a one-hundred year old house (Big Bertha) on a street that runs a few miles east, past the Clydesdales in their elegant stable at the Busch Brewery, to the Mississippi, where an arsenal used to dominate a river island. I face a twelve by six block greenage planned out before the Civil War by an entrepreneurial Englishman who did right well in hardware, and gave us the start of this Victorian park and its dozen pavilions, plus, on nearby blocks, one of the finest botanical gardens in the world.

Under the land of our neighborhood, there are sealed coal mines and clay pits. A miniature version of the Industrial Revolution was enacted under our feet, and before that, somewhat lackadaisical farming by the French, under Spanish rule. Before that it was prairieland of the Missouri and Osage Indians, land good for giant grasses, butterfly weed and buffalo. And once the sod was broken, growing food in this rich Mississippi mud. I'm sure it's native hyperbole, but a lifelong resident of my neighborhood told me that, if I could dig below the random rubble from building materials and the like, I'd find twenty feet of topsoil.

The people here, unlike my own, were never noticeably English or Protestant. Here came waves of immigrants looking to make a fortune, or just a living: French, Spanish, Irish, Welsh, German, Italian. And of course the Africans brought here by no choice. And in the last twenty to thirty years: Vietnamese, Thai, Bosnians, Mexicans.

When it was thought the Kosovars might be coming to America by the thousands, the newspaper editorial here said: Let them come to St. Louis. Ya gotta love that. There's a sweetness here, a friendliness, a low-key welcome, an open door, people unimpressed by bona fides, whether of credentials, origins, or money, and more than a little provincial. They're particularly hard on themselves, seemingly partly from little experience elsewhere. They seem surprised at praise, distrustful of wonder, and even-keeled about almost everything else.

Well it's a plain Heartland community, strong on family, church, neighborhood, sports and union. (Ya gotta love that it's still a union town, and that every square inch is identifiably some specific neighborhood.) Whether the Cardinals are hot or not, pumped-up mottos zip across the buses where bus stop names normally go, and people Dress Red. Oh yeah. (And when the Cardinals are hot, the games are piped into the grocery stores' sound systems: doesn't everyone want to hear?)

I've lived a zillion places, with grits and without, not all of them even faintly lovable. And I say you can leave it or live it, but ya gotta love sweet St. Lou.

THE LURE OF ANNIHILATION
by Colleen McKee

"We're pretty—pretty vacant."
—The Sex Pistols

The Continental Building was the skyscraping dream of a scheming banker, a rare combination of conspicuous consumption and taste. It is the stunning embodiment of Art Deco glamour, with a touch of the neo-Gothic. Twenty-two white-tiled flights at its tallest, countless turrets shoot down its dizzying façade. Its twelve roofs at varying levels make it appear even taller than it is, and enhance the sense of enchanting vertigo. It's the kind of roof a character in an F. Scott Fitzgerald story would fling himself from. The martini glass still in his hand would reflect the lights from Grand Boulevard in flight.

Who wouldn't want to put their money in such a beautiful bank?

The Continental had a kind of fairy tale allure—the forbidden tower, so conspicuously white in a city of crumbling rust-colored brick. Built in 1929, on the verge of the Depression, the building was doomed from the start by embezzlement, fraud, and a mysterious theft of one million dollars from its basement. That winter night in 1989, when our little pack of trespassers first wriggled our way inside, it had already been vacant ten years.

It was easy to get in. There were boards on the windows that led to the lobby, but they were so sloppily nailed, it only took a few moments for Peyton and Tom to pry them loose with a hammer. Nick and I leaned up against the corner in a way we hoped appeared casual, looking out for police. Nick took Grand and I took Lindell. The cops didn't come, so the guys pulled themselves inside, while I needed a bit of a boost.

I awkwardly landed on a floor slippery with shattered glass. But beneath the gray glass and dust was marble. The entire interior of the building—walls, floors and stairs—was made of marble, silver-gray and silver-white. It looked wet in the moonlight slanting through the windows. But it wasn't really moonlight. It was streetlight. Downtown the streetlight sucks up the moonlight, but that makes it no less romantic.

I was fifteen and drunk, as I was every night, not just on moonlight, or streetlight, but on Boone's Farm Strawberry Hill "Wine," (In case you've never tried it, it's as pink as cotton candy, twice as sweet, and fizzy. Need I say its cap twists off? Their target market's so obvious, they should include a free toy in every bottle.) I was at the Continental with my skeevy drug "buddies," all guys in flannels and ripped leather jackets, all eighteen, twenty years old. There was my twenty-one year old boyfriend Tom, whom I hate to really call my boyfriend because he was never so much my friend as my sleeping bag. He gave me drugs and a place to stay and in exchange I gave him blowjobs, regardless of how long it had been since he bathed. Any semblance of romance between us was shot down the day I refused to blow him and I was forced to sleep in the playground down the street. The bench was very hard, and I quickly relinquished my pride. I forget who else was at the Continental, besides Peyton and Nick, whom I'd also swapped "favors" for drugs, whenever we figured Tom was too drunk to notice. (The only drug I wouldn't do was heroin. *Naked Lunch* scared me too much. I thank William Burroughs for my only scrap of adolescent self-preservation.)

I'm not sure why I wasn't dead, what with all I'd ingested, but that night at the Continental, I was maddeningly alive. The guys liked to run up the stairs, faster than I could or would go. I liked to explore the building alone. Homeless men were rumored to live there, but I was fifteen and unafraid. Besides, I didn't see any homeless guys, just their Army blankets, food scraps and ashes heaped on the marble landings.

Pigeons cooed in every window and turret. Pigeon shit splattered the stairs—another good reason not to run up them. On one of the lower staircases, I discovered a tin of saltines that read, "EMERGENCY: Fallout Shelter Saltines, To Be Eaten in Case of Nuclear Attack." Somehow the mice had broken in, and there were crackers strewn across the stairs, with fearless mice gnawing on the crumbs. I guess the mice did not realize that the USSR had not yet fallen, that the Cold War was in fact still on, and that they should really be saving their saltines for Doomsday. But the mice were unperturbed by politics and my boots alike. I couldn't nudge them out of the way. I wound up tiptoeing over them.

The building narrows near the top, and the staircase does as well. At some point, the wide landings and elegant windows were gone, and I found myself in a stairwell hardly wider than my hips. Each floor was marked by a door whose cursive number I could barely make out. I worried each door would stick or lock. I began to grow claustrophobic, but curiosity carried me through. It was wonderful to push open each new door, 16, 17, 18. I must have been climbing for over an hour when it finally hit me, how tired I was. Only then did I feel the coldsweat under my boyfriend's black leather jacket, the ache in my lungs, the stray hairs that slipped from my ponytail sticking to my wet cheeks. I brushed the dust from my Danzig T-shirt, and collected my breath for the climb.

When I opened door 21, the stairwell began to grow light. One more flight and I was there. I was on the roof. It had begun to snow, snow dry as cocaine, skittering down from a sky that seemed so close. I walked across the icy roof to the ledge, looked down, enjoying the vertigo. I saw grids of gold streetlights, and headlights pulse down the streets between them in slow snakes of light. My breath was dry ice, little clouds of exhaustion and exhiliration. I was on top of the city. Up here, the air was thinner and all the usual St. Louis sounds—the whine and hiss of Bi-

State buses, the bang of busted tires, the softer bang of bullets, the groans of drunks and trains—up here, all that was gone, that soundtrack of my life. I only heard the wind.

In the center of the roof was an elevator shaft with no elevator in it, a completely black abyss. The guys poked around it, bending over it daringly, but I preferred the edge of the roof. I gazed down at the light outside, the new and strangely appealing light. But the boys had climbed all the way up here, just to stare into a hole. "Look, look!" they yelled, proud of their non-discovery. I ignored them as I had so many times before, which was half as often as they ignored me. I served a very limited, localized purpose for them.

I returned my attention to the ledge, surveying my city like a queen, a teenage queen, yes, and a queen of ruins, but beautiful ruins, beautiful lights in slow graceful motion. It was an unfamiliar feeling, to let go of the lure of annihilation. I didn't want to jump. I wanted to look at the world from afar, then reenter it some different way. Don't get me wrong—I didn't want to become one of Nancy Reagan's Just Say No types, and I never did. I just got an idea, no, more like a vague yet heady feeling, that there might be more to life than being fucked and getting fucked up, that life might not be best lived on one's back.

I could have stood up there all night, but the guys wanted to explore the basement. So we tromped down 2400 slick stairs to the darkest place I have ever been. The boys turned on all their flashlights. Still we could only see a few inches at a time. The basement was vast. It was once divided into rooms, but now the doors were gone. On one end was a safe, its door was wide open, empty. File cabinets had been kicked over and a layer of papers knee-deep covered the floor. The basement was like an underground swimming pool, like swimming in paper instead of water. The guys waded through the papers as though they were piles of fallen leaves, but I was not as intrigued by this lightless place. It seemed sad to me, all the women who spent years typing those documents, just to have them stomped on by brats in combat boots. I was thinking of row upon row of typists, hammering the keys, hour upon hour. I thought of the ache in their wrists as they typed and filed, typed and filed, darting their eyes at the clock. I did temp work myself, with the help of a fake ID; between the typing jobs by day and the hand jobs by night, I knew how it felt to have every muscle in my hands go numb then cramp in pain, as though instead of blood, there was salt water running through my veins.

But mostly I was thinking about the view from that roof. I stood in one place as the boys swarmed around me in the dark. I was lit from within by the city inside me. A city of coal dust and rail yards. A city of flickering light.

I write this in 2004. After many false starts, the Continental has been all cleaned up. Just as my life has been. I no longer go to work in a mini and a filthy bra held together by safety pins. Now I go to work in buttons and pleats. I save my safety pins for weekends. In a way, the rehabilitation—both of the building and my life—is a good thing.

Still, something has been lost. Once this building, one of St. Louis' most amazing architectural triumphs, was mine, if only by force. But now it is carved into neat little suites and I can only peer through the window at the listing of names and security codes where once I had been able to easily clamber up twenty-two flights of stairs to a strange sort of urban heaven.

St. Louis has more vacant buildings than any other city in America. This saddens me, but it is not an unmixed sorrow. Behind every cracked panel of glass, every chipped and fading brick, behind every board on every busted out window, I know there are possibilities. On the roof of that white locked tower, I knew I was no one's princess. No one would save me with a golden key, or a kiss, or a rehab program. But I, a fifteen year old whore, a "pretty, pretty vacant" little girl, began to sense how to save my own life.

THE GRANDMOTHERS
by Rick Skwiot
(from *Winter at Long Lake*)

We continue on, moving over a vast viaduct with scores of railroad tracks beneath, and through Madison and Venice, Illinois, two more factory towns.

I recognize the place where, on my weekly trips to St. Louis with my mother, we change from the bus to a streetcar that climbs a trestle and rocks us over the Mississippi River. The track then bends, the old flat-end car with its musty, brocade seats leaning over rusty scrap-yards on the Missouri side. Nose pressed against the glass, I feel my stomach rising and await our sudden, dark descent into the comforting tunnel that takes us under St. Louis skyscrapers to the 12th Street Station.

But today we ride in the black Plymouth with its itchy wool seats, rumbling across the McKinley Bridge, streetcar tracks down its center where the wheels of the Plymouth slip from side to side. We stop at the toll booth on the west bank to pay our dime and turn south toward downtown St. Louis, or The Mound City, as it is called, after Mississippian Indian mounds that once lined the river.

Grandma Mary lives by a small park with a baseball diamond and a fountain where, in summertime, children bathe. But on Christmas morning the air hangs clear and cold and the park stands empty.

My father kills the engine and without a word slides from behind the steering wheel. He moves across the herringbone brick sidewalk in his wine-colored letter-jacket and disappears into a narrow, sunless walkway between two redbrick buildings.

The rest of us remain in the car. I gaze up the street to the poultry shop on the corner, where geese, chickens, ducks, and turkeys stand waiting in metal cages for the white-bearded man with the blood-smeared apron, who reminds me of God as depicted in *The Storybook Life of Jesus*.

After some minutes my father returns, opens the car door for my mother, and releases my brother and me from the back seat. Together we march in file down the dank brick passageway between the buildings and mount the stairs in back, shoes hammering the wooden steps.

I no longer question this routine of waiting in the car, having done so once before and gotten a perhaps plausible if vague reply from my mother: "Your father needs to talk to Grandma Mary alone. We'll go up soon."

Only decades later—when my mother is facing death (just as she faced life, with good cheer and resignation) and no longer has reason for secrets—do I learn the truth. My father precedes us upstairs to chase away the man who shares Grandma Mary's bed and whose existence is hidden from us children for propriety's sake.

Now I think warmly of this poor man, whoever he was. Likely a Polish immigrant like Grandma Mary, who, after forty years in America, spoke no noticeable English. I think of him on Christmas morning being rousted from the widow's warm bed, or maybe rushing through his hot breakfast, taking a last gulp of steaming coffee before being sent out into the cold.

Where can he go? What could be open on Christmas morning 1953 other than a church or precinct house? Even drugstores and gas stations close on holidays and Sundays. Today there is no newspaper. It is a holy day, kept holy by most everyone keeping quiet and staying put.

I see this nameless man, my grandmother's lover, shivering as he descends the backstairs, walking hands-in-pockets across the treeless backyard, shuffling over the cold cobblestones of the alley, a hand-rolled cigarette in his lips, muttering Polish curses.

Maybe he has a friend he thinks to visit. But it would have to be a good friend to receive him empty-handed on Christmas morning, when most families are gathered around the tree exchanging gifts. So I see him roaming the streets, looking wistfully through tenement windows at warm hearths and lighted trees, and repeatedly passing by the watch-repair shop on North Market Street to glance at the clock in the window.

Stepping into Grandma Mary's flat I cross into an exotic world spiced with the odd sounds of her Slavic tongue and the familiar aromas of steaming kiska, warm Russian rye, and frying Polish ham.

She stands at the center of the shining, linoleum-covered kitchen floor not five feet tall, gaunt and silver-haired, in a prim gray gabardine dress, white lace handkerchief peeking from her pocket. The facial resemblance to my father (and ultimately to myself) always impresses me. Though I do not yet understand procreation and all that it entails, I can see that she is my father's mother and I my father's son. But while the strong jaw, deep-set eyes, prominent nose, and fine black hair make my father a handsome man, similar features in her make for an overly masculine and homely woman.

These are not northern Slavic features. No fair-haired, round-faced, blue-eyed Poles in this family. But dark, wolfish folks, perhaps descendants of raiders from the East. Or of Gypsies, for that is the look and the temperament: dark, taciturn, and suspicious; wary of institutions and the larger civic order; nomadic. Or perhaps descendants of the Neuri, militant Iranian nomads who inhabited Eastern Poland in the Fifth Century B.C. and who, according to Herodotus, turned into wolves at certain times of the year.

Today when I read of recently urbanized nomads who, after a few months of setting up home on a street in, say, Riyadh, will fold their tents and move across the street to another, identical plot of sand, when I read of these nomads I think of Grandma Mary. She seemed to relocate annually to an identical second-story shotgun flat with polished hardwood floors, checked linoleum in the kitchen, and mothballs in the closets, each apartment within a block or two of the poultry shop. I know I share those nomadic instincts and blood, whether Gypsy, Neuri, or Hun.

The rich Slavic tones, a mix of soft vowels and harsh diphthongs, come to me—though mostly in the words of my father. Even in her native tongue Mary is not talky, and my father is forever lecturing her and throwing up his hands in frustration over some stubbornness or another that neither I nor anyone else in the family can divine.

Polish is my father's first tongue as well, spoken at home and, at the time, on Cass Avenue, where immigrant Poles gathered in the early 1900's. Spoken too in the National Catholic Church, Piekutowski's sausage shop, the bakery, and the bars.

The foreign mother-tongue is both a curse and a blessing to my father, who views his ethnicity as the social handicap it truly was in his youth and early manhood. So he refuses to teach Polish to my brother and me, whom he thinks will thus better blend into the dominant Anglo culture. But he does not have the forethought or the heart to anglicize our name from Skwiot to, say, Scott.

But the blessing of the foreign mother-tongue is that he did not learn English until beginning public school, and then from rigorous and well-spoken English teachers instead of from parents and peers. As a result his English is grammatically precise, slang-free, and unaccented, his voice deep and commanding. To hear him speak you would think him a university-schooled radio announcer. It's what makes others think he would be a good salesman.

But Grandma Mary's English is another thing entirely. She takes a tentative step toward Eddie and me and presses a white envelope on each of us.

"Mahree Creezmos."

Most everything else she has to say to us boys or to my mother must be translated by my father, who after a while grows exasperated with much of it and refuses to translate.

"What did she say, Dad?"

"Naah, you don't need to know."

Mahree Creezmos.

But I do remember this much of what she said: the story she once told me of her childhood, in a village near Zawady, Poland, before World War I. I can't recall how much she actually spoke and I actually understood, how much might have been sign language, how much my father might have translated, or how much I may have embellished it with my own imagination. I wrote about it once in a short story:

> *Although it was a cloudless summer day, Maria and Kristina looked to the sky when they heard the rumbling sound, as if searching for thunderclouds. Then they realized their mistake.*
>
> *They ran over the mud road of their village toward the safety of Kristina's cottage. Maria, a lithe twelve-year-old, reached the cottage before Kristina, who was slowed by her infant, Piotr, at her breast.*
>
> *As Maria pushed through the plank door, she turned to see the only image she would ever dream of her native land for the next seventy years: Kristina on her knees, breast naked, mouth open but mute, gaping at the Cossack galloping away with Piotr hanging limp from the end of his saber.*

Then, when she was seventeen, her family somehow arranged her passage to America. Within a year she married my grandfather, Joseph, who was forty-five and from the same Polish town—but who had left for America two years after Mary was born. I suspect it was an arranged marriage of some sort.

Obviously life was vastly different and very difficult then and there for Mary, Joseph, and their kin. Which makes me reserve judgment of her and those involved in her migration, with the exception of the Cossacks. I see that my grandmother likely had her reasons for being mute, rigid, and wary, for never touching me.

But now it is Christmas morning and this is America, and I have an envelope with a new dollar bill in it and a Christmas card signed, simply, "Skwiot." At the kitchen table she places before me a plate with the fried Polish ham on Russian ryebread and a piece of steaming kiska—a heavenly sausage of blood, liver, and buckwheat groats spiced with hot pepper—alongside a fried egg. It is breakfast, and we all dig in.

There's little talk around the table except for brief and acrimonious exchanges in Polish between my father and grandmother. But the mood is bright, and the sharpness in their conversation is expected and not bothersome, as if a necessary ingredient in their close and emotionally charged relationship, like pepper in the kiska. We're a quiet family, who can enjoy our food and the pleasure of our own company without need to comment upon it. For me, eating kiska with eggs and watching my strange-bird of a grandmother sitting in her best dress drinking beer from a can at nine o'clock on Christmas morning is great fun.

My father winks at me and I nod back, acknowledging tacitly our shared appreciation of the rare food, which is nothing like the canned stews and soggy carrots served in my school's cafeteria. I understand that this is a privilege, a good, secret thing that few people know about and appreciate.

I know mine is a privileged and enchanted life, and that I have the unqualified alms and affection of the dark, handsome man and the quietly smiling and beautiful, fair-haired woman across the table. I know that later that night, after all the food and gifts, relatives and fun, they will wrap me in a scratchy blanket and carry me sleeping to the black Plymouth and then, at journey's end, put me to bed on the back porch that faces the frozen lake, with flames from the coal stove dancing in silhouette on the wall, like fairies.

• • •

Grandma Ida lives but blocks away from Grandma Mary, on North 14th Street. We make the short drive on largely deserted cobblestone streets bound by redbrick tenements. While either grandmother is forbidding to me in her own way, it is Grandma

Ida, the sour German Protestant, who most repels and scares me.

At Grandma Ida's an inhibiting tension always hovers in the air and grows tauter and tauter as the day grows longer. Whatever affection she may hold for me is tempered by a wariness, as if waiting for me to break a vase, spill my milk, sass my parents, or somehow misbehave. When such inevitably occurs, Grandma Ida is the first to condemn and correct me. Perhaps she sees something of her husband in me.

She and Uncle Harry, who sleeps on an army cot in her front room between marriages, are both silent, distrustful sorts. Not until much later do I understand that their silence and distrust—actually a distrust of words and thus of thought—likely lie in intellectual dimness.

Certainly my attitude toward them is influenced by the example of my father—who, conversely, is well spoken, humorous, and playful despite his mercurial Slavic soul and the funks it sometimes produces—as well as my father's assessment of his in-laws. Once, when I was three and being carried in his arms down the dark backstairs from Grandma Ida's and Uncle Harry's flat, I felt his breath in my ear.

"Thank God, Rickey," he whispered, "that at least you can choose your friends."

But this is the last Christmas we will share with Grandma Ida, who will die in June. My mother is to learn of her death when she visits her in the hospital after a minor illness and finds her bed empty. When she asks a passing nurse about her mother, the nurse, without pausing replies, "Oh, she's dead."

That nurse's comment still hangs like a black cloud over my family history, reminding me why I was so repelled my slow-eyed German kinfolk: They were nonentities. People who could be casually and disrespectfully dismissed, even in death. And worse, who confirmed and accepted their low status with a sullen slavishness.

Emerging from the Plymouth I inhale a steamy cloud of St. Louis sewer gas rising from beneath the city through the storm drain on the corner. It's an unmistakable odor of dark crevices and decay. The smell seems to permeate the red bricks defining this world: the redbrick streets, the redbrick herringbone sidewalks, the two-story redbrick tenements standing cheek by jowl down both sides of the block.

We move through another dark, musty, brick-enclosed walkway to the backyard, where a line of green-painted outhouses sit at the alley's edge. Although this is the United States of America, the richest nation ever known, and although this is the civilized core of one of its most populous cities with downtown skyscrapers not a ten-minute walk away, and although this is the second half of the Twentieth Century and the Romans had indoor plumbing two thousand years earlier, Grandma Ida still does not.

Rather, she lives in an antebellum coldwater flat with one lone faucet of chill water in the kitchen sink. A handsome but archaic Greek Revival building with jerry-rigged wiring added after Edison, it also houses generation upon generation of indigenous American mice despite baited mousetraps under Grandma Ida's bed and the living room sofa, where I occasionally spend the night. The mousetraps sometimes crack me from sleep, like death clapping in the night.

But notwithstanding the outhouse, lone faucet, mice, and second-hand furniture, I do not think my grandmother poor, though poor she is. For me her home only means a chance to explore—to examine dead mice, search the attic for relics, and linger in the glass-flecked alley behind the outhouse, which I scour for odd beer-bottle caps to add to my collection.

But by most all other standards Grandma Ida is poor and raised her children—my mother and my Uncle Harry—in poverty. Both of them were taken from school at age twelve and placed in jobs to help relieve that burden.

Although now as dour, silent, and homely as Grandma Mary, Grandma Ida was once a beautiful, straw-haired young woman, the daughter of German immigrants. She married a rakish and charming musician and dance instructor, Emil, who ran a dance studio in North St. Louis, at the corner of Easton and Kingshighway.

By 1919 they have two young children, not yet in school. While Ida already knows about Emil's weakness for the jug, this year she discovers his weakness of the flesh. She learns (how, we do not know) that he is having sex with his female students. (However, we do know that Ida once sends her five-year-old daughter to fetch her father from a tavern, and the girl reports back that he has a woman on his lap.)

But whatever she learns and however she learns it, Ida takes the extreme measure, in 1919, of divorcing her husband and refusing even one dime from him to help support her children. (Anyway, he would drink himself to death within a few short years, so any help she might have accepted would likely have been feeble and certainly temporary.) It is a time when women of her station do not divorce, for such a young woman cannot easily earn a living wage, much less support a family, and there is no government subsidy to encourage such independence.

So she goes to work as a live-in domestic at the German Children's Home while her own children sleep in the dormitory at the orphanage and are permitted to visit their mother for a few hours on Sundays. Such is divorce American-style circa 1920.

Some seventy-five years after the event, while researching family history, I find that the 1920 census lists my grandmother's residence as the State Mental Hospital on Arsenal Street and her occupation as "inmate." When I tell my aged mother of my discovery, she stares off for a few seconds, nods, and says, "Oh, yes. I remember Aunt Lennie saying Mom was having trouble with her nerves and that I would stay with her a while."

But soon Ida leaves the mental hospital and goes to work as a housemaid for well-heeled South St. Louis kin and eventually establishes her family in the cold-water flat on North 14th Street. And although it is a mean life—they often can afford no milk, no meat, no Christmas presents—it is not an unhappy one, by her daughter's accounts. They can still afford to laugh—at their plight if nothing else—and find neighbors and lifelong friends who are hardly better off than they and with whom they sit on the front stoop evenings and sing, which costs nothing.

But now, after enduring Grandma Ida's embrace and but a minute of the warm, cloying kitchen atmosphere, I rush again outside, where the sharp chill on my cheeks and fresh, cold air in my lungs please me. Down the wooden stairs to the backyard—this also covered in red brick. There I scout the coal chute that descends to the cellar, examine the incinerator next to the outhouse, and go to the alley to comb for treasure.

The alley is an alluring place. Although vendors sometime come down the street in front pushing their carts and selling vegetables, ice cream, or hot tamales, and people still sometimes sit on front stoops talking to neighbors or singing, the alley holds more secrets and more life.

In the alley on gray winter days you can see families in their lighted kitchens cooking, kissing, or fighting. You see them carrying out their garbage or running to the outhouse. And while the fronts of homes here all look pretty much the same—the same aged red bricks, the same swept sidewalk, the same sheer curtains—from the back you get a better idea of a family's nature by noting the state of their garden, the number of whiskey bottles in their trash, and the color and condition of their underwear on the clothesline.

The alley is also where, in summer, the men drink beer and play bottle caps, trying to hit a swirling and curving pitched beer-bottle cap with a broomstick.

I search for treasure there but rather gingerly, since I am wearing good clothes. Not my combat boots, worn trousers, and bomber's coat, but brown wool slacks and dark-green corduroy shirt (both sewn by my mother), the brown dress-shoes I wear to church, and a gray, hound's-tooth overcoat that was once my brother's.

Nonetheless I find two mills—the plastic coins that people used for money during the war—one green and one red, a Miller High Life bottle cap with the leggy blonde I secretly love sitting on a crescent moon, and a playing card, the King of Clubs, which I sense is good luck, for it resembles a four-leaf clover. I slide it into my pants pocket alongside my rabbit's foot, knowing luck is a good thing to have. But even if you are born with it as I was, I understand that you can lose it if you don't guard it. So I am forever touching my rabbit's foot, knocking on wood, and saying secret prayers to the gods that govern catching fish, winning at checkers, and shooting marbles.

Now I hear my mother calling—"Richard! O, Richard!"—and run back down the alley and up the gray-painted stairs to the second-floor flat.

Inside more gifts are exchanged. I share with my brother a leather football from Uncle Harry. From Grandma Ida we each receive an apple, an orange, and a red-net bag of walnuts—much the same as I got from the skinny, beer-breathed Santa at the Pontoon Beach VFW Christmas Party.

I want to return outdoors to play football even though I do not know the rules and can barely grip the ball. But I am told I have been outside in the cold enough already. Besides, the bricks will scuff the new ball. So while my mother helps Grandma Ida in the kitchen and my father and Uncle Harry drink beer and smoke in the front room, Eddie and I construct domino homes and long, curving files of domino soldiers that we fight to knock down.

Uncle Harry fetches photographs of himself in Paris, which I have seen before: Astride his motorcycle in dark wool overcoat and white M.P.'s helmet. Posing in front of the Eiffel Tower. Standing guard against German saboteurs before an elegant building with ornate, wrought-iron balconies, which I believe is Army Headquarters. Only years later do I learn from Uncle Harry that he is in fact guarding an officers' brothel, to keep out enlisted men.

Soon we ring the table in the stuffy, good-smelling kitchen and say grace in unison, the two women standing behind their chairs. Mother lifts the roast goose stuffed with sauerkraut onto the table. The sharp smell of the kraut and the thick aroma of browned goose-fat enfold me like warm, scratchy wool. There are mashed potatoes and canned peas, cranberry sauce, and finally pumpkin pie with whipped cream. Excellent fare, to my palate, excepting the peas, which I try to hide under a pile of goose bones. My parents catch me at this ruse but, since it's Christmas, give me dispensation, and this once I can leave the table without cleaning my plate.

Beside the kitchen cupboard stands a gray door. When my father goes to the front room to smoke and my mother and grandmother are at the stove heating water to wash and rinse the dishes (or "warsh and wrench" on Grandma Ida's Teutonic tongue), I pry it open and slip through.

Behind the door lies more grayness: dingy stairs that I mount soundlessly and that lead up to a colorless attic with grimy windows and gray slat floor. Gray dust-motes hang in cold, musty air, cold as a grave. Gray dust lies everywhere, a century's worth of indifference coating everything like a thin, gray blanket.

In the center of the floor sits a gray tin washtub and corrugated-iron scrub-board. Each Thursday the women boil water on the kitchen stove and carry it steaming up the stairs. I see my mother on her knees, bent over the tin tub, fists working a garment up and down the scrub-board as if grating cheese. Above, on crisscrossed clotheslines where the laundry is draped on rainy days, a few gray sheets and pillowcases still hang.

The colorless, airless attic smelling of neglect depresses and frightens me. But it lures me as well, for I know that here in this grim room treasure also lies. I steal toward it, toward the coffin-like steamer-trunk beneath the fly-specked window. My eyes are drawn up to the window momentarily by the cooing of pigeons, which I spy on the black-tar roof.

I lift the lid of the trunk slowly, as if fearful of releasing ghosts, and start when I see the arms and legs of Uncle Harry's army uniform resting there. Beneath the uniform in a shiny black-metal sheath lies a dagger with a swastika on its hilt. I slide it from its sheath with a tinkling, scraping noise that sends a ripple up my spine, and lay it across my palm to examine it for blood.

I discover more treasure: a tintype photograph of a young woman in a pleated dress buttoned up to her chin, wispy blonde hair curled atop her head. Grandma Ida on her wedding day, I have been told, but find it hard to believe. Grandma Ida is a heavyset, heavy-jowled woman with stringy gray hair and sad gaze, who ambles about uneasily on thick legs, and this is a slender young woman with a hopeful smile, a straight back, and vivid, dancing eyes.

My mother's voice comes lilting up the stairs: "Are you up there, Rickey? Come down or you'll get dirty. We still have to go to Maria's."

I close the heavy trunk-lid, careful not to catch my fingers, brush dust from the knees of my trousers, and rush from the grayness back downstairs into the warm, bright kitchen, eager to wash my hands under the cold kitchen tap, to rinse from them the feel of death.

Fido the Talking Dog
by Robert Earleywine

Some time ago a friend of mine who'd just gone through a divorce was feeling lonely at home in his studio apartment. I told him he ought to get a dog, for company, I said, but he pooh-poohed the idea.

Then one fine autumn day, perhaps bearing my words in mind, he went for a long walk. He walked far past his apartment in Dogtown, and was walking around in the posh Clayton neighborhood wishing he could afford a big house, when he saw a sign stuck on a lawn:

Talking Dog For Sale
$10.00

There was a man with a leaf blower blowing the fallen leaves away from the pathway up to his stately home. My friend went up and tapped him on the shoulder and the man silenced the leaf blower.

"Is it true you got a talking dog for sale?"

"That's what the sign says."

"Can I see him?"

"He's around back. Go around and talk to him."

It was a corner lot. My friend went around and saw a nondescript dog sitting in front of a big dog house, so big he could've have had cable in there. The dog seemed lost in reverie.

"Excuse me. Hello," my friend said. "Is it true you talk?"

"Sure, I talk," the dog said, looking at him, then looking away again. "I'm a talking dog. Talked before I whelped, talked when I was knee high. Learned a few languages, the usual Roman ones, besides Swahili, and Russian, thanks to my first master. A diplomat. Women loved him. Fed me a special diet. But withheld the treats, the scraps of red meat and pork fat till I'd conjugated my verbs. Then he sold me out, put me to work for the CIA. And then I became the perfect spy. They'd leave me in a room of world leaders. The usual dickheads of state. Who'd suspect me? What they said at their long tables, I reported back, nearly word for word. I have a remarkable ear. I earned respect. But it was a hectic life. All the time maintaining manners. No licking, no scratching."

The dog talked on, and my friend liked hearing the dog talk, a talk so unlike the talk of his ex-wife. "But if you can talk," my friend asked, "what are you doing here in Clayton?"

"What good is it?" the dog said. "Fame. Citations. Bright ribbons. Like my pa used to say, If you can't eat it or fuck it, piss on it. Not that I like it here. I hate it here. Corner lot, no fence, I'm on a chain. It's a dog's life. But there's a roof over my head. What about you? How's your life?"

Not only a talking dog, but a listening dog, he let my friend go on and whine and piss and moan about his divorce. The dog turned a sympathetic ear. They went on talking together, and the dog agreed to move in with him, if he could sleep indoors, if he could have a steak now and then, not a cheap steak but a good steak, and a bowl of cold beer.

My friend went back out front and walked up to the man with the leaf blower who had just turned it off. The path was clear..

"It's true, the dog really talks."

"That's what the sign says."

"But he really talks."

"You want him? Ten bucks."

"But he talks." My friend opened his wallet. "How can you sell him for ten dollars?"

"He's such a liar," the man said.

• • •

So my friend moved Fido into his studio apartment, and built him a bed, much like his own but smaller, and nights they talked into the wee small hours. Though the dog tended to tell tall tales about himself, my friend didn't mind. He didn't care whether Fido was lying or not, he enjoyed the tales Fido told, thumping his own tail on the wooden floor, for paragraph breaks, and as if to say, And then, thump. Thump, and then, thump thump. Fido's stories, when they weren't that interesting, helped put my friend to sleep.

Late one night, when they'd run out of beer and neither could doze off, my friend had an epiphany. "Fido," he yelled into the dark so loud Fido cowered. "I don't know if I believe this shit about you and the CIA. But we're out of beer money."

"Frankly," Fido said, "I prefer Scotch."

"Listen. I just thought of us a way make money. Fido, my friend, we'll be rich."

"Bow wow," my friend thought he heard Fido say and entertained a moment of doubt, and twirled his finger into his ear. "What?"

"But how?" Fido said.

"We'll start small. We'll do it for drinks. We'll go into a bar. I'll tell them you're a talking dog. They won't believe it. We'll make a bet. You talk. We'll drink all night for free."

My friend could picture it, phosphorescent images unreeling in the mottled dark.

"When your reputation grows, by word of mouth, we'll get a TV spot. We'll write a book. Sell it to the movies."

"I don't care a biscuit for fame," Fido said.

"Do it for me," my friend said. "Do it because, because you're my friend."

• • •

So the next day they go into a bar. Fido jumps up on a stool.

"No dogs allowed," the bartender says.

It's the middle of the afternoon. But for the bartender, the bar is empty.

"This is a talking dog," my friend says. "Will you stand us a round if he talks?"

"If this dog talks, you can drink all night on the house."

"Sure, on the house. Fido," my friend says, "what goes on top of a house?"

"Roof," Fido says. "Roof."

"Get the fuck outta here," the bartender says.

"Wait," my friend says. "Fido, who was the greatest baseball player of all time?"

"Ruth," Fido says. "Ruth."

"Get the fuck outta here."

My friend and Fido walk along the shady city street in silence for a while. It's a spring day, but they don't feel it. Head drooped, staring at the pavement, my friend is downcast. Tail between his legs. Hangdog. Fido's hangdog too. His back slinks. His ears droop. Another block and Fido realizes something and perks up, "I should have said Dimaggio."

About the time my friend is about to believe dogs aren't as smart as they're said to be, about three steps past a pause at a fire hydrant, my friend says, "Now look, Fido, we'll try this again. We'll order the first drink, and then you tell one of your CIA stories."

It's a neighborhood of bars. Churches at the end of every block. Long alleys cutting down the middle. At the next bar, they go in.

"I'd like a beer," my friend says, "and give my dog a scotch and toilet water."

The bar is empty but for the bartender. My friend says to him, "This is a talking dog."

The bartender serves, and goes back to wiping down the bar, "Sure, pal."

"Fido," my friend says, "tell him about you and the CIA."

Fido rests his forelegs on the bar, surrounding his drink. "It's true," he says, "I used to work for the CIA, but after a few years I resigned. Truth is, it made my conscience ache. And the traveling. Living out of suit cases. Dried chow out of suit cases. Dirty toilets. You never know who's been drinking out of them . . ."

And Fido goes on. Of course, the bartender is astounded.

His mouth hanging open, it never seems to occur to him Fido might be lying. He stands them another beer, another scotch and toilet water. On their third free drink, they're all having a good old time, Fido and the bartender swapping jokes.

A giraffe walks into a bar... A grasshopper walks into a bar... A parrot walks into a bar... A skeleton walks into a bar and asks for a beer and a mop... An Irishman walks out of a bar.

Fido doesn't much care for parrot jokes. They seem to make him a little jealous somehow. But the bartender has a celebration of them and Fido nods and feigns listening.

My friend has to pee, but he doesn't want to leave Fido alone at the bar, like a babe you're afraid somebody'll steal, but he has to pee, and so excuses himself.

"You wait right here," he says to Fido and, "Watch my dog," he orders the bartender.

In the crapper, he pees for an hour it seems, washes his hands, combs his thinning hair, tucks in his shirt. Looking in the mirror, he considers his future, his and Fido's.

When he comes back, his dog is gone.

"Where's my dog? Where's my dog? Where's my dog?"

"Relax," the bartender says. "He's such a hoot, I gave him five dollars and sent him up the street. My best friend runs the bar two blocks up. Wait till he sees a talking dog. So Fido worked for the CIA? Is that true? Here, have a beer on the house. He said he'd be right back. So a moose walks into a bar, and sees a moosehead on the wall..."

My friend is nervous. The booze doesn't help. Another beer and the dim barroom begins to sway. He can't take it any longer. He asks for directions and runs out into the street. He finds the other bar and goes in, opening a light screen door a Pekingese could push open. "You seen a talking dog?" he cries.

But for the bartender, the bar is empty.

"You mean Fido?" the bartender says. "Yeah, scotch and toilet water. Used to work for the CIA? I can't believe it. Left, I don't know, a little while ago."

My friend is frantic, he sees his future gone, but worse, it's like he's lost his best friend. It's like his dog died. He combs the streets, stops in every bar. You seen a talking dog? They look at him like he's got rabies. He looks in backyards where from behind fences dogs bark at him. He tries several alleys calling Fido's name. "Here, Fido. Fido? Fi-do. You want to eat? Here, Fido. Fi-ido."

The dogs bark.

It's getting dark and he's near tears by the time he crosses another alley and sees deep in this darkening alley his best friend Fido trying to mount a French Poodle.

"Fido," he calls. "Fido, what's got into you? What are you doing? How could you do this to me? What about our future? I've never known you to behave this way before."

Fido looks at him and shrugs. "I never had five dollars before."

Heman Park:
The Urban Tennis Jungle
by Michael MacCambridge

On a suffocating summer afternoon in St. Louis in the early '90s, some of the regulars were staying away from Heman Park, holding out for shade or breeze or darkness, anything to take the edge off the punishing heat. But Stan Webb, a rangy engineer with a serene countenance, was out with his new racket, hitting on the practice wall, diligently working on his game.

Webb did a double-take when he first saw the approaching stranger, a patchy-bearded black man of indeterminate age, traversing the shank of grass separating the parking lot from the tennis courts. Walking with a purposeful, pigeon-toed gait, he was dressed like a drifter, in a faded army cap with the brim turned up, cheap purple mirrored wraparound shades, a long sleeved shirt, faded blue jeans and weathered old brogan work shoes, dangling a lit cigarette from his mouth and carrying the first wooden tennis racket Webb had seen in years. The man sat on the bench just outside the court, eyed Webb for a few moments, then cheerfully asked, "You wanna hit some?"

A half-hour later, the stranger lit his next cigarette. But by then, Stan Webb—hands on his knees, victim of a thorough, 6-0, 6-0 whipping—realized he'd just received his Heman indoctrination. Once you've been taken to the woodshed by Jimmy the Shark, you either skulk away in quiet agony or recognize that lessons are being imparted, the first of which is: Out here, image and appearance count for nothing. You can roll up in all the designer tennis attire you want, but once we pop the can and twist for serve, all that really matters is: Have you got game?

Welcome to Heman Park, and the urban tennis jungle.

Across the country, tennis faces an identity crisis. After the populist promise of its mid '70s boom, the whole sport seemed to disappear into some sort of Federal Witness Protection Program. And in the public perception of today, it remains smug and aloof, held prisoner in the private clubs by nattering old codgers who enforce dress codes and arcane rules of etiquette, taken hostage on the pro tour by spoiled, intellectually-atrophied 16-year-olds with monstrously overbearing parents. It's child abuse, with millionaires.

But far away from the private clubs and posh resorts, a different reality is emerging. While tennis has been dying in the public mind, it has been resurrected and largely reinvented in the public parks, far from the game's traditionally cloistered centers of power. In St. Louis, the Dwight Davis Tennis Center in Forest Park remains the city's finest, most popular tennis facility. But not nearly its most interesting one.

For that, you have to go by Olive Blvd.'s busy stretch of strip malls and fast-food chains, in the multicultural jigsaw of University City. Out here on the eight cracked courts of Heman Park, the regulars return each year. They are a profane, prideful mass of hackers, hustlers and rogues, some coming from as far as 20 miles away to join in the vibrant, cutthroat scene that Bill Tilden would have a hard time recognizing.

This is tennis without the amenities. At Heman Park, where there are no ball machines, no pro shop, no clubhouse, no reservations. But there's Doughbelly Earl, a fleet butterball with a ponytail and a vicious net game; there's the voluble elder Roy Taylor, described by one regular as the Don King of tennis. There's Chinese John, who can run down lobs forever, laughing in his high-pitched squeal all the while; and there's the perpetually laid-back, obstinately old-school Lonnie, who thinks giving the score before each point is just so much honky nonsense. And somewhere in the midst of it all, you can still find Jimmy "the Shark" Kimple, always in jeans or work pants, these days brandishing a ridiculously archaic, 25-year-old T-2000 racket, and still whipping nearly everyone in sight. This loose, testifying mix of intermediate players long ago dispensed with many of the staid, priggish traditions of the sport—the dress code, the unctuous politesse, the residue of elitist snobbery that still exists at all levels—and retained that which is best about the game, distilled down to its sweaty, rowdy, hypercompetitive essence.

What has emerged at Heman is a vibrant tennis scene with an uncommonly egalitarian spirit, largely because the courts are dominated by middle-class blacks, playing what has for centuries been a white upper-class game. On summer nights, you can hear Cardinals' games emanating from a small transistor radio that the court attendant brings out, while gangsta rap and '70s soul blasts from the massive trunk systems of the softball players who do battle on the other side of the parking lot. When the weekend cookouts start on the stone-hearth barcecue grills just a few steps from the courts, the atmosphere is akin to an integrated outdoor house party, as close to idyllic as any you're likely to find in urban America in the late '90s.

But don't be fooled. Utopian visions aside, there remains a remorseless, Darwinian aspect to the game, especially in this setting, that is unsurpassed. No one who's serious about tennis comes *just* to have a good time. Points are being made, grudges are being built, scores are being settled. "There is no racial animosity at Heman," says Loren Watt, a freelance videographer and former stand-up comedian. "But that don't mean that there's no *personal* animosity."

• • •

The first thing you have to get used to is the constant noise.

From a doubles match on Court Two: "Hey, Butch! You know, the line is *in*!"

Out on Court Eight, a handsome, bearded man named Norman smacks a forehand approach into the net, and looks up in sweaty frustration. "Get it *out* of me! Wine, beer, all that s---!"

Jerry Fitch, bespectacled, mid-fiftyish, intense, sits among a group at a picnic table watching the action, separated by just a few feet and a chain-link fence from court one. The square table serves as Heman's informal grandstand, the gathering place for the Greek chorus of players, philosophers, hecklers and gadflies that are always present. Fitch is only a couple days away from hip replacement surgery, but that doesn't stop him; he's still handing out advice, chomping for a challenge, his mouth writing checks that his game can't cash. "Oh, I think I better get my tennis gear," he bellows, to everyone and no one in particular. "I see some fresh live bait out there."

Soon enough Fitch focuses on Earl Williams, the rotund, ever-smiling veteran of so many Heman Park wars. Dough-belly Earl—wearing a shirt of wide, fluorescent, horizontal stripes that makes his thin-necked racket look all the smaller by comparison—is pounding the ball on court one, ripping crosscourt forehand winners and sharp, angled volleys. But he makes one unforced error, and the litany starts...

"I *saw* that," shouts Fitch.

No response. So he continues.

"You got to bend your knees!"

Still nothing.

"Earl—you know I'm talking to you! So fat in that shirt, you look like a sunset."

This finally gets a reaction from Williams, who has to step back from his next serve, while his preposterous laugh rises up over all eight courts.

The raucous scene at Heman has been decades in the making, part of rich tennis tradition in St. Louis that hasn't always been a proud one. This is the hometown of Dwight Davis, after whom the Davis Cup is named; and Jimmy Connors cut his teeth just across the river in Belleville. But there are people here who remember what it was like when blacks weren't allowed on any public courts in the city; winters when the only indoor venue for them was the old Downtown Armory. That didn't change until the early '60s, when Sumner High teacher

Richard Hudlin brought in a black tennis prodigy named Arthur Ashe to St. Louis for his senior year in high school, and forced the issue.

It was a generation of players from the civil rights years, many of whom learned the game from Hudlin, who began the raucous, all-black scene at Fairgrounds Park in north St. Louis, where all-day tennis parties and cookouts became the norm. "Everybody would bring something," recalls one regular. "The cheap people would bring a loaf of bread." In the late '70s, a hail of gang-banging and drive-bys drove the tennis players to O'Fallon Park, an equally tough complex a few miles away. But after a few years there, they returned one spring to find the nets torn down, and broken beer bottles littering the courts.

That's what started the migration to Heman Park, which the core group of players now guard with a mother bear's ferocity. The park's clientele is a monument to both the burgeoning black middle class and suburban white flight. In 1960, there were only 88 blacks among the 50,000 people in University City; today blacks make up 50% of the 40,000 residents living here.

With all this as prologue, the atmosphere at Heman might have developed into one of chippy exclusivity, but instead the opposite has occurred—the place is a model of meritocracy. Don't worry about calling for a court, setting up a time or bringing a partner. Just show up. On Saturdays in the summer, the No. 1 court becomes the challenge court, held by whatever doubles team can keep winning. All challenges must be met: two lowly hackers can call out for winners, and they must be given their shot.

Unlike the mind-numbing baseline blasting of today's tournament-level tennis, the game that's developed at Heman is extraordinarily idiosyncratic, built on a slashing, attacking style and a keen sense for an opponent's weakness—rushing the net at the first short groundstroke. The best players possess daring net games and the raw athleticism to run down anything hit away from them. And even the old hands who can't run so well anymore have constructed their games in direct response to the standard, with most possessing a vast array of ancillary strokes—passing shots, drop shots, offensive and defensive lobs. There's a strain of quirky self-reliance that runs through the roster of Heman hitters. Remembering one hallowed victory, the ebullient Loren Watt describes his approach: "I went out there, and I was slicing and dicing, and hacking and whacking—the Veg-O-Matic had nothing on me. And, you know, sometimes that stuff would *go in*. I ran some balls down 'cause I got some pedals, and all of a sudden, I'm winning the match."

Like speed-chess or mountain-climbing, urban tennis draws a curious mixture of people. Most of its proponents are excellent athletes with pride and a sense of determination. They don't hike, they don't camp—they want to keep score. Though many of the blacks who play at Heman used to view tennis as a sissified endeavor, they've found through experience that it's the most strenuous competitive athletic exercise around that doesn't involve collisions. And despite the demanding physicality of the sport, there's enough strategy that people can keep honing their game for decades. There aren't many 50-year-olds playing their best basketball ever, but the tennis courts are full of middle-aged athletes at their competitive peak.

Also, in any objective real-world analysis, tennis has it all over golf. Both sports can be played for life, but tennis gives you more exercise, over less time, in less space, at less expense. The females are cuter. Granted, both sports feature a large assortment of jerks, but in tennis, you don't have to spend 4-1/2 hours making small talk with them. And at Heman, there is something that even in the Age of Tiger is rarely found on golf courses: genuine social integration, of races and classes. Airline pilots serve to garbagemen, and private investigators hit with security guards.

• • •

But even in this eclectic mix, one player stands out. Though you might get some decent stock tips at a private tennis club, you'd never meet anyone quite like Jimmy the Shark. Jimmy Kimple is a true American original, a man so authentically eccentric that he doesn't like eating meals in public. He doesn't practice, doesn't warm up, is able to hit forehands from either side, doesn't drink water during changeovers, and invariably plays, even in the dead of summer, in jeans or slacks. Kimple is the ultimate tennis hustler because it's not an act. Though he's playing with equipment that most would find obsolete, he's never let it bother him. "I bought all my stuff used," he says. "The only brand-new racket I ever bought was a K-Mart special. And everybody was saying, 'Jimmy, I don't know how you can play with a K-mart special.' I said, 'Well, I figure it like this: It *ain't* the racket.'"

Growing up in the decaying inner-city of North St. Louis, Kimple was so poor that his first bicycle had no tires on it. He used to delight in riding it down a hill after dark and slamming on the brakes, to see the sparks fly from the metal rims scraping on the pavement. These days, at 48 years old, he still works a job of heavy manual labor, moving 100-pound drums in a local plastics factory. That keeps him strong, and his first sporting loves—table tennis (where he's one of the top-ranked players in the state of Missouri) and roller-skating—keep him agile.

Other people have schedules and routines out at Heman. But the Shark just shows up, and when he does, there are no formalities. "Jimmy's out there smoking a cigarette and he's ready to go," says John Embry, the retired TWA pilot who is his friend, and fiercest rival. "If he's out there, he's playing. Doesn't want to warm up. Hit about three balls and Jimmy's ready to play. I mean, that's just being courteous doing that. He can just walk out there and never hit a warm-up ball, never take a warm-up shot."

You want urban myths? Everyone has their own Shark story.

"First time I saw Jimmy, Jimmy looked like a dead man," recollects Roy Taylor, the burly, heavy-browed doubles specialist—try to picture Muddy Waters playing tennis—who captains winning teams in seemingly every league in the city. "Blue jeans, mismatched socks, old dirty tennis shoes. He looked like a druggie, and he still looks like a druggie, when he go out on a tennis court. And I said, I'm gonna go out here and whip this boy's butt. And he went out there and gave me the whupping of my life."

But what makes Kimple so special and so beloved is his lack of pretense or condescension. In true Heman fashion, he takes on all comers—good, bad, white, black, male, female. And changes his game not a whit for any of them. Kimple moves his opponents around, wearing them down by sending them on a geometric frenzy of side-to-side rushes. And he keeps pounding, whether he's in a tight match or playing a woeful novice. By the second set of one of his ritual 6-0, 6-0 thrashings, one begins to appreciate the whipping, and understand. This is how it's done. No quarter is asked for, none given. Heman Park, to borrow a line from an old Bruce Springsteen concert intro, is "a land of peace, love, hope, justice... and no mercy."

• • •

So why do so many people still think tennis is so, well, dull?

"Tennis defeats *itself*," says Hal Cox, who works as a counselor for troubled youths, and has been a Heman regular for nearly 20 years. "Look, the sports that are the American sports—football, baseball, basketball—they go out there and they're loud, raucous, have a great time, party. How are you going to party when you're sitting up there and and the umpire says, 'May we have silence please?' Tennis isn't going to recover until they decide to go to the rock 'n' roll tennis. And that's one of the attractions of Heman Park. A lot of the parks you go to, you get out of your car, and all you hear are the tennis balls. It's most definitely not like that at Heman—we get down there and we have fun."

Maybe someday, tennis will catch up. But in the meantime, at Heman Park, they'll just keep playing their own game.

One Friday afternoon in May, I'm playing a doubles match partnered with Charles Gross, an aging man with a Fu Manchu mustache and a service motion so convoluted it looks like a witch doctor's voodoo incantation. Though his serve isn't hard, it's very accurate, and Gross has carried me through a closely-fought set that stands at 6-7, 40-30 with him serving to tie it once more. After a short rally, he hits a sweet spinning forehand wide that one of our opponents barely tracks down, mustering only a weak lollipop lob that floats harmlessly in the air toward our side of the net, where I stand waiting, locked and loaded.

In that split-second before I uncork my precise putaway, I experience a moment of clarity. The ball moves in technicolor slow-motion, and my mind strobes through everything good about the competition and the toil and frustration that goes into an evenly-matched set; of the exquisite joy and sense of accomplishment one gets from a single, crisply-executed shot. Carefully eyeing the ball's slow, steady trajectory, I draw back my Prince Longbody Thunderstorm, and let loose a furious blast—and, of course, whiff entirely.

Of all the skills that are cultivated at Heman, none are more valued than peripheral vision. In the wake of my spectacular display of physical ineptitude and grievous choking, everything freezes—points stop on adjacent courts, people drop rackets in laughter, a small fandango erupts right there. And as I move into position for the next point, head ducked in shame, eyes focused on the court beneath me, I can't help but hear the grating, teasing voice, from fully two courts away:

"Why don't you put *that* in ya' goddamn story?!"

And then sustained, louder laughter piercing the warm evening air.

What preserves me is not just the rueful realization that, after a year, I am enough of a Heman regular to be the object of joyous ridicule. Nor the fact that at a private tennis club, this entire scene would have gone quietly unremarked. It is that someday—tomorrow, next week, next year—there will be another all-important chance, and next time, the overhead won't be missed. Out here, that will surely be noticed as well. It's never too late for redemption.

So play continues, time passes, stereotypes die. A city is integrated. And the lights are on at Heman.

BIG MUDDY BLUES
by Charles Wartts Jr.

When Sam didn't show by bedtime Friday night—a full three days—what started out as a simple bout of restlessness, became a full-fledged case of mass insomnia. At a quarter past midnight, I was making my third trip downstairs to the kitchen for a glass of water and something to snack on when I noticed lamplight seeping from beneath my parents' bedroom door. I tiptoed closer, but couldn't hear anything but the tense warble of voices.

Back upstairs in my attic bedroom, I lay half-heartedly musing over *The Catcher in the Rye,* a book that had been practically forced on me by my high school counselor. It had come in handy over the past couple of days though, as I fended off dismal thoughts of Sam by slipping for moments at a time into Holden Caulfield's shoes. Did going away to school really work those kind of upside-down, inside-out changes on people? What would GWC University be like?

Just then a scream ripped through my revelry, causing the entire household to run riot. After a few moments, with everybody scurrying from room to room like rats in a maze, it was finally established that the screams had come from my baby sister, who'd had what we all hastily concluded was a nightmare. But in spite of all attempts by Mama and Daddy to reassure her, Ella Mae, who was only nine, stood her ground against the grown-up voices of reason and common sense. With big tears sloshing down her soft, caramel face, she insisted that she'd woke up to find a man with no head bending over her bed.

That's when Daddy, supported by me and my older brother, Frank, took pains to demonstrate that no one could possibly sneak into the house, let alone escape through the nailed-down windows and double-latched doors. But Ella Mae's bald-faced refusal to yield, even when confronted with such elaborate proof, began to gnaw away at everybody's confidence, until none of us could be sure that the flat's heavy-laden security could waylay a man with no head. In the crawlspace of doubt that stole upon us, Sam's absence thumped like a mad mammy-jamming bass man upon our last taut nerve.

There was no thought of sleeping after that, and Mama, rising to the occasion, whipped up a fresh batch of flapjacks, some spinach and eggs smothered in fresh shallots, two cast iron skillets full of the old man's homemade rabbit sausage, and we beat back trouble with a feast. Later, after everybody had turned in for bed, I trailed Daddy out to the front, where he sat bare-chested, coaxing a lonesome blues from his harmonica as his eyes scanned the deserted streets. I sat down next to him, as silent as a shadow, something I hadn't had nerve enough to do since I was a kid. It was near daybreak when our vigil ended, neither of us having spoken a word the whole time.

Thursday, the third day running, came and went, and that night found me and the old man still holding down the stoop together—but still no sign of Sam. By now Daddy looked like an aging barnyard rooster who'd just gotten the worst of it in a cockfight with a feisty, young challenger. His face was a patch of chicken-scratched delta earth, eyes bleary and sandbagged, his scraggly beard like half-plucked feathers as he sat there filling the air with smoke signals. Ever so often he drew a half-pint bottle of Old Granddad from his back pocket, unscrewed the cap and took a swig. He was on the verge of breaking up and I couldn't help but wonder if it was his last words to Sam that were eating away at his gut. Shortly before midnight, he drained the bottle, pitched it into the trash and shuffled off to bed. Minutes later when I peeped in through the cracked bedroom door, he'd fallen into a fitful sleep.

Without the benefit of a bedtime tonic, I wasn't so lucky. Once upstairs, I plopped down on my bed, grateful to be rid of my own weight, which seemed to have doubled. I rolled over on my back and stared up at the shadows crawling over the ceiling, wishing I could nod off. Not that I wasn't hip to warm milk and counting sheep from watching *Father Knows Best* on television, but sheep were pretty hard to come by in my neighborhood. So I lay there squinting, trying to count the number of insects that dotted the spider web high up in a corner, but soon gave up. The shadows cast by a dangling forty-watt bulb was too much competition.

Encouraged by a breeze from the open window, the ceiling shadows were putting on a grotesque peep show, conjuring up scenes of Sam, his bloated body bobbing up in some dark, lonely inlet of the Mississippi River. But in the very next instant, I would see him diddy-bopping across the ceiling, sporting that devilish grin that he reserved especially for late night entrances. I guess, deep down in the gizzard, there was no way I could believe that Sam was dead. I'd been in the world for sixteen whole years and nobody really close had ever died. That was proof enough for me. And besides, it just wouldn't be his style.

I lay there for the longest time, gazing up at the ceiling, fascinated by the easy collaboration of shadow and act, of matter and mind. After awhile I got my fingers and toes into the act, adding my own ghoulish effects to the cartoon-like drama. I was so busy skinny-dipping in the Twilight Zone that I didn't even hear the groan of the front hall door or the careless syncopation of Sam's footsteps on the stairway, and when I knew anything, he was standing there beaming down on me like the morning star. Even then I couldn't be sure that this wasn't just a signature edition of one of Sam's tall tales as he stood there clean as the board of health. Ragged down in a white silk suit, baby pink shirt, a burgundy tie with little twinkling stars that clustered round a diamond pin, he could've been Little Black Sambo just back from a jungle rumble with fresh tiger butter.

"Sam...? What you doing here?" I blurted out, still blinking, feeling halfway foolish for talking to a ghost.

"Sorry to disappoint you Sleepin' Beauty, but the prince had a little trouble keepin' up wid my stride. So here I be!"

I sprang up on my elbows, knuckling stardust out of my eyes. "Sam, where you been, man? Where'd you get those clothes? Everybody's been worried sick!"

"Whoaaaaa podnuh!" he shushed me. "I didn't just tip all the way up them stairs for you to go raisin' the dead. Put yo' jacket on and let's ride."

"But ain't you gonna let Daddy 'nem know...?"

Sam's raised hand was a streak of ruby-red light. "Not just yet. Now you make haste befo' somebody hear us," he squeezed my forearm with a freshly manicured paw, the big diamond on his pinkie raying rainbows in my eye. "We won't be long," he reassured me. "Now c'mon, let's rock and roll befo' dawn catch us!"

Minutes later we glided smoothly away from the curb after I, playing the fool, allowed myself to be coaxed inside the plush interior of a white convertible Lincoln Continental with Illinois license plates. Once inside, I sank down into the white satin softness of the upholstery, trimmed with smooth burgundy leather on the doors and dash. I turned a baffled gaze on Sam, watching him maneuver the car through the empty streets like he was born to this style of living. For a fleet-footed second we were back on Blackbottom Plantation, purring along in Sam's old Hudson Terraplane, about to run a raid on Jimmy Westland's prize cotton crop. I broke out with the giggles.

"Sumpthin' ticklin' yo' fancy, podnuh?" Sam shot an amused glance at me.

"I gotta hand it to you, Cuz, you got more tricks up your sleeve than Br'er Rabbit himself. Pardon me...make that *Cuz'n* Br'er Rabbit," I grinned back at him. Sam made a smooth turn onto Easton Avenue, and as if I wasn't already sufficiently impressed, he lowered the top on the Lincoln with a flick of the wrist as we cruised through the cool crisp air, still scented with the sweet funk of barrel bottom life. Meanwhile the white-gloved battle of the blues blared from the radio as Louis Jordan funked it up with "Saturday Night Fish Fry." Then there was Howlin' Wolf snapping at the seat of his pants with "Howlin' For My Darling," while Muddy Waters went off the deep end with "Ain't That A Man?" In between time, I was still trying to take it all in, trying to make all the pieces fit. How could all this be real and yet so damn *unreal* at the same time? The million dollar threads, the diamonds and rubies flashing signals I couldn't catch, this mean motor-scooter of a machine! *What did it all mean?* I'm scoping Cuz bigtime now as he delicately flicks the ashes from the fat Cuban stogie off his lapel. And I'm just about to yell, "Will the real Samuel Will Turner please stand up?" when it hits me like chunks of ice blue sky raining hickies down on Chicken Little's head. I hear a voice inside my head blurt out: *Goddammit! This is Sam the mammy-jamming Man. And all this time he's been playing possum on me!*

I let my head sink back into the headrest, a red ripe grin splicing my face as I sank deep into the feminine softness. Still a relentless pestering, like the buzz of my alarm clock, kept urging me to pinch myself just to make sure that Cuz was sitting beside me in the flesh, that all the fairy tale creature comforts were real. But I didn't dare. Dream or scheme, I wanted to be on the scene!

The Lincoln, like a sleek, sultry Siamese, was pawing its way onto Franklin Avenue (later to become Martin Luther King Boulevard), the heart of the strip, jammed with night clubs, beauty and barber shops, soul food restaurants, liquor stores and mom and pop confectioneries. Sandwiched in between were Jewish, Italian and Chinese food marts, fruit and vegetable stands, pawnshops, and clothing and furniture outlets. As we crossed Leffingwell Avenue, I cut a glance at the lifeless marquee of the Roosevelt Theatre, where, once upon a time, a freak sitting near me in the dark had gone for my crotch. After that I started frequenting The Criterion a little farther down, where I saw "Imitation of Life" with Lana Turner and Juanita Moore.

Axelbaum's Pawn Shop was still brightly lit as we cruised by, its booty of shiny trinkets leering out the windows at their prospective new owners. Outside the Pink Pussycat lounge, two sexy barmaids were swapping chitchat with members of the band, who were loading their instruments into a beat-up van. Most of the businesses were steel-latched and sombre at this hour, except for the glow of neon from Crown's and Southern Kitchen restaurants that challenged each other for first dibs on the night crawlers. We came to Jefferson at the end of the block and hung a right over to Washington. The thought crossed my mind to ask where we were headed, but somehow it didn't seem to matter.

The magic carpet ride ended abruptly as we passed underneath a viaduct, then almost came to a dead stop as the Lincoln crept onto the cobblestones that covered the riverfront. Sam was grooving to the beat of "Kiddio," one hand playing the air as he sang along with Brook Benton.

I wrote you a six-page letter
I called you on the phone
But you started talkin' bout the weather
Kiddio, don't you know that's wrong?

"Pay for your ride and get your rocking free, huh Cuz?" I parroted a line I'd picked up from Sam's cotton-running tales.

"You sho' got that right, podnuh," Sam called out as the Lincoln loped over the cobblestones, nosing its way toward the pier where a large boat stood docked offshore. Sam killed the motor. Then we just sat there taking in the silence against the backdrop of lights lining the bridge, watching their reflections skating across the current of black river water. Or maybe we were just overwhelmed by the hulking shadow of Eads Bridge, stalking us like the giant tentacles of some pre-historic river monster. Sam took a deep breath and let it out slow, his eyes plunged into the river's blackness.

"Well...?" I looked at him under-eyed.

"Well yo'self!" He turned toward me, shadows veiling his face and eyes.

"Square business, Sam, where did all this come from?" "After you claim heaven, Lil Buddy, earth is easy." He hit the door latch. "C'mon podnuh, let's walk!" he commanded.

I cracked my door. Then feeling the bite of the breeze, paused to zip up my light windbreaker. Sam was already tipping lightly across the cobblestones.

"Oh! I almost forgot," he pivoted on his toes like he was about to shoot some hoops. "Got me a little tonic for thin blood in the trunk," he said, leaning gingerly over the dashboard. The trunk opened magically. He hauled out a couple of army green blankets along with a small silver flask that he tucked away in his inside coat pocket.

We found a spot off to the side of the bridge, up against the stone wall that stood guard against the whims of the Mississippi. I spread one of the blankets for Sam and me to sit on and used the other to huddle. It was one of those clear, brisk May nights, and at this hour, the only sounds were those coming from the heavy metal chains marking the path to the pier as the breeze turned them into wind chimes, or from the low moan of a barge followed by the lapping of waves against the riverbank.

Draping the blanket over my head and shoulders like a desert Arab, I felt as warm and cozy as if I was back at home balled up on my own little cot. Looking out over the expanse of the river, lulled by the free-style riffing of the chimes, I found myself gazing dreamily at the headlights racing back and forth across the bridge. I watched, fascinated by the spears of light as they plummeted headlong into each other, glowing brilliantly for an instant as they merged. Funny, I mused, that the brightest rays always seemed to stream from the East.

Then I recalled the story of W.C. Handy from a book report

I'd done at school, and decided that Sam, blues buff that he was, should hear all about it. So I told him how Handy wrote his world famous "St. Louis Blues" all because of two down and dirty weeks he spent sleeping on these very same cobblestones. How the blues man's gift for gab made his saga come right off the page at you, as heady and full-bodied as Daddy's pear brandy at Christmas time. As I sat blinking bleary-eyed into the full moon, mercilessly bending Sam's ear, I could feel the scene surging inside me, cresting and spilling over upon the stones like brother-love, until even they yielded to the fraternal warmth, yeasting softly under us like fresh loaves of bread.

Meanwhile Sam sat squench-eyed against the wind, apparently listening to the lowing of the barges—as peaceful a sound as cattle put out to pasture. He sat quiet as I rattled on about the celebrated musician, who, from all indications, he'd never heard of. He seemed far off somewhere, slowly receding into the darkness along with the fading sound of the barges. Not that his mood mattered much to me, because my chatterbox was running on automatic pilot. Ever so often, he would rouse himself to take a medicinal swig from the silver flask inside his coat, but still he never so much as glanced in my direction or gave any sign that he heard a word I was saying.

That is, until I got to the part about how Handy's clothes had become lice-infested from sleeping in the open, a fact the blues man discovered one day while he was walking across the bridge flat broke and hungry. In a panic, he tore off his jacket and shirt, climbed up on the railing and started throwing his lousy garments into the river. At that point, somebody spotted him from a distance, and thinking he was about to jump, ran up and begged him not to do it, promising him food and shelter.

"Life is a hoot sometimes, ain't it Cuz?" I snorted. "Just when things look like they can't get any worse, all of a sudden they up and get better!" Just then I felt a gust of whiskey breath warming the side of my face and I turned to find Sam staring at me.

"What become of him after that?" he asked.

"Well, that little stroke of luck lifted his spirits some, and things started to get better right off. Anyway, he eventually made his way back down south to Memphis, got him a band together, and started on a whole roll of hits. But the strange part about the whole thing is that if he'd never hit *rock bottom*—get it?" I smacked the cobblestones for effect, trying to coax a smile. "He never would've written his greatest hit."

Sam grunted, his eyes blaring approval as he looked at me long and hard. I didn't know what to think, so I just eyeballed him right back without blinking, even if it did feel like any second my eyes were about to short-circuit like a cheap light bulb. I was surprised when he looked away, his gaze diving into the moonstruck river water as he spoke.

"What made you bring that up...'bout that fellah, I mean?"

"What...?" I asked, not understanding.

"About the musician fellah...him wantin' to commit suicide and all?"

"But that was the funny part. He wasn't really..."

"Yes he was!" Sam snapped, cutting me off. "He was gon' do it allrite...maybe he didn't know it at the time and maybe he did. But sho' as grits is grocery that's what he climbed up there to do!"

"But how can you say that...? There's no way for you to know that, Sam!"

"I know 'cause I been there myself...up on that bridge," Sam let drop quietly. I sat stunned as he went on. "You see, Lil Buddy, a man can't git but so low. And when it come time for him to bail out, it's like he playin' a game of mind jive wid hisself: he can't let his left mind know what his right mind is thinkin'." He placed a hand on my shoulder, melting my resistance with those moon-eyed bogies.

"You see...one mind told him the reason why he was up there on that bridge was to throw them mangy clothes over. But, all the time the other knowed different. And deep down in the gizzard, he knowed it too. But right then he had to lay on a little mind jive to help hide it from hisself 'til it was too late. Good thing somebody come along in time, else them "St. Louis Blues" might still be right down there at the bottom of the river along wid Lawd knows how many other dreams and schemes that ain't never gon' see daylight."

AWFUL
by Richard Newman

What bothered me most was not that Pam left me and Sophie but that a month later she took up with a woman. We both knew she wasn't happy—a house in the 'burbs, not working to take care of the baby, no community, no adventure. Clearly she wanted something beyond the life we'd chosen several years ago.

"She wants to run with the wolves," observed my friend Russell, "and here she is jogging with poodles."

I should've seen something coming soon when she took me to the Native American sweat. Those kinds of things aren't my kind of thing, but she wanted me along "to be supportive." She was nervous, so I left most of my snide comments at home. We all drove out there in the Blazer, Sophie sleeping the whole way.

I have to say, it was a flakefest: people camping in tents and teepees or sleeping in brightly painted cars and vans, people meditating or doing some kind of Tai Chi moves everywhere, various tables filled with rough-hewn pots for sale, incense, organic produce, wicca paraphernalia, books about finding your inner goddess, medicine sticks, and my favorite—free trial consultations in iridology, which, I learned, is the science of studying the colors of our eyes and what our irises tell us about our moods, our personalities, and our future. So much for Mendel.

As much as Pam wanted me to come along and be supportive before, she barely acknowledged me once we arrived, left me straggling behind her with a zonked-out Sophie on my back. She did introduce me to Jim Ponybone, a long-time friend of hers—also the guy who was in charge of the sweat lodge.

"This is my husband Jeremy," she said. "He teaches philosophy at the community college."

"Oh, a mind guy," said Jim Ponybone.

I smiled and shrugged. Pam said, almost under her breath, "closed-minded guy," then looked away, and I couldn't help it—I shot back, making a sweeping gesture at our immediate surroundings, "Well, at least I'm not so open-minded all my brains fell out."

The two looked at each other and smiled, then smiled at me, turned and walked toward the sweat lodge. Lynn was there, too, but I never noticed any sparks between her and Pam. If anything, I figured Pam would have ended up with Jim Ponybone, not Lynn. Who knows—maybe she had already been seeing him. While Pam sweated in the lodge, I spent the next several hours playing with Sophie, dishing out snacks, grading papers, trying to keep Sophie from mud-staining her sunflower overalls, and hoping Pam might sweat out her evil spirits.

"I think they should put Pam back in," said Russell the next day. "She still seems a little underdone to me."

Russell teaches in the English Department, but his office is right down the hall from mine. He's gay and can't understand Pam's sudden conversion.

"Whah, Hunny!" he said in his Southern Belle accent, "payple just don't wayke up gay. It's not naychural."

"Maybe women do," I offered. "I've heard this—"

"I know nothing about women," he said, back to his regular voice, "but I've always known I was gay. Even when I was a little boy, I had a huge crush on Johnny Quest."

So Pam moved out and started living with Lynn, who also had a child—Dugan, a year younger than Sophie. I'm not sure if Pam and Lynn started out as roommates and soon became lovers or what, but within a month they were holding hands in public. They seemed especially demonstrative when I came over. Pam acted like she'd finally found the love of her life. They both gave each other surprise birthday parties (a few months apart), cooed and squealed and hugged, and left sappy little sticky-notes for each other all over the house. Three years of dating and three years of marriage were apparently little more than an opportunity to breed. Had she been faking it with me all this time? Her current carrying on certainly seemed phony.

Sophie went back and forth between my world and Pam's. Pam always described her home as a loving, nurturing, family environment.

"Sophie is very well loved," she said. "There are so many other children and loving parents that come through here—our friends and their children, people stopping over while travelling. It's a little hectic, but it really feels like community."

I would have thought she'd be confused, caught in a parent's lifestyle tug-of-war, especially with the constant carnival-like atmosphere at her mother's, but Sophie seemed to accept it all at face value—and she seemed happy. All the little kids in school these days had broken homes, two sets of parents, and they seemed unfazed. Even in Sophie's three-day-a-week nursery school, half the parents were divorced. It looked like she would fit in just fine.

About a year later, I found out Pam was pregnant. It was supposed to be a secret, but Sophie told me. She was excited about maybe having a real brother. I called Pam that night as soon as I put Sophie to bed.

"Pregnant!" I said when she answered the phone.

"She told you already," laughed Pam.

"I thought you were gay."

"Don't be so simplistic," she said, in her most patronizing voice. "I loved the person, not the gender."

"Must have been a very deep love."

"I don't have to listen to your sarcasm anymore," she said. "That's one of the reasons we divorced."

In one of the few times in my life, I said nothing, which, as I rarely remember, is one of the best ways to obtain more information.

"There are many things I don't need to share with you, but if you must know," Pam continued, "Lynn helped me get to a good place—where I am right now."

"How does Lynn feel about all this?"

"Well, obviously, she's very happy for me, but things are a little strained right now. I'm going to be moving in a week or so—there's a house for rent a few blocks away."

I was stunned for days. I went into Russell's office hoping for wryness and consolation.

"Oh, God, I'm glad it's you," he said. On his computer screen there was a color picture of a naked boy with blue water streaming out of his ass.

"What the hell is that?"

"Close the door," he said. "Odd, isn't it? It's called Rainbow Boys. There seems to be a whole sub-culture of it. They have it in video too."

Russell clicked on a few pictures of different boys with different colored water coming out of their butts until he found a video attachment and played it for me—a boy wearing a cowboy hat, pink water coming out of his ass, then reversing back into his ass, then out again, back and forth in an endless loop.

"Kinda makes you feel good about humanity, don't it?" he said. He clicked the enema boys back to oblivion, then asked, "How's the semester starting?"

"Okay. Same."

I teach survey courses in philosophy. At the community college, we don't have a huge demand to study Nicomachean Ethics or, of course, Hume, my favorite. My job is to present each philosopher through the ages as objectively as possible. I defend their arguments against attacks by the brighter students and against apathy from the dimmer ones, and I defend them all equally, from philosophers I admire (like Mill) to the ones I hate (like Kant), though the longer I teach, the harder it is to defend them all against the apathetic students. Even the ones I liked were growing, as the students always say, "not relevant in our society today."

"I think I have a bright one this semester," Russell said, "though it's too early to tell."

"Good luck," I said.

I decided not to tell Russell about Pam's pregnancy yet. Suddenly, wryness wasn't going to work for me.

Meanwhile, Sophie's school finally started, and it broke my heart. All the other kids in her class group had been in this school's preschool together. They all knew each other and had their own little two's and three's. I made Sophie's lunch the night before—half a turkey sandwich, a pudding, some carrots, and one of those little bitty boxes of raisins—and packed it in her Mary Poppins lunchbox. I even drew her a little picture of a wildly tentacled, bug-eyed alien, the kind she likes me to draw, eating bananas, and put it in with her lunch. On the second or third day of school I stopped by to bring her Froggy, which she left on the bed that morning and would need at her mother's house that night if she was going to fall asleep—Froggy is a soft, stuffed comfort creature.

There was Sophie eating alone. Apparently, every day, they choose lunch partners, and no one chooses Sophie. Recess is no better. She spends it walking around the whole playground by herself.

Suddenly a window into my own childhood opened up, one I thought I'd closed and painted shut years ago, and I saw myself getting tripped as I walked down the aisle of the school bus, the bus lurching forward and my lunchbox sliding all the way to the back where the big kids sat, them opening my lunchbox and passing my lunch in pieces this way and that, all up and down the rows of seats, everyone on the bus participating, my eyes burning with pent-up tears. Other childhood windows flew up everywhere, the house overrun with ghosts. I saw the whole class invited to a classmate's birthday party except me. I watched myself get kicked in the face with soccer balls, whacked on the head with a tennis racket, and the bigger kids all lining up to piss on my street clothes, which someone had tossed in the urinal while I was in gym class. By the end of grade school, I was giving it back hard—even harder than I ever got it. Children are incredibly cruel, I remembered, but we never get any better when we grow up—we just get better at hiding it.

The second week of Sophie's school, she had finally found a friend in the other kindergarten group, a little girl named Hannah. Sophie told me how she waited every day at recess for Hannah to come out with her group. Every day after school, Sophie told me breathlessly how she and Hannah dug down to clay and were going to start a yellow dot club.

The next week when I asked Sophie how school was, she said "kinda weird."

Hannah had apparently told her she didn't want to play with Sophie that day, that she wanted to play with some new friends. When Sophie tried to play at their digging hole, they told her she couldn't, that she had to go away. I felt like feeding all the little brats to wild dogs.

"Oh, Honey, I'm sorry," I said instead. "I bet that really hurt your feelings."

"Yeah."

"So what did you do?"

"Walked around the whole playground. Every bit of it."

"You mean by yourself?"

"Of course."

"Sometimes it's hard to be a—" I stopped myself. I was going to say a kid, but then I remembered I should be more honest, that it never got any easier. I looked into Sophie's face, no longer a toddler's. She was a little girl now, and I could see in her eyes that she'd already been corrupted by the knowledge of fate. Sometimes the arbitrary hand of fate is full of jelly beans, sometimes it smacks you upside the head. It never made sense, and Sophie knew it in her bones at the age of five.

"Sometimes it's hard to be a person," I said. With all my training, all my education, all my skill in argument, all my years of experience, it was the best I could do.

"It's awful," she said.

Keough's Career

by Robert Randisi
(from his novel, *In the Shadow of the Arch*)

Keough's career with the New York City Police Department had dribbled to an end after a particularly messy case. He could have stayed on if he wanted to, but there was a lot of bad blood and it wouldn't have made much sense. Still, he might have hung on if he hadn't gotten an offer from a friend of his in St. Louis.

"Heard what happened to you, man," Mark Drucker had said on the phone one night. "Bad break."

Drucker was a minor politician or something in St. Louis—actually, the assistant to a minor politician—but he swore he could get Keough onto one of the smaller municipal police departments in St. Louis.

"There's tons of them here, man," Drucker said. "Every ten blocks you're in another city with its own police department, and they need experienced detectives."

So Keough had come to St. Louis, gone to the Richmond Heights Police Department for an interview with Chief Harold Pellman, and gotten the job—after answering some questions.

"I know what you went through in New York, Detective," Pellman said at that first meeting.

He was a tall, slender man in his early fifties who had stood to shake hands, and then reseated himself, inviting Keough to sit.

Keough didn't reply to the statement.

"Why would things be different here?" Pellman asked.

"I don't know that they would be, Chief," Keough answered. "I can only tell you that I would do my job."

"I don't need trouble here, Detective."

"I'm not here to bring trouble, sir."

"What I do need is an experienced detective," Pellman said. "I've finally succeeded in getting money from the city to increase the number of detectives we have on the force."

"How many do you have?"

"Three," Pellman said. "With the extra money we're going to hire three more. In fact, I'm going to promote two officers to detective. They're being tested tonight. I'll expect you to show them the ropes."

"Will I be in command?"

"No," Pellman said. "In addition to the three detectives there's also a detective sergeant, and he'll be in command. I will, however, need you to guide the others with your expertise."

"I understand."

"Even the detectives who have been here a while could benefit from your knowledge."

Keough nodded, but he was hoping he could avoid having any of the existing detectives resent him.

"Once you're here and we see how things go," Pellman said, "then we might talk about a promotion."

Keough shrugged at that. He just wanted to be a detective and do his job.

"Okay," Pellman said, "what do you say we try it?"

Keough had smiled and asked, "When do I start?"

They figured it would take two weeks for him to get settled. When he arrived in St. Louis with his belongings, he had taken a small furnished apartment in Soulard and then started looking for something more permanent. During those two weeks he also went to see the Arch, the Botanical Garden, the President Casino on the Admiral Riverboat, University City, the Central West End, just some of the things he might not have time for when he started the job.

Again, through his friend Mark Drucker, he found a place to live. A friend of Drucker's who owned one of the large homes in the Central West End was going to Europe for two years and needed someone to house-sit.

"Most of the house will be closed up," Drucker said, "but you'd have use of the living room, den, and kitchen downstairs, and one of the bedrooms upstairs."

There were twelve rooms, but four out of twelve was plenty for Keough and he liked the Central West End. It reminded him of Greenwich Village in New York, with its shops, bookstores, and restaurants and sidewalk cafes. That's how he came to live on Pershing Place, one of the West End's private streets.

On his first day as a detective on the Richmond Heights Police Department, Keough stopped at the Tuscany Café, the newest coffee emporium—nobody called them shops anymore—in the Central West End. He had coffee and a danish, never suspecting that in less than an hour he'd be in the station kitchen—he had to remember to call them stations and not precincts—with a three-year-old boy who had blood on the feet of his Dr. Denton's pajamas.

He sat the boy on the table and looked up when the door opened. A uniformed officer entered with one of the female clerks who worked in the city hall. One of the things Keough learned about St. Louis is that the smaller police stations like Richmond Heights shared a building with the city hall, and sometimes even with the fire department. Richmond Heights Fire Department, however, had its own building, right behind city hall. Behind that was the local library.

"Officer," he said, "would you go to the vending machine and get me some chocolate chip cookies, please?"

"You want cookies now?"

Keough stared at him and said, "They're for the boy."

"Oh, right..."

As the door closed behind the officer, the woman approached Keough and the boy. She was in her thirties, dark-haired, slightly overweight in an attractive way.

"What's your name?" Keough asked her.

"Joyce Wilson."

"Joe Keough. Do you have children, Joyce?"

"Yes. Three."

"Any boys?"

"One."

"Then maybe you can help me."

"You seem to be doing all right."

"I'd just like to have a woman present."

"Sure. Can we clean his feet?"

"No," Keough said, "not until we have another pair of pajamas. I've sent one of the men for a pair."

"God knows what he'll come back with."

"Is there any milk—" he started to ask.

"Not in the building," she said, then spotted the small refrigerator in the corner. "Unless there's some in here."

She opened the door, saw a quart container of Pevely milk. She picked it up and shook it, found a glass, and poured the milk out. There was just about a half a glass. She brought it to the table where Keough was sitting on a chair facing the boy, still trying to avoid his bloody feet.

"Are you thirsty?" she asked the boy.

He nodded and said, "Cookies."

"The cookies are coming, pal," Keough said. "How about telling us your name?"

"Brady." The boy dug at his nose.

"Brady," Keough said, "what's your last name?"

The boy didn't answer.

"Where are your mom and dad?"

"Gone."

"Gone where?"

The boy shrugged.

"How old are you, Brady?" the woman asked.

The boy thought a moment then laboriously displayed three fingers of his right hand. At that moment the door opened and the officer stepped in with a bag of cookies.

"Thanks," Joyce said, taking them.

"Any sign of the captain?" Keough asked.

"He's on his way in."

"Bring him in as soon as he gets here, will you?"

"Yes, sir."

The officer withdrew as Joyce opened the cookies and gave the boy one.

"Brady?" Keough asked.

"Yeth?" he said, with a mouthful of cookie.

"Do you know where you live?"

"Yeth."

"Where?"

The boy started to swing his feet and drops of blood flew from them, narrowly missing Keough. He put his hand on the boy's knees to stop him gently.

"In a houth."

"A house?"

The boy nodded.

"Yeth."

He pushed the rest of the cookie into his mouth and looked at Joyce, extending his hand.

"Swallow what you have first, Brady, and have a sip of milk," Joyce said. "Then after you answer Joe's questions you can have another cookie."

The boy chewed and chewed with great concentration, then Joyce gave him a drink. He wiped off the milk mustache with the back of his right hand.

"Do you know where your house is, Brady?"

"Yes."

"Where?"

The boy pointed, his index finger slightly bowed.

"Where are you pointing to, Brady?"

"My house," the boy said, reasonably.

"Do you know the address of your house?"

The boy looked confused.

"The number on your house, Brady," Joyce said, helpfully. "Do you know the number on your house?"

"No," he said, shaking his head.

"What about the street?" Keough asked. "Do you know the name of the street you live on?"

The boy nodded.

"What is it?"

"It's Wise Street."

"Where is that?" Keough asked Joyce.

"A couple of blocks from here."

"We'll have to do a house to house."

"Maybe not," she said. "Brady, what color is your house?"

He pushed at his nose with his palm, flattening it momentarily, and then said, "Yellow."

Keough looked around. There was a yellow lined pad on the other end of the table. He grabbed it.

"Brady, look at this, then look at my shirt and at Joyce. Point to the color yellow."

Keough's shirt was blue, and Joyce's blouse orange.

The boy touched the yellow pad with one finger, then looked at Joyce and asked, "Cookie?"

Joyce looked at Keough, who nodded, and she gave the boy another cookie.

This time when the door opened, the uniformed officer was wearing captain's bars.

"What have we got?" the man asked.

"I'll tell you outside," Keough said, and left the boy with Joyce to step out of the room with the captain.

• • •

Keough had been living in the house in the West End for only a week. The house stood on the corner of Pershing and Euclid, Euclid being the main street that cut right through the West End.

The Central West End was where St. Louisans did their shopping until stores like Saks Fifth Avenue and Montaldo's moved away in the seventies. Since then the area had been built up again and now sported all sorts of shops, cafes, and restaurants.

What impressed Keough about the West End were the choices available to him, and he was only too glad to house-sit the house on Pershing for as long as the owners wanted to be away.

He arrived home in the evening, when it was no longer necessary to put coins in the parking meters. He had developed the habit of parking on Euclid, instead of driving through the gates onto the private street. Somehow, he didn't quite feel entitled to that, yet.

He parked and got out of his car, a 1993 Oldsmobile Cutlass Supreme he had purchased when he first arrived in St. Louis. He admired the huge, ornate streetlights which belonged to another erea as he walked to the gateway that led into Pershing Place. The wrought iron was moored on each side to big concrete pillars, and to either side of each pillar was a small entryway. Once through there he mounted the steps to the house and let himself in.

There was no two ways about it, the house was a mansion. It had three floors, with two stairways, one which led to the kitchen and the other to the large entry foyer.

The living room was to the right and the dining room was on the left. The dining room, however, was one of the rooms closed off, the furniture covered with sheets. When he ate in the house he did so in the kitchen, which was large enough to have a good-sized table in the middle of it. He used the living room and kitchen on the first floor, and the bedroom and den on the second. He never used any part of the third floor. The den was actually one of the five bedrooms which had been converted into a den and office. He'd only been there a week and still had boxes in the living room, den and bedroom to be unpacked. He probably should have worked harder at getting settled during that week, because it was going to be slow going now that he was on the job. Truth be told, though, it had been too long since he'd been on the job, and he was anxious to get back to it. Of course, he didn't know that he'd be back in it five minutes after walking into the building.

As he entered the house, he went into the kitchen and opened the refrigerator. He pulled out a beer, a Pete's Wicked Ale, which he had discovered since moving here. One beer at home, he thought, and then he'd wander down the block for some dinner.

He popped the top off the beer and sat down at the kitchen table to drink it. He became aware of the phone book in his jacket pocket and pulled it out. The yellow lined sheet of paper he'd written the most often called phone numbers on was folded up inside.

He had not been able to locate any members of Mr. or Mrs. Sanders' families. Tomorrow he'd ask the boy, Brady, what he knew, but he didn't really expect to get much out of a three-year-old.

When he'd returned to the station the first time the boy had still been there, dressed now in new pajamas. Keough still didn't know the name of the officer he'd sent for the pajamas, but it was obvious the man knew nothing about kids because he'd brought back a pink pair. Joyce had removed the bloody ones and given them to Detective Haywood to bag, and then had dressed Brady in the new pair.

The second time Keough returned to the station the boy was gone. Tomorrow he'd go down to wherever they were holding him and try to question him further.

Meanwhile, he sipped his beer and leafed through the phone book, looking for some hint of whom to call. He wasn't about to start making long distance phone calls from the phone bill on his own phone. He'd do that from the station.

By the time he finished his beer, his stomach was growling. He decided to take the phone book with him to Dressels, where he'd have a few more beers with dinner.

Dressels was small, dark, and comfortable. They served food downstairs, while the upstairs was reserved strictly for drinking and, when they had it, entertainment.

The walls downstairs were covered with framed sketches and drawings of literary and theatrical figures, and there were similar sketches on the front of the yellow menu. Classical music played constantly, and a collection of cassette tapes was clearly visible behind the bar.

It was an oval bar, and it dominated the place, stuck right in the center of the room, with tables all around it. He grabbed a table toward the front and ordered a Newcastle Brown Ale from the waitress, whose name was Dawn. She was one of the reasons he liked the place. She was mature, attractive, and greeted him warmly the second time he had been there. This was now his fourth visit and she greeted him again like a long-lost friend—or, at least, a regular customer.

"How are you getting along in St. Louis?" she asked, when she brought him his beer.

"Just great."

"Finding your way around?"

"Well," he said, "I can get to work, and I can find my way back here to the West End."

"That's not bad for, what, two weeks?"

"Starting my third. In fact, today was my first day of work."

"How did that go?"

He looked up at her. She was slender, and he knew she kept herself in shape with exercise, from conversation he'd heard during his other visits. Although they'd talked a little each time he came in, she still did not know that he was a policeman.

"You don't want to know."

"That bad, huh? Maybe a good meal will fix that."

He ordered some of Dressels' homemade potato chips, and the contents of the crock pot, which changed every day.

Dawn brought the basket of chips and Keough worked on them and the Newcastle while going through the phone book again. He turned over the piece of paper on which he had written the long distance calls and wrote down three local numbers. One of them was for a Dr. White, another was for Jenny Rasmus, and a third was for a YWCA. The phone book was apparently Marian Sanders', not her husband's. If he was a businessman, it was likely he had a phone book at work, or even carried it with him.

Thinking of business Keough went through the book yet again, looking for a number that might be Mr. Sanders' work number. There were two in the book that looked likely, and he wrote them down just as Dawn brought his dinner. He tucked the book away in his pocket, ordered a second Newcastle, and devoted all of his attention to dinner.

    Keough left Dressels after dinner, saying good-bye to Dawn. He was well fed, but in the mood for coffee. He thought about crossing the street and going to the Tuscany Café but instead decided to stop at Left Bank Books, the Central West End's—and one of St. Louis'—oldest bookstore. There were two entrances to the place, one which led directly into the store, and the other into their coffee shop, which appeared to be a new addition. He decided to browse a bit, and bought a mystery novel called *Lukewarm* by a local writer. The book featured a private detective who lived and worked in Florida. Keough had never read this writer before, but the book sounded interesting.

    He read a couple of chapters over a cup of coffee and then left the store and walked home.

    When he got home he took a shower and went into the den. He was greeted by the sight of boxes stacked against one wall, small and medium in size. He decided to ignore them for now.

    There was a leather armchair there, which he had begun to use for reading. He briefly considered leafing through the phone book again, but decided to leave that for the next day, when he was at work. Tonight he'd do some reading for pleasure, before turning on the television to watch CNN or ESPN, or maybe even both.

    He could do some unpacking tomorrow, after work.

SAFE AT HOME
by Eileen Dreyer

My father was, I was afraid to admit to my friends, an accountant. Not just an accountant, he was quick to tell us all. A CPA. A man with a degree in a neighborhood of blue collars. A solid, unpretentious calling that put enough food on the table and afforded the extras that would enable a houseful of children to attend good schools and participate in the sports they so loved.

But to a six-year-old girl whose best friend's father drove the Clydesdales and whose Uncle Bob was an undercover narcotics officer, it was tough to cloak a CPA in romance or mystery.

He used adding machines, for heaven's sake. He drove a station wagon.

I was in agony. Every parents' day. Every time I found myself on the playground engaging in another round of one-upmanship. Maggie Stevens's father had ridden the rodeo circuit for years. She had a huge silver belt buckle she kept in her crayon box to prove it. Tammie Koch's dad drove a train. And not a zoo train, either. One of the big trains, the kind we used to walk right up to, just to feel the wind of it blow our clothes against us as it went wailing past on its way somewhere we'd never been.

My father had been to Missouri and Michigan, and once he'd gone to war. In the Pacific, he said. All I knew from the blurry scrapbook was that they must have fought that war in their underwear, which wasn't like any war I saw on television. I'm not sure that for years I even believed he hadn't made the whole thing up.

It didn't occur to me then to cherish the warm roughness

of his cheek as he tucked me into bed every night, the slightly smoky scent of his shirts, or the rich bellow of his unrestrained laughter. I didn't understand how rare a thing it was to have a father who held my hand all the way into church and watched my posture there even more sharply than my mother. I didn't know that my most pristine memories would involve afternoons playing catch on the lawn or the fact that spring would always be to me the sound of Harry Carey announcing spring training games on the radio as my father bent over our old yellow Formica kitchen table teaching me how to keep score.

Baseball. Oddly enough for a daughter, it was the language by which my father taught me. The language I still respond to. *Field of Dreams* and *Pride of the Yankees*. Old-fashioned heroism, team loyalty, and simple communion between a man and his child on a dirt lot as the sky turned a peacock blue at the end of a summer day. My mother was the person who used words well. She would have been a writer in a different age, maybe a different place. She was the storyteller, the family historian, who imbued old ghosts with humor and mystery and magic. She praised with effusion and pilloried with deadly accuracy. She knew, with that terrible understanding mothers have for their children's fears and insecurities, that the most fearsome threat she could deliver for bad behavior was: "Wait till your father gets home."

And my poor father, after a day spent unraveling other people's problems would step in the door to unravel ours. Without my mother's quicksilver epistles and trenchant parables.

My father couched his lessons in coaching lingo. And he delivered them to us all, sons and daughters alike, as if we were not simply his dependents but his team. His responsibility and his friends and his future, crouched before him with Neatsfoot-oiled gloves and bright, anxious faces. He ruffled hair and smacked butts and stole noses while we weren't looking. And always he preached the tenets of the team. He taught us, his seven players, that it wasn't one of us that mattered, but all of us. That more than him, we needed each other.

He taught us the lessons that had filled his youth with magic, and filled ours with order.

And, as these things happen, it was at a baseball game I finally realized how vital this all was.

Not a real one, of course. At those I just realized that more than two hot dogs made me sick and that real baseball players cursed a lot more than my dad.

This was at a block party for our neighborhood. We held block parties once a year in August, closing off our street and stringing Christmas lights through the trees. The local church lent tables and chairs, and one of the fathers who worked in a radio station managed to get a sound system. The mothers cooked and the children gathered games and decorations and looked forward to the night, when they could stay up under the stars that hung in their trees.

And the fathers, beer in one hand, spatula in the other, barbecued. Half-barrel, beer-marinated meat, pungent charcoal smoke that would have to be washed out of white shirts and khaki shorts. Laughing, gossiping, arguing over everything and nothing.

And in the afternoon, while the babies napped in playpens on front lawns and flies buzzed in the lazy heat, everybody would gather at the field at the end of the block for the annual baseball game.

I'm not sure why the game that particular year was different. Maybe it was because I was different, hovering uncomfortably between childhood and adolescence. Torn between the sweaty, dusty fun of shagging balls and the isolated, slightly petulant cool of standing in a group off to the side with the teenage girls.

The boys played ball until the day they died. The girls began rolling their hair and shaving their legs, and suddenly willed their ball gloves to a younger sibling. I was rolling my hair. I'd been casting covetous glances at my mother's razor. But I wanted to give myself up to the rough and tumble of a kid's game, a kid's game the fathers still played, especially on the afternoons when they barbecued in the middle of the street.

As it sometimes still does, the game won out. I untucked my new white blouse and exchanged sandals for tennis shoes and trotted over to the field that Mr. Stewart the old rodeo star was marking with base paths.

"Aw, does she have to play?" my brother Tommy asked.

My father looked up from where he was pounding home plate into the scorched grass of late summer. "And why shouldn't she?"

Tommy scowled. "Because she's a girl."

My father grinned. "Not because she's a switch hitter and bats three-fifty?"

"Three-fifty?" Mr. Stewart asked, his voice a little slurred as he stepped closer to me. "Really? You must have some arms, little girl."

For the first time I could remember, I stepped back from one of my friend's fathers. "My dad taught me," was all I said.

Mr. Stewart was really handsome. Everybody said so. He looked like the Marlboro man, with a strong chin and light blue eyes and a swagger when he walked. We all saw him on that horse like Little Joe Cartwright or somebody, even though he just drove a truck now. But for the first time that afternoon, I noticed that his nose was red all the time. He smelled like stale beer, and his eyes, those light blue eyes that had seemed so romantic, tended to focus on places that made me nervous.

It could have been worse, I guess. I could have been on his team. But I was on Mr. Koch's team. Mr. Koch the train engineer and Mr. Stewart the ex-rodeo champ were the two managers for the day. I thought my father should have been, because, after all, he'd coached all our little league teams. He'd played baseball in high school and college, and for a while pitched for the Pat's Bar and Grill adult league team until, he said, there were too many kids for him to take the time out for weekly games.

But Mr. Koch insisted, and my dad smiled and offered to help coach. That frustrated me. After all, what good was it to have a father with one really good talent, and him not use it?

Especially since Mr. Koch was such a yeller.

It might have been because he was used to needing to be heard over a train whistle. But, boy, did he yell. At everybody. He yelled at kids in the street when he was trying to get into his driveway at the end of the day. He yelled at Mrs. Koch when his dinner wasn't ready. He yelled at everybody on the grass ball field, whether they were on his team or not. But he especially yelled at his son Timmy, who Mr. Koch decided should be pitcher.

Timmy was my friend. He was funny, and he was a great drawer and could burp the national anthem on command. But Timmy was not a pitcher. The kids on the other team cheered when they heard the news. We groaned. My dad ruffled my hair and said that wasn't the way to help a team member.

"Timmy can only pitch better if you guys all help him out," he said quietly so Mr. Koch, who was yelling at Timmy to try harder, wouldn't hear him. "Timmy needs all the encouragement he can get. So let's hear it."

Mr. Koch started assigning other positions. My brother Eddie to first base, my cousin Joey to third. Ellen Peters to right field, Mary Casey to left. Mr. Koch turned to me and began to point. "I play shortstop," I told him, pounding my hand into my glove just like I'd seen Julian Javier on the Cardinals do it.

"Uh-huh, I'm sure" he said, already looking toward the weedy patch of the field that made up center field.

Oh, no, I thought, the pleasure of playing the game dying like frogs on a driveway. I'd be sitting out in the middle of nowhere making daisy chains while the rest of them played ball, just because I was a girl.

No, I thought, catching Mr. Stewart's eye, sliding my way at a moment when my dad wasn't looking. Because I was a girl who was getting breasts. It was just like school, where they seemed to think that breasts sucked out any ability to learn science or math. Well, I could understand math and science just fine. And I wanted to play shortstop.

No, what I really wanted to do was make a play at shortstop

that would so surprise Mr. Koch he couldn't yell for a straight five minutes, just so he and Mr. Stewart forgot that breasts set me apart from the rest of the players.

"You'd be wasting her out in center field," my dad said to Mr. Koch as he took a sip of beer. "She's the best shortstop I've ever coached."

"That's softball," Mr. Koch said.

My dad smiled again, in that quiet way he had that made him look almost invisible, so people didn't even realize that sometimes they were doing what he wanted them to. "Try her out. It's only a game."

That was when Mr. Koch got red. Everywhere. But Mr. Koch was a redhead, and my mom said that redheads blushed faster than anybody in the world. Well, he did then. But I ended up trotting out to shortstop, right between my cousin Joey and Freddie Marston, who wore braces and carried an old Roy Rogers lunch box to school.

Mr. Koch yelled at me, of course. I was too far left, or too far right, or I wasn't crouched down low enough and might let the grounders sneak through my feet. I probably would have let it bother me if I hadn't looked over to where my father stood on the sidelines with his arm around my mom's shoulders. Because when I looked over, my dad winked. And when he winked, I remember his biggest coaching lesson: "It's only a game." Mr. Koch, he was telling me, would never get that rule. Mr. Koch didn't like to lose. He would do anything to pull that game out. Well, anything but take out his son Timmy from pitching. But with that one wink my dad was letting me in on the joke. Mr. Koch was wasting all that energy on the perfect team for the perfect game when we were just a bunch of kids wasting time till the babies woke up and dinner was served.

"Who's gonna umpire?" my Uncle Bob asked from where he was lying in the grass, watching the sky.

"What about you, Dad?" my cousin Joey asked.

Uncle Bob waved a hand and stayed where he was. "A Man with a gun should never umpire."

We all thought that was terribly cool. I saw my mom frown and walk over to her older brother. There was some short, quiet, intense discussion that ended with Uncle Joe sitting up and my mom walking over toward the field.

"I'll umpire," she said.

All the kids cheered. My mom was a great umpire. She was always more than willing to arbitrate on the street games we'd pick up after school. And she usually never made anybody mad.

Mr. Koch looked like he was going to have a stroke, but he didn't say anything. Mrs. Marson said that Mr. Koch was afraid of my mom. After surviving my mom mad at close range more than once, I couldn't say I blamed him. But you'd think a train engineer wouldn't have much to be afraid of from a five-foot-tall housewife with seven kids. On the other hand, my dad said he was afraid of her, too. But my dad never acted like it.

"Play ball!" she yelled.

I pounded my glove a couple of times and rested my hands on my knees. Timmy reared back in the most bizarre windup anybody had ever seen and wafted a pitch a foot above Max Camper's head.

"Ball one!" Mom yelled.

The other team hooted from the old log that served as the bench. Mr. Koch started screaming. Our team, even seeing disaster loom, started chanting.

"Weenie batter, weenie batter, come on, Tim. Get this guy outta there!"

My dad, sipping his beer, smiled at my mom. My mom, who had a baby of her own on the lawn next door, smiled back. They were forever touching, my mom and dad. Hands, butts, lips. Nothing big or fancy, no sweeping anybody into a passionate embrace. Not in front of us, for sure. But they couldn't seem to walk by each other without making contact. I noticed as I watched Timmy walk the first two batters that when my Aunt Jackie bought out Uncle Bob's baseball cap, she tossed it to him from about ten feet away and then turned on her heel. I liked

Aunt Jackie. I liked Uncle Bob. But I'm not sure they liked each other. Joey was forever at our house, showing up a lot right before meals so that he'd sit down with us to eat. "There's always room for one more," my mom would say.

"Joey's on the team," my dad would answer. "And a teammate is always welcome, Right Joe?"

And Joey, who always looked a little nervous, like he was waiting for somebody to catch him without his homework, would take off his ball cap and sit down.

"Weenie batter..."

"Strike one!"

We all yelled really loudly, my dad loudest of all. Timmy had that kind of grin on his face that said he was more surprised than anyone.

"Strike two!"

Mr. Stewart was yelling now, and Uncle Bob, back to lying on the grass with a Cardinals cap over his face. And Max, finally getting the idea that Tim wasn't going to just walk him, too, swung at the ball. And hit it. Right back to Timmy, who threw it to me. Which would have been great if there'd been a runner on first.

Maybe I was the only one who noticed, but it was my dad who kept Mr. Koch from storming the field. At his own kid.

And this was just the first inning.

I didn't get my big play. Mostly what happened was that kids walked, or balls slithered by unprepared gloves into the outfield, and kids ran bases around their moms, who trotted over for congratulatory kisses. Timmy pitched, and then Eddie and then my best friend Katie, which made Mr. Koch nuts all over again. Until Katie started striking people out.

But then Katie had spent almost as many nights in my backyard as I had. Her dad was the one who drove the Clydesdales, which was really cool, because every Thanksgiving we'd all gather around the TV to watch the Macy's Thanksgiving Day parade and wave and yell to Mr. Brady, like he could hear us. He'd even invited us all down to the stables once, where they kept the horses in St. Louis, and let us sit up on top of one of the Clydesdales as if we were riding them. From that moment on, I would have been the wagon dog just to ride with them in a parade, even though that was just something else a girl couldn't do. But Mr. Brady was gone almost every day, at some parade around the country for Corn Festival Rodeo Days or Veterans Day or something where they'd need the horses to make an appearance. Mr. Brady loved his horses. I know he loved his Katie, too, but it was my dad who taught Katie to pitch.

So I didn't get my big play. I did, however, get a big home run. It wasn't one of those mythical moments, when we were tied in the bottom of the ninth. That would have been too perfect for words. It was just in the bottom of the seventh, and we were behind three runs. Paul Bigelow was pitching for the other team, and he hated me. Which was okay, because I cheerfully hated him back. He was the neighborhood bully, and more than once he'd tried to hurt my little brothers. I'd had to knock him down. Then he'd knocked me down, of course, but the next time he tried to pull me off my bike, I ran him over. He still has a scar over his lip from where the pedal hit him.

Which meant that when I got up to bat, he tried to bean me. It didn't bother me, really, because I knew it was coming and ducked. My dad, on the other hand, wasn't amused. It wasn't just that Mr. Stewart thought it was funny. It was that it was one of Dad's kids. Heck, he got madder than my mom, and she was umpiring. She was also the one who'd cleaned out Paul's lip after he'd tried to run me down.

But Dad settled down when I laughed, too, because he knew that if I was okay, I'd get my evens by simply ignoring Paul's dumb move. It was sure better than clearing a bench. At least, that's what my dad thought. I just knew that laughing hurt a heck of a lot less than one of Paul's rabbit punches. I really got my revenge on the next pitch, though. There was one man on, and Paul pitched me a perfect strike. I wound up like Stan the Man himself and corked it out into the street. I'd really like to say that nobody had ever hit a ball farther. That would be silly, since I was playing with my brother Eddie, who would go on to play for the Cincinnati Reds. But, as my dad was heard to say as he smacked me on the butt when I rounded first, "not bad for a girl." I laughed. My mom smacked my butt again when I came home. Then everybody smacked my butt. Everybody was laughing and yelling, even Mr. Koch, who for once seemed happy.

It probably would have been my best memory ever, especially since Paul looked like he'd swallowed a bug, standing out there on the pitcher's mound. But then, as I went past home, I ran into Mr. Stewart.

He'd had a beer in his hand all through the game. He had one now, and his nose was redder. His whole face was redder, and he wasn't running back and forth anymore. He seemed to move pretty fast when I jumped on home, though, because, just after my mom congratulated me, he was right in front of me, and I smacked face first into his chest.

His beer slipped and sloshed all down the front of my white shirt. His hand came out to steady me, but he seemed to need to steady me right on my left breast. And his breath was in my face, all fast and fuggy.

I bounced right back, suddenly breathing way too fast myself, but he seemed to be there, too. My stomach was upset, and I wanted to cry, even though I wasn't sure why. He was smiling. He was smiling, and his eyes had that look in them again, and suddenly everything was wrong. The day and the homer and all the people crowding around. There in the sun with my friends and my neighbors and my mom and dad, I felt crawly and afraid.

And I didn't know what to do.

So I looked over to my dad.

He must have seen something, because he was there even before I got away from Mr. Stewart's reach. His face was red, too, all of a sudden, his happy smile as gone as dinosaurs. Mr. Stewart never saw him coming, because he was looking down at me, at my shirt where the beer had splashed so you could almost see my very first bra beneath.

He didn't get the chance. Suddenly he was spun around and shuffled away, and nobody but me knew why. Nobody but me knew why he never came back out to dinner, or why he had that big bruise on his face at mass the next morning.

But I did know. I knew for sure when my dad came back ten minutes later to find me still standing there at the edge of the field, wondering what I'd done wrong. My dad walked over to me and just put his arms around me and said that Mr. Stewart had been kicked out of the game. That Mr. Stewart was no longer welcome at our home. That Mr. Stewart would never bother me again if Mr. Stewart knew what was good for him.

"I'm sorry," I whispered, reassuring myself with the slightly smoky scent of his shirt.

My dad made a funny sound in his throat, and seemed to wrap his arms around me more tightly. "No, honey. Mr. Stewart is sorry. It's his fault and his fault alone. He forgot for a minute that you aren't an adult. He won't forget again. And if anybody... *anybody*... ever makes you feel the way you felt today, you just let me know. That's what I'm there for."

I pulled away a little, so I could look up at him. Just to make sure. To see that my mom was waiting for her turn just past him.

"You mean it?" I asked, all over shaking again because, for the first time in my life, I saw tears in my father's eyes, and that scared me almost more than Mr. Stewart's hand on my breast.

"Oh, yeah, honey," my dad said, and kissed the top of my head. "After all, I'm the coach. I watch out for my team, don't I?"

And in that moment I realized that CPAs were cooler than cowboys, than train engineers. Even than the guys who drove the Clydesdales. Because standing there at the edge of my childhood, with summer behind me and my dad's arms around me, I felt safe. I felt secure and warm and cherished. And I knew that no matter what else my dad did or didn't do, what clothes he wore or people he knew, he knew how to raise a team. And that his kind of coaching was all I needed to take me on, and take me through.

A STORY TO TELL
by Ryan Stone

Lakland doesn't think of himself as Peter anymore. It's a direct result of his job in a corner cubicle, working network security for a construction company. He rides the number 80 bus each day, stares out the window, and watches the stops move by. Mexicans get on, headed for job sites on St. Louis' north side. They smell like sweat and work not yet done. Lakland thinks of them as where he starts each day; they make him tired. There are times he worships his little cubicle with no window and fourteen-inch computer screen. He's worked there three years now, and the constant job hunting finally tired him out. On his living room floor were cut up pieces of the Sunday Post, leafs of possibilities, scattered and blotted with dark red ink. He'd even considered selling insurance over the phone for a brief time. The ad, circled with a red marker made black by the shave-thin newspaper, said he could make twelve bucks an hour, less than he makes now, but more than then. He still had the little scraps tucked away somewhere in his file cabinet because Lakland never threw anything away. Never. His baseball cards, his limited stamp collection, his over-zealous stacks of *Playboy*, every old tax return, all of these are piled in the back room of his three-bedroom, second floor apartment, which stares out over a park loaded with peeling ash trees. When he stands at the window, he can feel the past smoldering behind him, a low fire, one he can barely feel or see.

One morning, a woman boards the bus, a dark woman with swishing hair. She sits in front of him; her hair drapes over the back of her seat. He notices the Mexicans don't look at her while they speak Spanish to each other, saying nothing he can understand. He'd tried a foreign language once; it made his head hurt. The woman leaves at the next stop. She could've walked the distance easily, but such a beautiful woman should never walk anywhere. For a woman like that, the laws of public transportation should bend and break every time. Lakland leans forward to get a look at the view. He tries to figure out his location. He's missed his stop before; the last time because he overheard an intriguing conversation between an overweight man and some college kid about one of the local sports teams. He can't remember which team, only that the man had a good point. The bus stops, and he gets off, makes his way to his office. There, the ceiling-tile lights are lit all night, and the windows glow fluorescent against a city background. He can see them from his apartment window and often wonders about the electricity bill. He asked someone about it once, whether there was a master switch somewhere that could shut the whole thing down, but they had told him no. When he pressed further, they said something about the building's height and an airplane's flight path. The airplanes, they said, fly right over the city as they come in to Lambert Airport. Everything, they told him, has to be seen at that height. Those little red dots, those are nothing when you're up there. He'd heard this from a man who works on the second floor who flies biplanes on the weekends out of a small airport across the river. The man sounded competent, but Lakland only knows him from the elevator, and then only until the second floor.

Hatteburg & Wylend Construction operates out of the twenty-first floor of the Wagnor building, situated opposite B&B Brokerage with a coffee shop between. The construction folks and the brokerage folks meet at the little coffee shop and talk while the coffee shop folks pour coffee and serve stale pastries. Employees mingle and, sometimes, even sleep together. There's a woman, whose name is Delores, sleeping with a vice-president from B&B, whose name is Bert—Bert from B&B, and the employees hide what they're talking about, mostly for the fun of it, by saying, "BBB." This is the talk of the floor. Lakland has found himself on the edge of some of this talk, but never thrust in full fold. His name's been mentioned in a few water cooler incidents, one where the water ended up in Mr. Wylend's office, and another where the water cooler was mysteriously stolen. He was involved in neither, but knows why suspicion surrounded him. Hanging out by the water cooler became a sort of hobby for him. Lakland never went very long without refilling his water glass, and soon it went from a nice hobby, a quick walk down the hall to escape his cubicle, to a necessity. He found himself needing the water, the way Jenny, the little secretary with the big voice, always needed the bathroom at two-thirty each day, and Marty, the graphics designer for the Web page, always had to have a Snickers bar around three. They would find Marty scarching through his desk, asking anyone he could find for eighty-five cents to buy a candy bar. Lakland, it seemed, was always at the water cooler.

So this, he often thinks, is the world I've plopped myself into. He sits down in his chair and fires up his computer to check the system for bugs. All he does all day is look for little bugs, things no one else would see, and he catches them, stomps them before anybody even knows it. In fact, if it weren't for his little cubicle, they would all go to hell in a hand-basket. What if they couldn't access their e-mail? Then the world would surely end. And when they have little problems, like their computers freeze, they call him, and if he can't fix the problem he has a friend on the other side of a one-button-speed-dial cell phone who can. He feels, at times, like a savior, and that makes him feel good, and at other times like a glorified, modern exterminator. But, he's glad he got this job, glad he became the man he is with his pudgy middle, perfect for the part of a computer man, and Birkenstocks. He is the only one among them who wears sandals. The rest are clad in thick-soled loafers or mid-range heels, nothing tripping, but just high enough to scrunch the calf muscle into a ball.

The evening after the dark woman boarded the bus, on the ride home, he sees a few Mormons standing at one of the stops just outside the city. They are in a group, about six or seven of them, in their ties and limp, white shirts, hard collars, and creased slacks, all black, and black shoes. Lakland thinks they must have little jokes amongst themselves. When they set out, do the adults throw parties for them? Does some uncle tell them how many doors were slammed in his face? Is there some ritual? Lakland feels as if he's never touched religion. He hasn't been to church since he was seventeen when his parents made him attend St. Peter and Paul, a monstrous black and beige building three blocks from his boyhood home; he could see the steeple from their small, insufficient porch. The Mormons climb aboard and gather in the seats around him like a calling. They are very tired looking, worn out. All those people they must talk to, all those souls to heal and each one looks as if he would rather ball up, fetus style, and sleep it all away. They can't change a thing, Lakland thinks. They are so small. One of them leans forward as if praying but then begins to snore.

There's a girl in Lakland's life; a small, pretty thing who works for B&B at the reception desk. She smiles at him each morning and raises her coffee mug in a mock toast.

"Another day, another dollar," she calls out, and it has this funny ring to it, like a bird he's never heard before. Her voice surprises clients who come up to the desk. It is, Lakland believes, the reason they keep her around. Not that she's a bad receptionist. She isn't, but that voice nails the job down as much as anything. Lakland smiles back, waves his briefcase in the air, returning her toast. Yes, he thinks, another day, another dollar. He doesn't know if he could sleep with her or not. He's never been great with women anyway. Not that there haven't been success stories. When Wylend invites him and Marty for drinks, he has a few to share, but they are far between, the gaps between them like big silences in his life. There was Marcy, a girl he dated in high school, the one he took to the prom, and that story's so boring he could tell it sober. There's Billie, a girl with a boy's name, who acted like a boy some of the time, and he often wonders if anything ever could have come of that. She had straight hair, like the Beatles, and thick legs. She threw the shot put in college, and Lakland was afraid of her. Billie had the ability, he found, to crack crab legs and lobster pinchers with her teeth and hands. Not the thing he found attractive in a woman, and when he told this over beers, it got a few laughs. Then there was Gabby, short for Gabriella, who was ten years older than he was, she was thirty-six, and more experienced in just about everything. She was the last one. That was three years ago. Gabby didn't leave him; she simply stopped showing up. They'd make plans, a dinner or a movie, and she'd never show. A call would inevitably come, some excuse, one thing or another, until he confronted her about it.

"I just like my time," she said. "I've worked for it. Now it's mine."

And that was it. She disappeared. Something has to happen to people who drop off the face of the planet, Lakland told one of his co-workers. They must go somewhere. The co-worker had said, "They go to Montana," and walked away.

The next morning, when Lakland boards the bus, he's the only passenger and it's both loud and quiet at the same time. He can hear the driver's radio crackle, can hear the engine rumble and wheeze, but he can't hear anything else. Lakland is so used to the morning murmur that it's part of the routine. They stop only at the stops where people are waiting; if no one, the driver moves on, pointless in his transportation. A giant woman climbs on, and the bus sways with her as she steps on board. She's tall, taller than he is, and heavy. Strange to see such a tall, heavy woman. Her shoulders are wide and pulled back, her hair is cropped short. She is what Marty would call "butch," and she is coming down the aisle. Lakland has never seen such a woman before. Her arms are thick and solid looking, not doughy like other heavy people. She looks as if she could kill something. Her face all scrunched up that way. Eyes hid deep in their sockets below big bushy eyebrows. She's a mistake, Lakland thinks. Somebody screwed up and gave her the wrong body. The bus moves forward, lurching as it does, and gains speed through a few green lights. There's no one at the next stop, nor the next, and the driver, apparently behind schedule, lays the pedal down, pushing the heavy bus up to what feels like its maximum. It vibrates as the driver pushes north on Hampton Avenue past flower shops and rows of shotgun houses with small porches. When they see the man on the bike it's too late. Lakland notices him coming from the side, propelling along with a front bike basket full of bright, yellow flowers. When the bus hits him, he must jump because his body hits the window, the smack is gruesome, and the window shakes and splinters in three lines, radiating out from where he hits. They feel the resulting bump of his body rolling under the tires, and the bus never jolts, never feels as if anything's happened, except for the driver slamming on the brakes and the butch woman screaming, a high-pitched scream, irregular and, Lakland thinks, very unlike her. The driver comes out of his seat. His face starched white, whiter than the color of the painted street lines. He holds onto the guide rail, leaning forward.

"You saw it," he says to them, looking down. "You saw him ride out in front." Then he vomits on the floor. Lakland can hear the liquid running down the stairs as the driver vomits again, then again, heaving as he does. There's blood on the window behind him; it streaks the three cracks. "Someone should call," the driver says.

No one has a phone. Lakland had left his cell phone at the office, the only place he ever uses it anyway, something he now regrets. He stands up and moves toward the front, the smell of vomit covers him, and he feels nauseous himself, seeing the blood, and he can't imagine what it will be like to see the body. Before he can say anything, he hears distant sirens, someone has made a phone call, and he notices, gathering around the outside of the bus, a small group of children with backpacks and brown paper sack lunches and lunch boxes, standing and peering under the bus. He touches the driver's shoulder.

"You saw it," the driver says, spitting. "You saw him. I had the green light. I had the right. You saw." Lakland doesn't say anything, but looks at the control panel. It's covered with green and red buttons, some flashing, some not, and none labeled.

"Which one opens the door?" he asks.

"You saw," the driver says.

"Yes. I did."

The lady appears over his shoulder and begins pushing the buttons. One after another, and a horn sounds, then an alarm goes off, the blinkers flash, the door opens, then shuts.

"I'm new," the driver says. "I'm new. I didn't see him. You saw."

"Yes," Lakland says. He's patting the driver's shoulder now. The driver is still leaning over, but Lakland can see a name tag. It reads "Ed." Not Edward, but Ed, as if this was something he requested, something to make him more familiar so his co-workers could relate to him. Good old Ed. Damn shame. The giant lady is still frantically pushing buttons. Outside, the school kids have gathered at the door, their faces pressed against the glass. The sirens are louder now, and an ambulance and fire truck move through the light, early morning traffic. Lakland moves over and nudges the lady away from the buttons.

"It was this one," he says and pushes it once. The door comes open and the lady runs off the bus and down the street, flinging her arms around and screaming and crying. Lakland takes the driver by the arm, helps him down the stairs and onto the sidewalk. When he steps down, the kids step back. There is blood on the pavement, on the grass, on one of the kid's shoes. The man on the bicycle is underneath the bus. His body is twisted in a way that everyone can see he's dead. Lakland looks down at the children and says nothing. They look back as if they expect something, some direction. Their little eyes begging for it, but he hasn't any.

The fire truck arrives, then the ambulance, then the police. The police ask questions and call the bus company over the bus radio, which the driver didn't think to do.

"I'm new," the driver keeps saying.

The cops ask Lakland questions. What's your name? Where do you live? What did you see? Lakland tells them exactly what he saw. He saw a biker and some flowers, and a green light, although he's not really sure he saw the green light, it might have been yellow, or red for that matter, but he doesn't say this. He saw a green light, and the man rode out, and the bus driver tried to stop, which he's not sure he did, but he says he did, and then there was the smack and the window broke, and then the bump. He can't be sure of any of this, he thinks. EMT's are pulling the body from beneath the bus and stuffing it into a black bag. The kids are gone, probably sent home, and Lakland is late for work.

He catches a ride with a small police woman, whose last name is Hamlin. She drops him off in front of the Wagnor building, and as he climbs out, he looks around hoping to see someone who will know him, someone who may ask why he's arriving late, in a police car of all things. He does see a few people from the twenty-first floor, but they all work for B&B and wouldn't ask. They are running, dodging through the street-level fountain, their shoes making sloppy clopping noises. They are all late. He thanks the police woman, who has been telling, the whole time, of her two sons, one a football player, the other a musician, twins, who will be heading south for Grambling in the fall. She's excited to tell someone this. Lakland could see it in her eyes as she talked back at him through the rear view. Her eyebrows wiggled. He says good luck. Good luck to those boys, he says, and makes his way to the twenty-first, up and up, the elevator feeling sluggish, and the whole time him trying to hack out how to tell the story to the little chirp of a blonde receptionist. How to break in? So, I was on my way to work . . . That felt boring, soft and boring. I saw an amazing thing today . . . But it wasn't amazing. It was sickening, he thinks. He's on the twentieth floor when he realizes he's forgotten his briefcase on the bus. There's a perfect platform. So, I've forgotten my briefcase today . . . It's subtle, quiet, nothing you'd expect, but the reasoning is so sincere. Of course he would've forgotten the briefcase. It makes perfect sense. The bell dings and the door opens. He comes out into the hustle bustle of the day. The lights are bright; he smells coffee. The receptionist is at work, answering phones and greeting people as they pass, each with a smile. She pauses when she sees him.

"Another day, another dollar," she says, same as always, same tone, same lift. How in the world can she be so precise? Lakland nods and begins to walk toward her, swinging his right arm casually as he does. He's at the desk before she looks up.

"I forgot my briefcase today," he says, a little smile comes over his face. He hopes it will show her there's more.

"That's too bad," she says with her little chirp voice, not smiling now. She probably practices that voice in the mirror, he thinks. She probably records it. Her blonde head is back down, staring into a fleshy mound of paper work spread out before her like a creed. The phone rings, and she answers, "B&B Brokers. This is Laura. How can I direct your call?" Lakland's lips purse up. He goes away then, to his cubicle, and notices his name, etched on one of those black and white plates, pasted to the cubicle just higher than his head when he sits. He finds his water glass, a small thing, a juice glass really, and he places it on the floor, near the opening, hoping he'll remember to take it home. Marty will be by soon. Marty will have something to say about some sporting event, or perhaps a big business deal, don't pass it up. You always pass it up, Peter. You always wait on things.

Marty's wearing a dark navy blue sports jacket and a pair of khaki pants, and Lakland has never noticed this about Marty before, how he dresses like he's about to go on the air for some afternoon talk show. Marty sits down and begins talking. He begins telling about his wife and their son and how their boy will start playing lacrosse this year. They went to one of the big sports stores to buy him all the equipment he needs, and do you know, Marty is telling him, how much that shit costs? Lakland is listening, but only with a half ear. He's staring past Marty, out to where the reception desks are, and waiting his turn. Waiting for the right moment to jump in and swim.

HER SECOND LOVER
by Margaret Hermes

When my husband walked out and left me with two distraught kids, a crumbling turn-of-the-century house, and an empty bank account, I wished for many things. I wished he and his inamorata would, arm-in-arm, fall down an open manhole, resulting in multiple fractures in three or four legs between them. I wished I would win the Publishers' Clearinghouse Sweepstakes. I wished I could get somebody to live on my horrible third floor and pay me some rent.

We lived only a few blocks from the university and several of our Parkview neighbors had installed graduate students in their empty nooks and crannies. Some had taken in students in exchange for rent money, others for household help. One couple was receiving monthly rent and *au pair* services for their toddler. Of course they did have a renovated carriage house to offer, but their previous grad student had painstakingly restored it. I wanted to get me some of that indentured slavery—or, at the very least, a little extra cash. So I called the university housing office and they sent me some forms. I filled them out but nothing happened. Students drifted into town for the fall semester. Apartment vacancy signs disappeared as though a sign fetishist was stalking the neighborhood. The sidewalks became cluttered with autumn-gilded dead leaves and summer-bronzed young bodies. But nothing happened to me.

I felt disheartened. No, I felt like guano. Rejected by my husband for a dental hygienist who is two years *older* than I am. Rejected sight unseen by every single grad student at the university. Surely there had been some mistake, some filing error in the housing office. I thought my application revealed stupefying tolerance: I would take any nationality, any religion, any sex with any sexual preference. My only suggestion was that they should not be appalled by children and my only caveat was that I preferred that there wouldn't be lots of noise lots of the time. I had listed my occupation as writer so this graduate student should know that s/he was coming to a house where brain waves thrived. No one came. No one even called.

I set about doing what I often do when I feel helpless over something. I wrote about it. I take a kernel of the real thing and I slap fiction all around it and this way I gain some kind of control over whatever is eating at me. I know this isn't how all writers operate. It isn't even how I operate all the time, but it is therapeutic and sometimes effective as well.

When I finished the story, I showed it to my best friend Colin who is also a writer, a poet from Liverpool who teaches in the English department at Wash U. His verdict was, "It's not so much a short story as an exercise in wishful thinking."

That stung. Not the wishful thinking part but the bit about it being not so much a short story. I bit my bottom lip to keep it from sticking out.

"The way I see it," he went on heedlessly, "is that you're ready for some kind of relationship but you're still afraid to trust."

"Pul-lease," I said, feeling vastly superior, sulking no more. "Are you transfixed by American daytime television? Reading books like *Women Who Run With the Wolves So They'll Stop Feeling Like Dogs?* My God, you sound like a talk show host."

"We were talking about you."

"*We* were not."

"I'd say you want a man in your life—don't we all?—but you just aren't ready to deal with all the *Sturm und Drang* that goes along with investment in the three Cs: caring, communication, and commitment."

"This is a whole new side to you, Colin, not your best one, I'm afraid."

"This is not about me. What is the perfect solution to your particular dilemma? A mythological grad student who rents a room in your house and a small niche in your heart. Someone who's not on equal footing. Someone who, by definition, will be moving on. A limited partnership for a limited time only."

"Maybe I'm on to something. Maybe you should try to get one too."

"Ah, but I'm sure there's only a limited number available."

"Maybe we could share."

"Very kind of you, but I think not. I've always deplored your taste in men."

So there I was on an unseasonably warm afternoon, several weeks into the semester, several months into feeling sorry for myself, sitting on my charming, crumbling tiled front porch reading Doris Lessing's *Summer Before The Dark* and thinking about coloring the emerging gray in my hair, when a head appeared above the top of my tentacled spirea bushes. He looked something like a lion, his large head fringed round by a tawny mane. "Oh!" I said, startled by this invasion of my property, if not my privacy. "What do you want?" I added ungraciously, once more acutely aware there was no man about to call upon for protection. "Well?" I said, standing to show I was a no-nonsense type, someone to be reckoned with.

"Excuse me," he said. "Is this the house of Frau Voolf?" He was squinting at an index card snugly bracketed in his big palm.

"Wolff?" I said. "Yes. Yes, it is."

"I am come," he said.

"Good for you," I said. He frowned. "Look, I'm sorry but I think you're looking for some other Wolff Frau. I'm not expecting anyone."

He handed me up the index card through the tops of the bushes. There it was: my name and address, the names and ages of my son and daughter, and a sum of money to be paid monthly—black type on white card, incontestable.

"You have already somevun living on your third floor?" he asked sadly.

"Well, no," I said with some reluctance now that I was face to face with the prospect. "You're from Wash U? But classes started weeks ago."

"Yah, vell, I come here vith my girlfriend and ve are living together by the Loop in vun apartment for two people but ve are having a fight and she is going back to Chermany and I cannot stay any more in this apartment for so much money." He shrugged.

All my imperiousness and irony melted away. I knew what it was like to be impoverished and abandoned. I came down the steps and thrust out my hand. "My name is Annie Wolff," I said. "You'll have to call me Annie. No one ever calls me 'Frau,' not even in English."

And so arrived Hubert—or Hoo-bairt, as he and therefore we pronounced it. He was a model boarder. He paid his rent promptly. He agreed to rake leaves/shovel snow/mow grass according to the season and in return I agreed to edit his philosophy papers and correct his spoken English. He cleaned up the kitchen as soon as he was finished eating. He never left his clothes to ferment in the washer. He didn't own a radio or CD player or anything that made noise and he only played mine when I was out. He always knocked politely—even on open doors—so as not to startle us with his presence. He would occasionally ask to join us if the kids and I were watching something on television. He even seemed to like my kids, but not enough to make him suspect. He never complained about the peeling wallpaper and cracked plaster on the third floor or having to share the bathroom on the second floor with the three of us. And he never entertained, even though I encouraged him to.

"You *live* here, you know," I would say brightly. "Invite your friends over. Just give me some warning if you're going to have a party or something so the kids and I can be elsewhere or rent videos and be invisible."

"Yah sure," he would say. "I don't know so many friends here yet that you should be inwisible."

"Well, feel free," I would say vaguely.

"Yah, sure. Thank you wery much."

I didn't ask him to join family dinners with us but I had taken to inviting him to dessert whenever I had friends over for dinner. I felt that a dessert invitation was hospitable enough yet still allowed me to maintain my distance. I didn't want him to feel snubbed, but I did want him to find his own circle of friends among his peers.

One night following a dessert of coconut-raisin bread pudding with rum sauce, Hubert was helping me clear the table after the guests had left. Our hands reached for the sauce bowl at the same moment and then his hand closed over mine. He gave me a gentle tug and spun me into his embrace, my back snugly fitted against his chest. "This is not a good idea," I said. Suddenly every part of my body was remembering just how long it had been since I'd been this close to flesh I wasn't mother to. I could feel his breath on my hair. "Hoo boy," I gasped.

"'Hoo-bairt," he corrected. "It is the best idea."

"No," I said firmly. "It would make everything so . . . so difficult." I sounded resolute but his hot breath was daunting. I had to extricate myself before he happened upon the back of my neck. "You live here," I said as stiffly as I could manage.

"That is vhy it vill be so easy," he said, holding me tighter. "Ve are living here together." Then it happened: he began to nuzzle the nape of my neck. The eternally cold stone that I carried in the pit of my stomach instantly dissolved from the heat coursing through me from the hot spot at the back of my neck. Like a kidney stone zapped by a laser. I was his. For the night. Well, for a portion of it.

We had an arrangement. There were to be no public displays of affection, no proprietary airs, nothing to give us away to children or neighbors, friends or foes. We would meet discreetly on the third floor for periodic releases of sexual tension. The way I saw it we were both lonely and we weren't harming anyone, just helping each other get through a difficult period. Hubert agreed readily to all my stipulations and abided by them. I think, for both of us, the coolness of our social commerce lent a degree of heat to our private commerce.

He was a refreshingly eager—the word robust comes to mind—if not wholly satisfying lover, and his compliments were more than generous. "No Cherman girls know to do these things that you do," he would say as I dressed to return to my downstairs life.

"I'm sure German women do," I would pat his hand, slightly annoyed. Feeling more like an experienced madam than one man's Frau for the past ten years, I would steal down to my own bedroom, which, by unspoken compact, he was not to enter. I never slept beside him, not even on those nights when the kids stayed at their father's.

We perked along, clumsy and yet comfortable—we were comically polite to one another—with what we called our "tutoring sessions" until one night Colin came over for dinner.

Colin was shooting off little barbs here and there. He was in a snit about something his department chair had said to him and was determined that the whole world should feel equally prickly. I was feeling sated and self-satisfied so his needling wasn't getting under my skin, but then Hubert came downstairs to join us for dessert.

"Here, my good man," Colin rose to his feet, acting out some cocktail scene from an old movie, "by all rights you should have my chair, head of the table and all that."

"Pip, pip, Colin. Cheerio," I said warningly. Colin, the stinker, was the only one who knew of our arrangement and had been immensely but quietly amused these last weeks. He gave Hubert an enormous wink and shifted to an empty chair.

"Thank you," said Hubert, clearly puzzled but probably assuming he had lost something in translation. "You are wery kind."

"An American trait, wouldn't you say, old chap? Must be something I've picked up over here. Always willing to share. Especially the women. Quite noble when you think of it."

"Oh, shut up, Colin," I said.

He ignored me and gave Hubert his full attention. "It's an interesting case of the American spirit of generosity and the German willingness to experiment. Very cutting edge of you, Hubert."

"Vhat is?" Hubert said, jumping headlong into Colin's snare.

"To be made use of so unconventionally and then to find oneself made use of as a literary convention as well."

"A literary conwention? I am sorry. I do not understand," Hubert said.

"*I* am sorry. Colin is being a jerk," I said. "A complete *schweinhundt*, who is just now going home."

"Without dessert?" Colin said, looking longingly at his mounded plate.

"Goodnight, Colin."

Colin departed and I resumed my place at the table opposite Hubert. He was looking at me expectantly. "Wait a minute," I sighed and stood up. I came back to the dining room with the story in hand. "Colin thought he was being funny. He was referring to this. It's a story I wrote. Almost a month before you moved in. You'd better read it." I cleared away Colin's dishes from in front of him and set the manuscript down in their place.

When he finished the story, he kept his eyes on the last sheet. Hubert's large leonine head hung over the dining room table, his paws no longer turning pages but now outstretched, sphynxlike, on either side of the stack of papers. His forehead was so furrowed and buckled that I wanted to inspect his fists for a thorn.

"This is wery strange," he said.

"Don't I know it," I said, rolling my eyes. "Imagine how I felt when you showed up in my yard and you were a German. I mean you could have been from Nigeria or Scotland, but you weren't. You could have been a female, but nope. It was as though you were following my script. Not that I planned to follow it any further. You do know that, don't you? I mean I was resolved not to even think about messing around with you, and I didn't. Really. Until that night. For me it wasn't even a possibility. But maybe deciding that something isn't a possibility makes it possible after all. I mean in order to rule something out, you first have to bring it into the realm of possibilities, don't you?"

Hubert was looking up at me now, rather intently.

"Hey, you can't think it's any stranger than I do," I said. "You know, there is something, well, metaphysical about words set on paper."

"I did not know you vere such a rich voman," Hubert blinked.

"Me? I'm not. Oh. You're talking about *her*." I rolled my eyes again. "Look, Hubert, I know the language thing makes this even more complicated than it would be anyway, but you have to understand that this is fiction.

"Just because a writer uses something real, usually from the past, people think that it's all real, that she—he didn't invent anything." I snapped my fingers in the air to make something, some comprehension, magically appear. "People think you're just a court reporter and you don't get any credit. And then they think that they suddenly *know* you."

"I don't get any credit?"

"Not you. Me. Sometimes when I've written something that sprang from something real, taken an incident and tugged at it, pulled it in a particular direction as far as it would go," I said, suddenly eager, remembering that this was a student of philosophy I had cornered here, "when it's finished, when it has set a while and I go back to it, I can't tell any more where the real leaves off. And the longer it sets, the more blurred the line becomes." I sighed profoundly, took a breath, and continued.

"About two years ago Colin said something, well, unkind to me. I was really hurt by it. So I made a character out of him and put him into a story and had him behave very much worse than he had that night. I had him say *terrible* things. Later I let Colin read the story. I was a wreck while he read it. I thought the story worked pretty well but I was afraid he'd be furious with me. Instead he *apologized* for all those terrible things he hadn't said." I lifted my shoulders, still surprised by the memory. "I couldn't quite believe it. It was a miracle, you see? I had created Colin's past. He accepted himself as I had written him. And he's a writer, for Christ's sake. He of all people should have known better. But he didn't. I guess writers are just as willing as anybody else, maybe more so, to let a writer play God."

Hubert was looking into my eyes now. It was clear that he had considered what I'd been saying and had finally come to some conclusions he was ready to reveal. I prepared myself to be enlightened by my philosophy graduate student.

"I do not vant to be a playball for your writing!" the lion roared.

"Hubert, I wrote that before you came to live here," I reminded him primly.

"Maybe."

"And it was your idea that we go to bed together in the first place."

"If you wrote this before I come to live here, then it vas your idea in the first place," he said, making me think of a fox and a block of wood at the same time. "If Colin had not been a jerk tonight, vould you have showed to me this?" He studied my face.

"I don't know." He was taking every word I said and translating it. Who knows how I was coming across in German? "Probably not."

"I vill go to my room and vork now."

"But you haven't had your dessert. Nobody's had any dessert."

After a day of pouting, Hubert asked if I had any time "awailable" for tutoring so we resumed our sessions.

One morning, after the kids were safely in school, I was lying beside Hubert, daydreaming. He was tracing little circles on my breast, a habit of his after making love. "There is chust vun thing I vant to know," he said softly. "Who is this Verner?"

"Hoo boy, Hubert! Yiminy Cricket! There is no Werner. There never was any Werner!"

"Then I am Verner." He smiled to himself so broadly that I

expected him to thump his chest with his free hand.

There isn't even a family resemblance, I thought to myself.

A few days later he asked offhandedly, "How many years you have been in this therapy?"

"I've never been in therapy. Not that I don't need it. Not that I am not thinking about getting some very soon."

"I think you should talk vith your therapist. It seems to me that this is vhat they call denial."

"Look," I said, trying to sound patient, feeling like Jane Goodall chatting with a different species, "that was *Elaine* who was in therapy. Maybe that's hard to believe because I had her say the thing about self-abuse in the basement which *is* something *I* would say. Colin told me to cut that line out, that she never would have said that."

Hubert eyed me strangely but he didn't say anything more then.

Another time he asked me about the two men I had sex with, after my husband and before him.

"What two men?"

"I do not care so much about the first man, but I am vondering if I have ever sometime met the second vun at dessert."

"The second man at dessert?"

"The vun you vere so sexy vith, the vun who vanted to go to church vith you."

"There were no other lovers, Hubert. Pay attention now: I made those up. Fiction. Get it?"

"Yah, sure," he said. "I get it all right. If you don't vant to talk about this lover, no vun can make you. It is your business."

"And what about my other son, Hubert?" I screeched. "Don't you ever wonder what the hell I've done with him?"

While the formality, the distance between us, had rapidly diminished since he'd read the story, the gulf between us was now a chasm. One of those little paradoxes.

"Vhen I stood up this morning —" he began one evening as I was gathering my clothes from the floor of his bedroom.

"'When I got up,'" I amended.

"Vhen I got up, I vas thinking of how your Verner slept in her room but you never sleep in this room and I never sleep in your room."

"But that's what we agreed to at the very beginning," I said, feeling a little panicky as I pulled on my jeans. "We made rules."

"You made rules. You think because you play God vith your writing you can play God vith my liver."

"I think you mean 'life,'" I stifled a snort.

"And that's another thing. Everyvun outside you—"

"Everyone *other* than you."

"Everyvun other than you is alvays telling me I am speaking wery good English. Only you is telling me—"

"*Are* telling me."

"That my English are—"

"*Is*."

"Alvays wrong. You vould never talk this vay to Verner," he muttered, barely audible.

"That's not fair, Hubert. You do speak very good English, but you asked me to correct you when you made mistakes. You said you wanted to improve."

"Everyvun outside you think—"

"*Other than* you *thinks*," I said gently.

"That I *have* improved!" he shouted. "And you know vhat? I think I only make so many mistakes now vhen you are in the room. Vhat do you say to that?"

"I say that it's obvious that the way for you to avoid mistakes is for me to stay out of the room." I stomped downstairs, my shirt still unbuttoned, my shoes dangling from my hand. "Vell, vell, vell," I sneered to myself behind my closed door, "that's the end of that chapter."

Hubert came to me a few days later and suggested that we had both been too hasty, that we should not let a momentary "explosive" destroy what we had between us. I said that it was really better this way, that I realized now that our "tutoring sessions" had left him feeling bad about himself and prevented him from forming any real attachments. He was free, I said.

For the remainder of that semester, Hubert did not exercise his freedom. Instead he took to presenting himself in some state of undress whenever the kids were not around. After he would shower he'd appear in an open doorway with only a towel girding his loins. I had once told him that I found freshly bathed flesh to be nearly irresistible. On mornings when the kids had stayed at their father's he would arrive in the kitchen wearing only his tiny European underpants in primary colors. "It is a fine morning," he would say as though decked out in a three piece suit and bowler hat. "As soon as I stood up this morning I knew the day vould be fine."

Every morning Hubert fixed for himself the same breakfast without variation: a container of plain yogurt mixed with a cup of dry muesli with a banana sliced over the top, two pieces of toast with butter and jam and a large mug of hot milk. He always used exactly the same dishes each morning—the same small serving bowl for his breakfast sludge, the same handpainted dessert plate for his toast, the same big Christmas mug with the fastidiously coifed Santa Claus on it. I had once thought the sameness of his breakfast endearing, the ritual of the dishes sweet. I now found the rcpetitiveness maddening. I would look away as he spooned the thick, yogurted muesli and imagine him shoveling cement into his mouth. I wanted—I *yearned* to smash my son's Santa-face mug with its marcelled beard and symmetrical spiraling locks.

The more Hubert posed, the easier I found it to embrace celibacy. I recognized that I had depersonalized Hubert—I was even grateful to Colin for he had recognized it first—and turned him into a character. And now, somehow, he had become a caricature.

Finally he stopped. But it was too late. I already loathed him.

Colin came by a couple of weeks into my loathing. He was sympathetic: he had once witnessed Hubert eating breakfast. I told him that Hubert had been deaf to my suggestion that he might find more suitable housing elsewhere. Colin said, "It's simple enough. Just tell your grad stud to pack his bags. After all, it's your house. It's not like he has a lease. Give him two weeks notice if you're feeling bountiful."

"I can't do that. I'd feel guilty," I looked at Colin pitifully. "I can't chuck him out"—I was hoping to persuade him by aping his own patterns of speech—"after having slept with him."

"But there'd be no reason to chuck him out if you hadn't slept with him," Colin said impatiently.

"You see, if we'd been equals and I'd slept with him, then I could tell him to get out. But it wasn't a partnership." I appealed to his native sense of fair play, "It wouldn't be cricket. It would be like sacking the underparlormaid once the earl had his way with her."

"I see," said Colin, seeing my irritating scrupulousness. "Well then, Annie, you'll simply have to endure his breakfasts and his underwear. That's what nobility does—it endures."

About midway through second semester Hubert began entertaining—one young female after another, until he finally settled on a fraulein from Munich who was here as an exchange student at U City High School. I never learned how they met. She had just turned seventeen and Hubert was twenty-four.

"When you said German *girls* didn't know how to… do the things I… used to do," I managed to say icily despite my embarrassment, "I see now that you *meant* girls."

"I think you are maybe jealous now that I got a girlfriend and you vish you vere not so quick to say 'Bye-bye, Hubert.'"

"On the contrary. I just think she's awfully young for you."

"She is less young for me than I vas young for you."

"Whatever you say," I shrugged. "And however you say it." I saw that I was not the most credible adviser on the subject of moral turpitude and discrepancy in ages, so I stopped speaking to Hubert altogether.

Lying in bed, I could hear the creaking directly overhead.

Sometimes I would hear their voices, hers hushed and submissive, Hubert's jarringly loud. I was startled each time by the authority in his.

I'd shut my eyes, shut out their sounds, and concentrate on that second lover, the one whose touch had thrilled me so.

Passing Through
by David Carkeet

I was brand-new to St. Louis, driving south on Hanley Road toward Clayton. I picked up a hitchhiker, and he asked to be dropped off near Famous Barr. I told him to let me know when we got there. Then I asked him what made this particular bar so famous. He stared at me for a while and finally explained that it was the name of a department store.

I've come a long way since then, approaching St. Louis nativedom but not quite achieving it. I've never called St. Charles Rock Road "The Rock Road," for example. In fact, long ago I vowed to get out of town before I ever said "The Rock Road." I think I'll make it just in time.

I grew up in northern California and lived there to the age of twenty-two. After four years of graduate study in Wisconsin and Indiana, I moved to St. Louis, where I have stayed put for thirty years. Next month I'm completing the trek east with a move to Vermont. I just picked out my new phone number from one of five offered by the local service there. I took my time with the choice, mumbling the numbers, testing them for rhythm and retainability. "Bear with me," I said to the phone lady. "I plan on having this number for the rest of my life."

I didn't feel nearly as permanent about St. Louis when I got here in 1973. In my first month on the UM-St. Louis campus, a student asked me, in a practice interview for a journalism class he was taking, where I expected to be in five years. "Not in this office!" I said boldly. I suppose I was thinking like a young person. I was restless, passing through. Or perhaps I was already thinking like Vincent Price, who, when asked why he left his native St. Louis, said, "Oh, everybody does." In my early years here I tried to get out, applied for jobs elsewhere, got nowhere. Then came a wife, a house, children. So I stayed. To my surprise, there came a day when a Lambert touch-down on return from vacation made me feel good instead of bad.

The novels I have written chronicle my gradual acceptance of local citizenship. I pined for Indiana in my early, unhappy years here and set my first novel in the land of Hoosiers in the nonderogatory sense. My second novel mentions St. Louis only twice, both times to complain about the summer heat. I planned on having a subsequent novel take place in Chicago, thinking it sexier than St. Louis, but I didn't know Chicago and fell back on St. Louis, in fact on the University City house where I lived at the time, half a block behind Blueberry Hill. I set my next novel in my Clayton neighborhood without even thinking about it.

What great virtues of the region made me finally embrace it? None. My life simply happened in this place, and I was committed to that life and thus to this place. But in fairness to St. Louis, there is virtue in its easiness, its dead-averageness, its suitability as a bland backdrop to the private dramas of one's existence. It stays out of the way. To a writer, whose life is relentlessly internal, this geographic quality is especially prized.

Writers measure an environment solely according to how well they write in it. St. Louis has provided me with just enough agony to fuel my novels. A nasty tenure battle at UM-St. Louis filled my first book with useful outrage, even though it treats entirely different subjects. My second novel was about depression and baseball because I experienced both here. What would it have been about if I had gone elsewhere—if I had taken the competing job offer from Florida State? A depressed alligator wrestler, perhaps. I met my east coast wife in St. Louis—she too fancied she was passing through for social work graduate school—and I've raised children here, and my last two novels treat the joys and agonies of marriage and fatherhood. Another book was about a Missourian, Mark Twain, whose geographic footsteps I seem to dog—California Gold Rush country, on the Mississippi, wives from the same small town (Elmira, NY). He died in New England, by the way.

As a comic writer, I've been conscious of my milieu as a traditional and conservative one. Whenever I played with religion or sex, I felt like a bad boy, something I doubt a writer in San Francisco or Los Angeles feels. I'm not a particularly aggressive humorist, and St. Louis' conservatism is of a flexible variety, so the degree of tension has been mild, just right for me, sort of like being bad at the dinner table and making Mom giggle in spite of herself. Of course, things have changed. Now, when I drive by an intriguing phone-sex billboard on Delmar, I wonder that I ever worried about offending local readers.

When I first came to St. Louis, I was an outsider in relation not just to the town but to the writing community as well, which seemed as established as Mt. Rushmore. I knew them all by sight. Howard Nemerov, walking down Westgate with his green book bag over his shoulder, used to greet my kids drawing on the sidewalk with a baritone "hello." He was able to give this simple word a poetic ring. Stanley Elkin lived a block down the street, and it made me feel good to know he was writing funny stuff while I was trying to. William Gass lived around the corner. I avoided him, afraid he might say something I wouldn't understand, but he was friendly, and his twin girls babysat my twin girls. I observed these writers from a distance. In time, I published. The writing program at my own university grew. I now feel part of a vibrant, varied group of regional writers—a community I am perversely giving up to retire and move to a state containing the likes of John Irving and David Mamet. I'll have to claw my way to respectability all over again.

In order to write full-time, I've had to make one of the most difficult decisions a worker of any kind makes: when to pack it in. In my case, the job was college teaching and some departmental administration, and the signs were many—growing impatience with co-workers; the onset of procrastination—a quality I hate; a sense of being overworked so great that I felt breathless, as if my lungs were too small for the job; a mounting feeling that the work was mechanical and didn't involve people; and boredom resulting from the absence of surprise of any kind. Above all, I wanted to be elsewhere. You know it's time to retire when you are so mentally somewhere else that as you walk to the men's room outside your departmental office, you begin to unbuckle your pants even though you are still in the hall. Clearly this man should be working at home.

A former student of mine, retired himself, beamed when I told him of my plans and said to me, "It's like childhood, only better!" He might be right, provided you leave out the hourly financial calculations, which I don't recall from childhood.

I already know that retirement is like something else. We spend much of our lives preparing to leave it. It's horrible to contemplate, but we must. I'm here now, but there will come a time when I am no more. *Everything will go on without me!* This outcome sours the whole deal, as far as I'm concerned. But by retiring—and, even better, retiring and leaving life as I've known it for thirty years—I am dying and not dying. I am experiencing roughly half of the sourness (I'm not sure of the percentages here), leaving behind lots of people, most of whom I like, and everything will indeed go on without me. But—here's the other half—I get to go on living. I jumped ship as it was crossing the River Styx. I beat the system.

Raymond Carver, known best for his short stories, wrote a wonderful poem celebrating the time between the day he stopped drinking (and thus saved his life) and the day that he sensed lay not far ahead when he would die of the brain tumor with which he had been diagnosed. He saw those extra years as "Gravy"—the title of the poem. I feel I understand what Carver was up to. Milestones help us carve life into individually precious segments, and if we cherish each one, we get more out of the endless bargain with death.

One of the strangest aspects of retirement is the sense of waste. If you leave your job before incompetence sets in—or, as in my case, before it becomes obvious that it has—you are taking with you knowledge that others will need years to acquire. If you work in a bureaucracy, you know which procedures must be followed and which ones you can ignore like an anarchist. You know shortcuts. You know who matters and who doesn't. When you're new, everything matters, everybody is a force to be reckoned with. Retirees thus have the feeling, as they leave the workplace, that things will fall apart. Some retirees are cocky about this, even sadistic. Others feel guilty for ceasing to be a true "human resource." The guilty ones need to remind themselves that just because they *can* do something doesn't mean they *must* do it.

 A student of mine once did a very odd thing in the classroom, and what she did illustrates the other side of the equation, the necessity of retirement. After a middling performance and many absences all semester, she dropped a linguistics course. But she needed the course to become a teacher, so she retook it when I offered it again. She brought the notes to class that she had taken in her prior attempt, a sensible move to cut down on duplication of effort. The odd thing was that as she followed along, she anticipated where I was going in my lectures by calling out the ends of my sentences. I would say, "Four examples of Old Norse borrowings into Old English are *skill, skin,* . . ." and then she would tiredly drone, " . . . *freckle* and *fellow*." Her behavior must have puzzled the other students. "She's *good*," I imagine them thinking.

 Who knows what was going on in this student's mind? My guess is that she anticipated my words mostly in disgust with herself for having to repeat the class. But for my part, each such moment expressed the essential fact that teachers ignore, and that they have to ignore, or they would go mad: we say the same things over and over. How can we do otherwise? This particular course was in the history of the English language, a history that certainly didn't change between my offerings of it. And if I'd found, after years of experience, what I considered the ideal way to teach it, how could I not do it that way again every time? But here is the paradox that dogs the profession: while it is efficient to say the same thing over and over, doing so means that knowledge that once quickened the teacher's pulse now brings it to a dead stop.

And I'm sure I'm not the only literature teacher to whom something like this has happened: I'm preparing to teach a work, let's say a short story, and as I read it in the class text, I excitedly make marginal notes of my new discoveries. Then I happen upon a copy of the same story in an old teaching file or in a book that I used and annotated decades ago, and I find marginal observations I made then that are exactly the same as those I've just made. I must face the truth: I am one limited brain capable of only so much growth, and it is time for a new brain to move into my office.

As I point my Cardinals cap to the northeast, I know there are a few little things, unique to me, that I will miss about this place:

I'll miss enjoying former UM-St. Louis students on the airwaves: reporter Kevin Killeen on KMOX radio, sports reporter Frank Cusumano on KSDK-TV, medical summarizer John Schieszer on KFUO, and *a cappella* nut Margie Kennedy on KDHX. I didn't teach them to do what they're doing, but I did teach them.

I *won't* miss students who say, "I really want an A in this course" or "I'm not going to be in class next time—you're not going to do anything important, are you?" But I *will* miss all the other students.

I *won't* miss the summer suburban cacophony—leaf blower to my left, weed-whacker to my right, cicadas at twelve o'clock high. But I *will* miss those alternating feathered harbingers—the tail-twitching slate-colored juncoes that bring us winter, and those stoned flyboys of summer, the chimney swifts.

And, to conclude where I began, with Famous Barr, I'll miss their bra ads in the *Post-Dispatch*, but not just for the reason you think. A friend and colleague of mine, a transplant who grew up in Maine, once called them "Famous Bahh brar ads." In linguistics classes that utterance provided me, over and over, with a perfect example of the eastern New England deletion and intrusion of "r," though my students were probably distracted by the thought, "Why were two English profs talking about bra ads?"

BIOGRAPHICAL NOTES

RICHARD BURGIN is the author of ten books including the novel *Ghost Quartet* (Northwestern University Press) and the story collection *The Spirit Returns* (Johns Hopkins University Press), and his stories have won four Pushcart Prizes. He teaches at Saint Louis University where he edits the literary journal *Boulevard*.

DAVID CARKEET's newest work *Campus Sexpot* recently won the Creative Nonfiction Award given by the Associated Writing Programs, and will be published in September, 2005. He is the author of five novels *Double Negative, The Greatest Slump of All Time, I Been There Before, The Full Catastrophe,* and *The Error of Our Ways* . For many years he taught linguistics and writing at the University of Missouri-St. Louis and edited its literary magazine *Natural Bridge*.

EDMUND DE CHASCA's fiction has appeared in the *Green Hill Lantern*, *Aethlon*, and elsewhere. His book of literary history, *John Gould Fletcher and Imagism*, was published by the University of Missouri Press. He is senior editor of *Boulevard* and pianist for St. Stephen's Church in the Central West End.

EILEEN DREYER has 29 books and 7 short stories published under her own name and her pseudonym Kathleen Korbel. She is an Anthony nominee in mystery and a member of the Romance Writers of America Hall of Fame. A native St. Louisan raised in Brentwood, she worked as a trauma nurse for 16 years at local hospitals. She sets all her medico/forensic suspense novels locally, the latest being *Head Games* from St. Martin's Press.

ROBERT EARLEYWINE teaches fiction writing and literature at Washington University. Some of his publications of fiction have appeared in *Epoch* ("The Sentrydog Section," 1980) *Webster Review* ("Ryder" 1980, "Faith Again" 1982, "Roy" 1985) *Delmar* ("Spirits" 1999) *Natural Bridge* ("The Lone Ranger" 2000 — available online).

WILLIAM GASS is the David May Distinguished University Professor in the Humanities (emeritus) at Washington University. His most recent book is *Tests of Time* from Alfred Knopf. Other works include the long-anticipated *The Tunnel*, as well as *Reading Rilke, Willie Masters' Lonesome Wife, Omensetter's Luck,* etc. He was also the director of the International Writers Center at Washington University.

MARGARET HERMES's work includes a novel *The Phoenix Nest,* and book and lyrics for an adaptation of an Oscar Wilde fable *The Birthday of the Infanta,* staged by Metro Theatre Company, which premiered at the Edison Theatre in St. Louis. A story of hers has been selected for the upcoming anthology, *20 Over 40,* a collection of fiction by 20 writers, published by the University of Mississippi Press.

A.E. HOTCHNER was born in St. Louis and grew up in the Westgate Hotel mentioned in "Christmas Canaries." A Washington University graduate, he is best known for his biography of his good friend, Ernest Hemingway, *Papa Hemingway.* His novel about growing up in St. Louis *King of the Hill* was a popular film in 1993. He has written numerous books, plays, musicals, and television dramas. He currently resides in Connecticut.

JAMES M. HUGGINS is a native of the Saint Louis region with publications in *Thema, Timber Creek,* and *Heartland* literary magazines. A full time writer, he also has one novel in search of an agent and another nearing completion.

HARRY JACKSON JR. is a journalist of more than 30 years experience including 21 with the *St. Louis Post-Dispatch*. He is an adjunct professor at Lindenwood University where he teaches narrative feature writing and documentary history. He has won more than a dozen journalism awards of one sort or another. His freelance work has been published widely and has appeared in dozens of publications across the United States.

MICHAEL A. KAHN is the author of *Trophy Widow, Due Diligence* and five other suspense novels starring savvy St. Louis trial lawyer, Rachel Gold. His short story, "The Bread of Affliction," won the 1999 Readers Award from *Ellery Queen Mystery Magazine*. He wrote his first novel *Grave Designs* on airplanes and in hotel rooms while working on an out-of-town lawsuit. Mr. Kahn is a trial lawyer.

JOHN LUTZ is the author of over forty novels and 200 short stories. His awards include the Edgar, Shamus, and Golden Derringer Life Achievement Award bestowed by the Short Mystery Fiction Society. One of his novels became the hit movie *Single White Female*. His latest book is the suspense thriller *Darker Than Night*.

MICHAEL MacCAMBRIDGE is the author of *America's Game: The Epic Story of How Pro Football Captured A Nation*, and two other books. He worked for eight years as a columnist and critic at the *Austin American-Statesman*, writing about movies, music, and popular culture. An adjunct professor at Washington University in St. Louis, he lives with his wife, Danica Frost, and their children, Miles and Ella, in University City.

COLLEEN McKEE, from Times Beach, Missouri, now lives on the city limit. She's finishing her MFA in Creative Writing at the University of Missouri-St. Louis. Her writing has appeared in publications such as *Confluence, Delmar*, and the anthology *Without a Net: The Female Experience of Growing Up Working Class*.

RICHARD NEWMAN is the author of three chapbooks *Greatest Hits, Tastes Like Chicken and Other Meditations*, and *Monster Gallery:19 Terrifying and Amazing Monster Sonnets!* His first full length book of poems *Borrowed Towns* will appear in 2005. He teaches at St. Louis Community College in Florissant Valley and edits *River Styx*. He and his nine-year-old daughter live in Soulard.

ROBERT RANDISI is the author of the St. Louis-based Joe Keough series of books, the most recent of which was *Arch Angels*. He was awarded a Life Achievement award in 1993 by the Southwest Mystery/Suspense Convention, and has been nominated 4 times for the Shamus award. Originally from New York, he has lived in St. Louis for 12 years.

SUZANNE RHODENBAUGH won the Marianne Moore Poetry Prize for *Lick of Sense* (Helicon Nine, 2001). Her poems have appeared in chapbooks, anthologies, and many journals, including the region's *Boulevard, New Letters, River Styx* and *Sou'wester*. Her essays have been published in *The American Scholar, Michigan Quarterly Review, Salmagundi* and other journals. She reviews poetry for the *St. Louis Post-Dispatch*.

RICK SKWIOT, a St. Louis native, won the Hemingway First Novel Award with his Mexican mystery *Flesh*. His second novel *Sleeping With Pancho Villa* was a finalist for the Willa Cather Prize. In 2003 All Nations Press of White Marsh, Virginia, published his critically acclaimed childhood Christmas memoir *Winter at Long Lake,* set in St. Louis and nearby southern Illinois.

DANIEL STOLAR was born and raised in the Central West End of St. Louis. His first book *The Middle of the Night* (Picador), a collection of short stories set mostly in St. Louis, was a BookSense 76 Pick in August, 2003. His fiction and creative nonfiction have appeared in a number of publications including

DoubleTake, The Utne Reader, Bomb, and the *St. Louis Post-Dispatch.* He teaches Creative Writing at DePaul University in Chicago.

RYAN STONE earned his MFA from the University of Missouri - St. Louis. He has lived in St. Louis for three years and is the former editor of *Natural Bridge* and is currently the Managing Editor for *River Styx.* His fiction has appeared in *Natural Bridge* and *Wisconsin Review.* His mother is originally from Valley Park and grew up here, yet another connection.

MARY TROY is the author of three collections of short stories—*Cookie Lily*, *The Alibi Cafe and other stories,* and *Joe Baker is Dead.* She has won a Nelson Algren Award from the *Chicago Tribune,* and has been nominated for the PEN/Faulkner award. She publishes her short fiction and essays widely. She teaches writing and directs the MFA Program for the University of Missouri-St. Louis.

CHARLES WARTTS JR. is a novelist, short story writer and teacher living and working in St. Louis. He is a graduate of the Iowa Writers' Workshop and has published articles and stories in *River Styx, Drumvoices Revue, Black American Literature Forum, African voices* and *Conjunctions* among others.

DAKIN WILLIAMS is the co-author of *His Brother's Keeper: the Life and Murder of Tennessee Williams, Remember Me to Tom, Nails of Protest* and other books. He calls himself the "professional brother." Dakin is presently a practicing attorney, he was a candidate for office (for senate, governor, and President with Jane Byrnes as V.P.), and a spokesman for his brother, Tennessee. He grew up in St. Louis, and graduated from Washington University.

Cover artist, **JENNIFER ROUSSIN** is a local St. Louis artist who appreciates the older architecture in the city of St. Louis. She currently works in pastels, oils, colored pencils, and graphite. She has won several awards at national juried art shows, and was just recently given an honorable mention from nationally acclaimed pastel artist Doug Dawson at the Gateway Pastel Artists' 2004 group show. Her website is www.chameleon-arts.net.

• • •

FRANCIS G. SLAY, mayor of the City of St. Louis since 2001 lives in the same south city neighborhood where he grew up. A graduate of St. Mary's High School, he received his law degree from St. Louis University. He served as an alderman and president of the Board of Aldermen before assuming his present position. Much progress has taken place in the City of St. Louis during his term, including the renovation of Forest Park.

• • •

PAUL THIEL, editor of this collection, founded Antares Press in 2003. His poetry is published in *Natural Bridge, Extensions* (New York City), *Poetry Review of Tampa,* etc. He has promoted poetry events in St. Louis for the last ten years, noteworthy being the "Day-of-the-Dead-Beats" readings and a reading from the writers of the Delmar Walk-of-Fame at Blueberry Hill. He is a several-generation native of St. Louis.

ACKNOWLEDGMENTS

Antares Press gratefully acknowledges all the writers, their representatives and publishers for permission to use the works in this book.

William Gass's "Winston Churchill" from *Literary St. Louis: A Guide* published by Missouri Historical Society Press ©2000

Dakin Williams's "Tennessee in St. Louis" from *His Brother's Keeper* published by Dakin's Corner Press ©1983

Richard Burgin's "The Park" published in *Fear of Blue Skies, Stories by Richard Burgin* by John Hopkins University Press ©1998

Eileen Dryer's "Safe at Home" published in anthology, *Fathers and Daughters* ©1999

James M. Huggins's "Pete Gray" ©2002

Harry Jackson Jr.'s "In Remembrance of Terry" ©2004

Michael Kahn's "The Caves" from *Due Diligence* published by Dutton ©1995

Colleen McKee's "Lure of Annihilation" ©2004

Robert Randisi's "Keough's Career" from *In the Shadow of the Arch* published by St. Martin's Press ©1998

Daniel Stolar's "City Map" published in *Double Take* ©1997

Rick Skwiot's "The Grandmothers" from *Winter at Long Lake* published by All Nation's Press ©2003

Michael MacCambridge's "Urban Tennis: the Heman Park Hustle" published in *St. Louis Magazine* ©1999

Suzanne Rhodenbaugh's "Ya Gotta Love It" ©2004

AE Hotchner's "Christmas Canaries" originally published in *Collier's Magazine* ©1955

Mary Troy's "The Alibi Café" from her book of short stories, *The Alibi Café* ©2003

David Carkeet's "Passing Through" published in the *St. Louis Post-Dispatch* ©2003

John Lutz's "Second Story Sunlight" published in *Most Wanted* c2002

Edmund de Chasca's "Shopping Day" published in *Portland Review of Literary Journal* ©2004

Robert Earleywine's "Fido" ©2004

Margaret Hermes's "Her Second Lover" ©2004

Richard Newman's "Awful" published in *Laurel Review* ©2003

Ryan Stone's "A Story to Tell" ©2004

Charles Wartts Jr.'s "Big Muddy Blues" ©2001

Thanks

The edititor wishes to express his gratitude to the following individuals whose help was invaluable in preparing this book for publication:

Ken Allen
Amy Debrecht
Matthew Grayson
Jeffrey Fister
Jasmina Kusuran
Bryan Lane
Ellen Light
Carolyn McCandliss
Seth Raab
Peg Redelfs
Suzanne Rhodenbaugh
Mary Troy
Eric Winters